SABOTEUR

J. TRAVIS PHELPS

The following story is true.
Proof is forthcoming.

G. C.

PART I

CHAPTER 1

A VERY STRANGE MAN

The thunder and lightning crashed with a wail, and his wife who lay next to him sat up in the bed. Through the blanket he could see the light play across her worried face, revealing that she had not slept. As always, when he was not well, she had watched over him. But tonight her worries had been near hysteria. He had slept poorly while the fever had worked through him, watching silently as the shadows danced across the ceiling of their bedroom. There was a light sweat still on his brow, and the sheets were soaked through. Finally, the fever had given way. He had fallen into dreams he could not remember. As always, even an hour of uninterrupted sleep refreshed him. Now he peered sideways through the sheets, almost like a child, feeling momentarily protected. He was no child though. His body ached palpably all of the time.

"Go back to sleep," he said, trying to calm her. "I have to get up soon anyway."

She glared at him, swiping her hand across his forehead, and for a moment he felt truly as a child must when a parent comforts him. He thought of his own mother, now gone for so many years. One look from her had always made his fears evaporate. He allowed himself to indulge the emotion only momentarily, peering out through the canopy of the blanket, finally rolling himself away to the edge of the bed.

"You will work today then, even after all I have said?" she said with irritation. "Please don't go; just this once."

"No," he answered, "I will eat and come back to rest as you wish. Look there," he said, his face suddenly becoming animated, "the light is breaking through."

And through the window, they both could see a beam of sun. The low clouds blew speedily past, seemingly headed to some faraway place, as though time was of the essence.

He walked silently down the hall to his bath, stopping only to catch his reflection in the mirror. It was a jolt. He had become old. His eyes were now permanently rimmed in red that no sleep could erase. His hairline was gone, only wisps of curls still clinging to his ears; there was nowhere left to comb it for protection or for artifice. *When had it happened? In Spain? No, earlier.* It was too late to care. He looked at himself and, as he had for years, started to make exaggerated and ludicrous faces at himself in the mirror. Each expression was ever more ridiculous: an old man chewing gumless at his food, an old man smiling proudly, then aghast with horror, then his tongue wagging in mockery, but always an old man. These expressions were all meaningless now. He felt almost none of those things any more. Every emotion had quotation marks. But the faces made him laugh inside. The only place left for him really.

"Fuck you, old man!" he said to his reflection. "No, fuck *you!*" he shouted, and it was funny because in real life he almost never swore. He burst into laughter, but then tears came without warning. They leaked. Emotions came over him suddenly and for reasons he could hardly explain. A condition of old age, not real feelings mind you.

His eyes would stay red for days now, but it felt good and wise to let some of whatever it was out. He thought of his younger friends and how they would talk behind his back.

"The old man is turning to crust," they'd mock, "outlived his usefulness."

They had said worse, no doubt. He stared at the scar near his throat, a gift from the war. Wouldn't it have been better to die there so many years before? He thought of the blood he had seen so many times pouring from other men. He secretly thought it was a sign of weakness to bleed. He had never even once considered that anyone could kill him. And no one ever could. Sometimes he had almost strangely longed for it, but none would release him, as he had for them. It was unadulterated intimacy to take a man's life with your own hands. You had to love people to kill them, and that he had. It was possible that no one had ever delighted in people more. The raw intimacy of a slaying was the pinnacle of that love, and there were a great many men he had made better through the killing. He had completed their lives in a way that no other act could. It was the very last thing you could give a person. He had never killed without feeling the sweetness in life though, the deliverance. It was beyond poetry, beyond books, and even beyond sex. Yet, if given the choice, he would never have killed anyone. He sometimes fantasized about turning himself in. But to whom? To men lesser than himself, who were guilty of far worse crimes? That would never do. It didn't matter now. He wiped his face, hoping it would improve, but he only looked more disheveled, more pitiable.

He wouldn't work today then. The worst of his fever had already broken and as always was in retreat. No sickness could take him; that much he knew. He endured illness quietly, barely letting out a moan, no matter how wretched he became. The business would be a bore, and today that was indeed too much, for his vanity at least. Still, at home, there would be no books to read either—not that he had not already read anyway—and no company that could bring him delight, nor a concerned wife, nor woman or man, nor food no matter how well prepared. He thought of running away for just a moment, and in his chest came an erratic purring. *To start over. Where to? There was nowhere to go.* He had been looking in the mirror for maybe thirty seconds now, no more. The agility of his mind sometimes astounded even him.

"Where are you going to go, old man, huh?" he said to the mirror.

A knock came at the door, jolting him.

"Yes?"

"Sir, I am terribly sorry to interrupt you." It was his servant Apollon. "I wonder if I may have a word."

Abandoning the mirror, he slid his head through the doorway slowly while pulling the bottom half of his face down. "Yeeeeesssssssss?" It was the expression of an imbecile. Apollon, after all these long years, never quite knew how to respond to his jibes.

"Sir, your nephew is at the door."

"So early?"

"Yes, indeed, sir."

Apollon's face drew up in a look of concern.

"He is not alone, sir; there is another man with him, a very strange man."

CHAPTER 2

THE GOOD PROFESSOR

I f there was one thing Professor Noah Downy despised, it
was lecturing in these damned auditoriums. They always
reminded him of his own school days, wasted in crowds of
other lost students just passing the time. Even worse, it was
utterly impossible for him to get the feeling in a place like
this. The feeling was the moment, the instant when everything was settled, when he conquered his audience, when
they submitted to him. It did not always happen, of course,
but it was next to impossible with a crowd of this size, in such
a room. He was at best a tour guide in a place like this,
pointing to glass cases full of dead mummies and artifacts.
Here lies Rameses, now a skeleton like the rest of us, so
mortal. So boring. He was at his best when he forgot he was
teaching and just started talking. He thought silently of his
early years as a part timer, running from campus to campus,
just trying to cobble together a living. It was better back then

in some ways, when his classes were always small and intimate. He could get the feeling easily. It was absolute exhilaration for him. He could make people swoon with his storytelling; it was the only thing in life that truly came easily to him. Downy wasn't your usual academic though. He never spoke in platitudes and suffered mightily in the company of pretentious intellectuals, which was pretty much all of them. He preferred to be direct, clear. Most days the company of fellow academics was simply more than he could stomach. It was his only complaint about the job really. Today, in his History 301, though, he was busy injecting the story of how Mark Antony and Cleopatra, despondent over their pending defeat and probable execution, had started their own drinking club called The Royal Academy of Outstanding Livers. Most didn't catch the double meaning until he announced that he had briefly been a member of the club in college himself. It was an old joke made up on the fly when he had needed to wake a sluggish afternoon class. He hated retelling jokes, but even real comics recycled material, didn't they? Today he was definitely too tired and knew the feeling wasn't going to come anyway. Looking around the room, he realized many of his students were probably already hung over, or headed that direction, since the college weekend always started a day early. It never ceased to amaze him that on exams students could remember almost nothing of importance about Mark Antony's political career but always remembered that he was a terrible drunk. He had thought of making it a test question, briefly. Today though, it was all Cleopatra, and she was an easy sell. The young female co-eds in the audience really lit up, and the guys too. The questions were always the same. What did she really look like? Had she really committed suicide by cobra? He took pains to clear up many of the myths about her.

"The only reliable likeness of her was a picture on an old coin face minted during her lifetime," he explained. "The pronounced hook of the nose was hardly beautiful, not classically anyway, which must have meant her powers of seduction— her mind—were the real work of art. She spoke five languages." Every plain Jane in the room plucked up her antennae at once.

"You could be marginally hot and still end up a queen in the first century," he explained. The young women in the room grimaced at the expression "marginally hot" as the guys all went wild with laughter. He hadn't meant it as a sexist comment. He marveled at how little things had changed between the sexes. It was still a girl's job to be beautiful, but the homeliest of boys considered themselves absolute judges and jury over such matters.

"The story that she simply committed suicide was probably a necessary fiction," he went on to explain. "With the ever ambitious and utterly ruthless Augustus waiting to take Egypt and her fabled riches, Cleopatra's continued existence was the greatest and only threat left to him. His soldiers may well have put her to the sword. She was a loose end that had to be sewn up in any case."

A hand went up, breaking his concentration. He knew the face and hand already. It was McGuire. It would undoubtedly be a dull comment.

"Yes, Mr. McGuire?"

"Wouldn't death by a sword be really painful and like—messy?"

Downy considered this brilliant inquiry with a slow rub of his chin, while other members of the class snickered.

"Mr. McGuire, you raise a serious concern here. Let me think on it a fortnight and get back to you." McGuire's hand went up a second time, this time more slowly.

"Uh, how long is a fort—"

Before Downy could answer, everyone burst into laughter. Kevin McGuire followed suit; he really liked to hear himself ask questions more than he cared to think about whether they made any sense.

"But I do get your point, Kevin, definitely not as poetic as death by cobra, is it, which is why I am suspicious of the myth-making elements of such a story—the cobra, of course, being a symbol of both royal power and immortality for the Egyptians."

Downy had a way of making people feel good even at their dumbest moments. He could also rescue a class from a pointless comment.

As the laughter finally died down to a murmur, a voice came from the back of the auditorium.

"It is quite a beautiful way to die as a matter of fact, elegant even. Killing meant something in such a time. It was a hero's trade. Now it is merely a common, wholesale slaught—"

The voice was low and clear but trailed off. People turned

in their chairs, somewhat taken aback by the interruption. Downy couldn't find the face out of the crowd.

"I am sorry, Professor, to interrupt your beautiful rendering. Please continue."

In the back row sat a man, wearing a floppy tourist hat like the ones you could find for sale in almost every gift shop in Southern California. His dark features were offset by two almost-piercing black eyes, and even at a distance, Downy could tell there was something unusual about him—the way he held his chin upward with a look of wild amusement or disbelief, he couldn't tell which. Something in the man's manner of speech sparked a note of caution. It was too formal. Weirdo groupies of history abounded in his classes unfortunately. There was the reincarnation crowd, of course. He had met more than his fair share of those who claimed to intimately know the details of Cleopatra's life because they in fact *were* Cleopatra in a previous incarnation. There were scarce few reincarnated *peasants* unsurprisingly. It was an occupational hazard unfortunately. His students used the interruption to start for their bags, and he realized he had spoken well past the allotted time.

He yelled as they departed: "Don't forget to read pages one hundred ninety-eight through two hundred sixty, covering the period of the proscription of leading Romans, including Cicero, *and* be kind to your liver—" Most had already disappeared though, so he simply waived his arms, "Have a nice weekend."

Today, it was he who would surrender. He looked through the crowd for the brown-faced man but couldn't find him in the melee. Out of the corner of his eye, he saw a student still sitting in her seat. Her stare lingered as she packed her things very slowly.

He tried not to notice her legs as she uncrossed them to sit up. "Professor, my father used to say your take on Cleopatra's death was pure speculation, not history."

He paused, squinting to confirm what his eyes couldn't believe.

"Your father was a rigid, unimaginative old Irish bastard, young lady, and God, do I miss him. Come here."

He was beside himself with joy to see her. His eyes unexpectedly watered. The girl before him was none other than Samara Lee Patterson. He recognized her immediately but had completely forgotten she might be there. The last time he had seen her she was barely a teenager. He had called her Sam then. She had loved his storytelling and sat at his feet like a young disciple, hanging on to his every word. She, in turn, had loved making strong, dark coffee for him and her father while they talked endlessly in the garden. It had been an ongoing contest to see how black she could make it. She would arrive at his side like a servant and offer it to him in her hilarious, mock British accent: "A glass of mud for the distinguished gentlemen?"

They had their inside jokes as well. He had taught her when she was just a kid the first and most important rule of archeology, which was "always watch your step." She would burst into a fit of uncontrollable laughter, seeming to understand even at such a tender age that this was sound advice.

He could never forget the look on her face when he had

decided to leave that final summer at Charlie's. She had been so angry she wouldn't even come out of the house to say her last good-bye. If he had only known then how little time he and Charlie had left together, he would have stayed. So here she was, finally on her way to college after a few years of "playing the world traveler," as her mother had described in the e-mail. She had her father's eyes, a deep coral blue, and like him, they were full of desire and mischief. For a moment he thought he could feel Charlie peering out at him. It bothered him. This was the man who had insisted that Downy must teach and that he should write, even when Downy argued no one gave a shit about history anymore, if they ever did. His books had certainly proven that wrong. He had practically watched Samara grow up, and now he couldn't believe she was sitting in his own classroom, nor that his dear friend, her father, was really gone five whole years now.

Out of the corner of his eye, he suddenly saw the man in the floppy hat walk past the door in the back of the room. His head was down, but he looked sideways in a flash. Downy tried not to break his concentration with Samara.

"Come by our place as soon as you get settled in," he heard himself saying. "Naomi would love to see you; she simply won't believe it."

He realized he had made the invitation out of absolute fear of the way she was looking at him. She was positively beautiful and knew it. His mind wandered to all those beautiful busts of the Persian princesses he had seen in Alexandria, each forever set in marble. He sometimes imagined they might come to life and speak to him. They had nothing on

Samara Patterson. The sooner his intentions were clear, the better. She seemed to wince a little at the mention of his wife Naomi. Was it a sign he had been right to feel the attraction and to try to interrupt it? He was imagining things, of course, and chided himself silently.

"We should get coffee, Mr. Professor," she said playfully, "something with mud in it, as I recall?" She slipped effortlessly back into the old accent, and he laughed out loud, throwing his hands to his face. He wanted to hug her again but was afraid of the feeling.

He could already see that coffee turning into a beer and then a second, just as he had done a million times over with Charlie, when they had been drinking buddies. But then the boundaries would disappear. He decided instead to put Samara Lee Patterson in a glass display case with a warning sign that read, "Daughter of a Dear Old Friend, Absolutely Off Limits." Samara glared at him a bit crossly, and it seemed to him she could sense what he was thinking.

She smiled at him almost disappointedly and insisted, "Coffee soon, you and me. I've really been looking forward to seeing you, ya know."

As she walked away, he feigned no principles and simply watched. The view only made matters worse. Goddamn, he hated being a grown-up sometimes.

CHAPTER 3

THE NEW GUY

In October, San Diego was quite simply the perfect place to be—endless days of dreamy-blue sky and warmth at a time when most states were experiencing the first chills of fall. It was crisp and clear, but in Southern California, the frigid winter simply never arrived. It would be Nick Sullivan's first year off the East Coast and the beginning of a job he was sure he'd hate. San Diego? OK, every city had crime, fair enough, but he had hoped to end up in New York or even Chicago. That was full-time work for a real detective. So this was his punishment then. This was how a career fizzled, and all for what?

He simply couldn't believe his luck. The chief had been irate enough to show up at his apartment with a baseball bat. He was wise enough not to answer the door of course. Small-town police force—a complete rumor mill. In a town like

Richmond, cops didn't really have to follow the law anyway, especially not with each other. Dickson would have certainly used the bat too, at least until he took it away from him. It would have been ugly. Instead Dickson's nephew, a deputy, had called him in on a Sunday and told him he was the best detective he had ever seen and that he was awfully sorry to see him go, but Richmond just wasn't big enough for Carl Dickson and the man who had slept with his beloved niece Caroline. Never mind that Caroline was probably even now moving on to the next deputy who caught her fancy, or quarterback or whoever. Still, it had been his fault, in as much as a man can be faulted for falling victim to a horny southern girl's charms when he was five shots into a bottle of Jack Daniels. She had done the pouring and was twenty-five, for God's sake, hardly too young for him by much. He could have made a thing of it and refused to resign or quit, but he thought it would be better to just move on.

A change sounded good in fact, and in some ways at least a transfer to San Diego was an upgrade. So he'd made the drive all the way from Richmond to Dallas in one night of nonstop-coffee-drenched driving. It had made him awfully thirsty though. The beer in Dallas had lasted for three whole days plus the one new, though very temporary, girlfriend. He'd simply slipped out of the cheap hotel while she slept it off. He'd almost missed his first day on the job and had to drive like the devil to make it to San Diego in time.

He looked up as he pulled into the parking lot of the San Diego Police Department. In the dark the building looked like a fancy hotel with soft-green track lights cascading against the ribs of the structure. But inside there were hardly any lights on at this hour. He had arrived during the biggest horse race of the year, and it turned out there wasn't a single vacant room available anywhere. It wouldn't be the first time he had slept in his car, but frankly as exhausted as he was, he could have slept anywhere. He might have flown, but flight attendants weren't at all what they used to be, screaming babies, and even a good stiff drink did nothing to calm him during turbulence. There was no safer place than the confines of his old banged up El Camino. At least he had a good parking spot. As he turned off his engine, he was sure he could hear the sound of the ocean breaking against the seawall only a few blocks away. It was dark still. The sun wouldn't be up for another hour at least, so he stretched himself across the seat carefully, but before he managed to roll over on his back, he fell into a dead sleep.

He awoke to the beeping of his trusted Casio calculator watch, now so old it beeped out of key like a drunk slurring his speech. He loved using the calculator in front of people. It sent a clear signal that he was old school and proud of it. That was true in some respects at least. He peeled his face from the seat leather, grabbed his bag out of the floorboard, and then slowly wandered into the station. He headed for the nearest bathroom, where he would have to imitate a quick bath. A few cars were now in the lot, but he was still plenty early. The e-mail had stated he was to arrive promptly at 6:30 a.m., and it was now exactly 6:27 a.m. Luckily, the restroom was just inside the door of the main entrance, so he slipped in unnoticed. He wanted to make a good first impression after all. Minutes later he emerged, looking largely unchanged except for a poorly tied tie and an extremely wrinkled shirt. They were nice clothes but so badly disheveled he looked like someone who had been on one long bender—a member of the Rat Pack perhaps.

Sullivan was forty now, but his raffish good looks had suffered none. His nickname "Ice Man" had been both an acknowledgment of his detective skills and of his uncanny resemblance to the character from *Top Gun*. He looked like a young Val Kilmer gratefully, and his appearance caused almost everyone not to take him very seriously. This he liked. Being underestimated was always the best position from which to operate, and so to become a cop, he had offered to take the most dangerous undercover jobs first. He hadn't really had much of a choice after the bust, of course. He might have seen twenty years for the amount of cocaine they had found in his house, his parents' house actually and, of course, their cocaine. They had started him dealing at fourteen, and by nineteen he was the go to guy from Richmond all the way to the Tennessee border. He would have ended up dead like both of them too, if not for some instinct of self-preservation, which had caused him to turn himself in. He wanted to make the people responsible for his parents' death pay for it, so he decided to become the law instead. In the process, he'd helped the police bring down an entire drug ring, reaching all the way to Juarez. It turned out pretending to be someone else was a skill he had an undeniable gift for; a gift he had been cultivating all his life in fact. He'd always been able to blend in easily because he had spent so much time as a kid surrounded by shady people. As a boy, making predictions about how drug addicts were likely to behave was simply a self-defense mechanism; as an undercover cop, it had become an invaluable skill. His instincts bordered on the supernatural. Still, because he had continued volunteering for the most dangerous stings with little or no training, everyone had said he'd be dead in a year; there had even been a pool around the office. He was at the top of everyone's list, but he had proved them all wrong and in the process finally got himself clear of the law. He'd spent exactly half his life breaking the law and the other half prosecuting it.

Thirteen years later to the day of his arrest for cocaine possession, he had become Richmond's most recognizable detective and a minor national celebrity. He had solved the city's most infamous case, the first and only serial killer the town had ever known, dubbed "The Red Neck Killer" by the media. The brutal murders of four college co-eds had set the town on fire with suspicion and fear for two sweltering summers, and for two long years, there hadn't been a single tangible lead, not until Sullivan had followed one of his famous hunches. The final clue was so unbelievable that he still couldn't understand why he had chosen to follow it. But that was part of the nature of his gift. He knew what to pay attention to and what to ignore, especially in people. How many times had he watched an interrogation and known instantly who to believe and who not to? So what if he hadn't been exactly forthcoming about his instincts when those media vultures had swooped in after he had single-handedly caught the Redneck Killer.

"Sullivan, you make the goddamn lie detector obsolete," Dickson had disgustingly acknowledged. "I'm just glad you're on our team," he'd always said and then mockingly, "You are on our team, right?" Some men could never forgive a man his past. Now Dickson had pissed all over his future too. Well, he thought, at least the weather was nice.

Sullivan peered down the hallway to room 717, which opened into the main gallery of the investigations' unit. It was an old room by west coast standards, full of antique mahogany, with a long corridor of separate interrogation suites set up against the adjacent wall. It looked right out of Dragnet and had a kind of retro charm that made him feel somehow at home. It was huge though. The biggest police station he'd ever seen. As he surveyed the room, he saw to his left row after row of phone operators, all typing furiously while talking into headsets. It could have been a customer-service call center in India for all that. He stretched his neck to find the end of the row, but as he did he heard a commanding voice shouting in his direction.

"You. Blondie! You my new detective or ya looking for the beach volleyball courts?"

Sullivan opened his mouth to speak, but before he could do so, the bulldog of a man grabbed him by the arm, leading him toward the interrogation suites. The man's face was beet red, and an unlit cigar dangled precariously from his mouth, which he did not need to remove to shout apparently.

"Sullivan, right?" the man grunted.

"Right, that's me."

He had seen angry police sergeants before, but this was ridiculous.

"Sullivan, I want you to take a look at the verminous collection of wasted potential standing before you."

The man pointed to a small group of detectives huddled against the wall, obviously the ones in question. Each was looking shamefacedly toward the ground.

"These are the best my city has to offer apparently, and right now a woman who brutally murdered her husband is in that interrogation room, as guilty as the cat that ate the fucking canary and then bashed in its goddamned head with a hammer; and not one of these geniuses can get a word out of her. I've heard you're some kind of damn prodigy. Your boss recommends you so highly in fact that I'm absolutely certain you must've shot a little old lady crossing the street right in the fucking back to get transferred with such a glowing recommendation. Carl Dickson hasn't had a nice thing to say about anyone since the day I met him. But, Sullivan, you're in luck. I want you to get in that room and prove to me you are worth the goddamn paper your recommendation is printed on. Enlighten us all with these super-fucking-natural powers of yours. And don't dare come out until she has signed this confession, or you just might end your career as a beat cop writing muthafuckin' parking tickets in El Cajon. I'm Tackett," he said, pointing a finger in his chest. "She's in there. Now go!"

"Don't forget your pen," he said, holding it only inches from Sullivan's face.

He stood dumfounded for a moment.

"What are you waiting for? A tour of your new goddamned office. This is it, kid. Get in there, or get back to Richmond or wherever the hell you came from. And knock twice when she signs it, or get the hell out of my precinct!"

He wasn't sure he could stand there any longer without throwing a punch, so he tiptoed around the sergeant carefully. Tackett was solidly built, but he was an old man, and Sullivan never listened to abuse for very long before taking a shot. He slid silently into the interrogation room and heard the door lock forcefully behind him. *Goddamn, this place was intense.*

He hadn't known exactly what to expect at his first day on the job, but he sure as hell wasn't expecting this. In the corner of the room, behind the desk, sat a woman with straight black hair, pulled back into a headband. She was smoking. She barely looked up when he walked in. The room was spare and even more strangely had no windows or glass. Somehow, someone had clearly forgotten the value of double-sided mirrors. He was truly alone with her then.

Old school. Wow. OK, he thought. *This is make or break.* He could always apply somewhere else. *Mall cop, maybe.*

The woman suddenly looked up, seeming to notice he wasn't quite prepared.

"Boy, they are really scraping the bottom of the barrel now, aren't they? Did all the grown-ups go home, honey?"

The woman was probably in her thirties, late thirties— maybe even forties—but her clothes, jewelry, and not to mention attitude were all Beverly Hills. Since he knew absolutely nothing about the case, he decided to play right along.

"Yeah, they did give up actually. My sergeant just sent me in to entertain you until the place closes."

The woman drew from a lit cigarette seductively, like something right out of an old black-and-white movie. It made him crave a smoke badly; he thought he could taste it. As she exhaled she placed her tongue on the tip of her lip before speaking.

"You must be fresh out of the academy, huh? No, wait. There's something else—ah, you just act young. I see it now. I know a Botox doctor who could fix those crow's feet. That forehead. You've done a lot of worrying in your life. Let's see I put you at about forty-two. No, wait—younger, just forty."

"You're a good guesser," he said, flashing a toothy grin.

The woman laughed.

"Would you like to smoke too?"

"Can you really smoke in here?"

"I can do whatever I want, wherever I want, Detective."

"Speaking of th—"

"Nice transition, Detective," she said, interrupting before he could get a word out. "But look, I have already spoken to all the idiots in charge, and there is nothing left for me to share, I'm afraid."

The woman tilted her head and looked at him with a squint, adjusting the cross around her neck on its chain. She let her hand slide slowly down to her breastbone.

"Tits like these take you places, Detective, help you out of all kinds of messes. But there's something about you. It's odd.

We've just met, but I feel...I don't know how to explain...I feel I can't lie to you. You're almost as good-looking as a movie star. Do you know that?"

"Well," he said, chuckling nervously.

"Are you a real cop," she said, staring directly at him for the first time.

"Look," she whispered, "they locked that door behind you, I think, and I'm feeling kind of hot in here—bothered really—as there are no windows, and we are completely alone. I'm newly single, and if I confess will y—"

The woman started to put her hand inside her black, sheer blouse, almost panting. Sullivan's face flushed as she started to climb over the desk, pushing her chair to the ground.

"Put me on that table," she said pointing, "and I'll tell you absolutely anything you want to know, Detective."

She put out her cigarette in an empty cup, which sizzled, and now she was practically on top of him. He had no idea what to do. He stumbled backward in his chair but fell instead, knocking frantically on the door. No one was there. He pounded now as the woman's hand reached inside his buttoned shirt.

"I'll sign anything you want me to, stud," she purred.

She was now pushing up against him breasts and all. By the time the door finally flew open, he fell through to the other side directly on his face. All around him was laughter. The bulldog sergeant was giving high fives, and people were doubled over in fits, even the detectives, and now the suspect, who was rebuttoning her blouse, reached a hand down to help him up.

"Name's Rodriguez. Undercover squad, Prostitution and Narcotics. Sorry, man, they made me do it."

Sullivan laughed the laugh of a man taken by complete surprise.

"If you're half as good a detective as your boss says, that will probably be the last time any of us will have anything over on you. We couldn't pass on the opportunity," she shrugged, smiling.

Tackett's drill-sergeant demeanor suddenly evaporated; he sounded like someone's sweet old uncle as he reached out his hand to shake. Everyone was now lining up to shake hands and do a proper introduction. The last in line was a guy near his age, who looked him over closely, squinting as they shook hands.

"Ok, Ice Man," he said, imitating the film, "we told you to knock twice. I'm Sheppard. I'll be seein' you around. Try not to solve all the tough cases, OK; save some for us mere mortals."

His reputation had clearly preceded him here. Dickson must have really wanted rid of him after all. Tackett threw an arm around him bear-hug style and pointed.

"The chief's office is all the way in the back, but don't let that guy put you to sleep. He comes across dry as a bone, but he's a barrel of laughs after a couple of shots of Jack Daniels; know what I mean?"

Actually for Sullivan, "dry" sounded pretty good right about now. The morning had already been stressful enough.

Rodriguez strolled by and without looking, under her breath, whispered, "Meant what I said about that movie-star thing."

He watched her walk away admiringly.

"And the Botox," she snickered.

Maybe San Diego wasn't going to be so boring after all.

CHAPTER 4

INCURSION

S he had never seen such a look of concern on Apollon's face in all the years she had known him.

"Please forgive the intrusion," he said, "but it is your husband, he has left this house under very odd circumstances. I fear something dreadful is afoot, madam. He was with his nephew and another man. His face, the second man, stayed most conspicuously hidden, but I caught a glimpse; he looked like a relative, though one I've never met. I have been with him for twenty-four years, and in that whole time, he has never once departed without explaining exactly when he would return."

"I need no convincing," the woman said, throwing on her clothing hurriedly. "My dreams have been full of great terror these last few nights, as if the whole of the heavens is screaming out a warning, but what man listens to a woman?"

She sped down the hallway with Apollon following

rapidly behind. He shouted instructions to their messengers, who then scattered with great haste.

"Apollon, you must tell me everything you saw."

"Yes, I observed through the causeway, madam, because there was something suspicious about the early hour of this appointment, and that...that other man wouldn't let his face be seen, not completely. Though, of course, his nephew being family, I could not protest out of respect. He sent me for drinks after greeting them, but I delayed so as to see for myself what they wanted. They talked for only five minutes, no more. They seemed in good humors, and your husband laughed several times; therefore, I felt it safe to do as he asked. But when I returned, they had vanished, leaving only this."

It was a piece of very old-looking parchment.

"I hope I have not failed him, madam. I pray."

"You have always served him well, Apollon, always."

The woman held the paper in her hands, and they began to shake uncontrollably.

"But this is his own writing," she gasped.

"Yes, madam, it is most strange."

She handed it back to Apollon. The words written clearly:

Your murder is planned this very day by those closest to you. I beg you to depart with us immediately. You are safe nowhere else.

A.

"Is it a forgery?"

Apollon stared at it intently.

"The ink has been on this parchment for some time. It must be very old. But why bring it now if it is to be a warning? If it is a warning, it is a very old one."

"We won't know until we find him."

"I'm right behind you, madam."

"Tell every guard to stand at the ready. I fear they will be needed before the day is done."

———

The man stood over the edge of the bridge, and vomit poured from him until only the bile from his stomach was left. He continued to heave, nevertheless.

"I told you I should not take off my hood," said the man in the cloak to the boy. "You can't imagine what a shock it is for him to see my face."

The man collapsed now onto his knees, too weak to stand. He could vomit no more.

"We can't stay out here for very long, I'm afraid. I need you to get back inside, both of you," said the man in the cloak.

In a weakened voice, the man muttered in response, "I cannot."

They lifted him to his feet and put him back under the cover of the carriage.

"Ey'e but you will. We will need some time in the country. The fresh air will serve you well, my friend. Time is no enemy to us, but being seen even on the city's edge is very dangerous to our cause."

"This is some trick of the gods, the black arts," groaned the man as he heaved yet again.

The boy suddenly spoke, though his voice quivered.

"I'm sorry, sir, but this is the only way to save you. You won't understand any of this for some time, but later it will be a tremendous relief, I assure you. You know that I love you as my own true father, sir. You must trust me and trust the gods."

"You deceive me, boy, with some sorcery," he replied and then wiped his mouth with his sleeve. "I'll have your head on a pi—"

The man's eyes fluttered like loose marbles in their sockets, and then he lost consciousness yet again.

"It's much better this way," the man in the cloak said, consoling the young boy. "He may sleep for days now. The shock is tremendous. Many die from it alone or never fully recover their wits. He will, though. Trust me, trust me," the man said, laughing. "Now put him in the back quickly," he demanded of the boy.

There was much noise in the city behind them, more than usual, but nothing but empty countryside ahead. Above them the last vestiges of the storm clouds that had been brewing since early morning sped past. To the man in the cloak, they looked like ragged soldiers marching off to war, an army of ghosts. He pulled the hood of his tunic up just slightly to see them better. The boy sitting in the carriage looked out at him and thought he saw a fresh tear suddenly race down the man's cheek, and then another.

"Are you injured, sir?" the boy inquired. "Are you hurt?"

"I'm not injured, but I am hurt. I will survive as I always do. It is you I rather worry about, my son."

And with that the man in the cloak wrapped his hands around the boy's throat, almost lovingly and, in one sudden spasm, snapped him at the nape of his neck. The boy's eyes rolled back in his head as a gush of blood poured from his mouth and nose. The man squeezed with all his might, until the last of the air escaped the lungs, and the boy's frail body went limp. It had taken no more than a few seconds. The man walked to the back of the carriage, pulling out a large rug, which he methodically unrolled. The boy's body fit perfectly, and once rolled, no one would never guess anything or anyone was inside. Leaning over the edge of the bridge, he thrust it over, where it smacked against the slow moving water below. He looked to his left and to his right again slowly. An old woman sat perched in filth very near to the bridge's edge. He hadn't noticed her before.

She yelled in his direction, "I seen what ya done. I knows what yer up to."

The man simply ignored her and stared out instead across the point on the horizon where the river disappeared. The sun blazed a crimson red, but a razor-thin slice of moon could be seen low in the sky.

"No, I doubt you do, old woman," he muttered. "I doubt you do."

CHAPTER 5

CASE 1032

S ullivan walked into the office, which had "Chief of Police, Robert P. Tierney" inscribed in gold lettering on the door.

"Detective Sullivan, welcome to SDPD," came a voice from across the room. "Have a seat. I'm Bob Tierney." He began to sit, but Tierney extended a handshake, bringing him to his feet again. "I hope they weren't too rough on you out there. A little hazing is good for everybody's morale around here from time to time. That Rodriguez is a piece of work, isn't she?"

Sullivan managed a half-hearted smile.

"One of the best we have, to be honest."

Tierney slid a pair of bifocals up the bridge of his nose and pulled at a stack of papers, which he had clearly been reading.

"Says here and I quote, 'you have been the most decorated officer on the force and your skills as a detective, your intuition are unrivaled.' Now I have to ask myself what would compel a curmudgeon like Carl Dickson to say such a thing if it wasn't true? And yet here you are. Page two is brief, but far more telling if you ask me," Tierney said, raising his eyebrows and tilting his head. "I'm quoting again, 'has serious self-control issues, and though they haven't had direct bearing on his work with the force, risks seriously compromising the moral and civic values expected of all officers in the city of Richmond.'" Tierney chuckled. "Sounds like a pretty personal beef to me, especially if I know Carl like I think I do. I'll bet you got into his cookie jar and stole some sweets, huh?" An awkward pause followed. He started to speak, but Tierney cut him off.

"Have you read your Emerson, Detective?" Tierney shifted in his seat, looked up and pointed to a framed picture on the wall. It was one of those ancient and faded frames filled in with old yarn cross-stitching, which read, "A man must never be too moral, lest he miss out on the finer things in life."

"I don't know, sir; I don't read much, to be honest," he answered.

"That's too goddamned bad. A man who won't read is a fool. Reading improves the soul and teaches refinement." Tierney seemed to reconsider for a moment and then waived his hands through the air with a groan. "I never read Emerson either, to be honest. My mother had a thing for sewing and for making sure I remembered to have some fun. Look, let me level with you. I don't care much about your past

—any of it. You make for an interesting read on paper, and I'll bet you are what this recommendation says you are, more or less. Out here in Southern California, we have just two threats to police work: criminals and the press. Both are equally dangerous. If you make me, or the force, look bad, I'll make it hurt for you in ways you can't imagine. I know every police chief from here to Kalamazoo, and if you think this job was a demotion, just you try me." Tierney finally looked up from his papers. "A cop has to be disciplined to be effective, and I can tell just by looking at that goddamn suit and not to mention that piece-of-shit car of yours that was sitting in the lot that you have very little of either."

He thought the car would go unnoticed. *Damn.* Tierney sat up in his seat.

"Tell me something, Detective. What could you tell an investigator about Bob Tierney after only one meeting? Please, you have permission to speak freely."

Sullivan's gaze suddenly hardened, losing its boyish playfulness. He went into an almost primal state, the trance that overtook him when he was keenly observing. *It was a test then.* He brought his fingertips together to a point before speaking, his pupils appearing to almost dilate.

"Well, go on," Tierney said, chiding him.

"Frankly, sir, Bob Tierney is a true professional, but he plays his cards very, very close to his chest. He uses his eyeglasses as a prop to imply thoughtfulness, not from necessity, and shitty wall art to distract people from his real motives. He claims the art was made by his mother, but this is very doubtful since the Salvation Army price tag is still clearly visible, from underneath, on the back. Probably his mother is still alive, though his use of the past tense suggests he has a poor relationship with her." Sullivan pulled his hands together behind his head and leaned back in his seat. "He has family working in the department and, based on a strong physical resemblance, is related to one detective— Sheppard—whose name was changed to his mother's maiden name to avoid any suggestion of nepotism. Sheppard is subpar, since talent would erase the need for subterfuge, and endlessly seeks the approval of his father, causing him to take needless risks on the job. Bob Tierney feels guilt over both of these issues, naturally, but he genuinely respects cops, which suggests he used to be one, so he's worked his way up through the ranks. This is why he doesn't make eye contact when hurling threats against them, because he knows they are empty. He is actually very well read, though he likes to pretend to be more superficial than he is, probably to preserve the sense that he is still just one of the gang, though in his current position as chief, he knows he most certainly is not." Sullivan suddenly looked up, stopping himself. Tierney's face was unmistakably flushed, drawn, but he did not seem angry exactly.

"I can see why Carl Dickson didn't want you around. That's remarkable."

He had been right on every point, it seemed. Tierney sat back down and picked up a large manila folder from his desk.

"Here is your first case," Tierney said, holding it out with a chilly look in his eye. "It's from the basement, a cold case, eleven years ice cold. This should keep your self-control issues at bay for at least—oh, I don't know—the next year or two, but do take your time."

He grimaced as he took the folder from Tierney's hand. "With all due respect, sir, I think my abilities clearly demonstrate that I can handle something mo—"

"More what?" Tierney snapped. "Take every case I give you seriously, Detective Sullivan. "You were right about my reading habits though," he said without looking up. "Tell me, have your read your Sherlock Holmes, Detective?"

"No, sir, but I saw the movie—I think."

"You know, there is no such person actually," Tierney said ruefully. "He's only a figment of Conan Doyle's imagination."

"OK, sir, if you say so," he said sheepishly.

"Holmes says when you have eliminated all the possibilities, whatever remains, however unlikely, must be the truth. I would think a man like yourself would have read some of it—your powers of analysis being what they are. Every man has a blind spot, Detective. Try not to forget that."

"I won't forget it," he said dryly.

"One last thing. How could you see the resemblance after meeting my son just once? That's incredible."

"There's a picture of you two playing golf together right over there on the wall," he said pointing. "It says, *Father Son Golf Tournament*."

Tierney sniffed, "So it does." His patience had clearly run out though, and he rose from his chair, escorting him to the door.

"Enjoy the city. This town can be a lot of fun for a young guy like yourself."

"Sir, if I may ask?"

"Yes?"

"Earlier you said my car *was* parked in the lot? That's an unusual shift in tense."

"Yeah, I had it towed; you were in my spot. You can pick it up at impound for about four hundred and fifty bucks, I think. It will give you a chance to learn your way around, meet people. Think of it as a self-guided orientation," Tierney said, laughing out loud. "And don't forget to close the door behind you."

CHAPTER 6

THE GLASS CASE

Downy stared at the view across the campus quad with his arms crossed. Students seemed to move in packs silently; through the tinted glass, from his fifth-floor perch, they looked orderly and thoughtful. They weren't. Like cities at night, they looked rather beautiful at a distance. Up close though, in the light of day, they were full of pathos, curses, and complaints. Not all of them, of course. Not Samara Lee Patterson. He looked at his phone, the message light was blinking, and he thought it would be wise to phone his wife. Her voice would help cancel out some of the uncomfortable feelings at least—help calm him down. Randomly, he thought of her thighs, his wife's, and, of course, the short black skirt that she wore when she wanted to get his attention. But then there was Samara. It was *Samara* who had him all charged up. He allowed himself a moment to think about her too—the simple dress, which hung so perfectly off her shoulders, the soft nape of her neck, the olive-colored skin. Perfect lips. And, of course, that tattoo across her back left shoulder, a Latin script. He'd barely made out the word: *veritas*. Truth. Lots of kids wrote things like that on themselves these days—reminders perhaps of what was important. Samara, of course, was a scholar like her father though and was already reading Latin by the time she was twelve. It had been their secret language so many years ago. His imagination finished the daydream, placing some beads of sweat on her chest and the hungry sound of her voice in his ear. He interrupted himself and pushed the blinking button, almost punching a hole in it.

"Uh, yello. Professor Downy, I need a moment of your time some day this week; I wonder if...well I'm calling from the prec—"

He punched for his secretary, ignoring the voice and the rest of the message.

"Janine, could you put all my messages through until tomorrow? I'm feeling a bit of a fever coming on, and I'll be heading home for a nap."

"Of course, Professor," came the voice on the other end.

"Janine, could you stop calling me that, for God's sake?"

"No, Professor, not when I so enjoy how much it bothers you."

"Thank you, Janine."

"I hope you feel better, boss," she replied.

He slipped down the back staircase, which he always used when he wanted to avoid getting held up. His car waited only a few feet from the back entrance. He would have been a professor for the parking alone, never mind the paycheck. He slid into the bucket seat of his Porsche Roadster and sped off like a banshee, hair blowing in the wind. He knew it was imperative to get home to his wife, who he hoped would be willing to get a drink and wear a certain piece of clothing that he could then carefully remove. He never grew tired of that routine. But today, as he turned the volume knob all the way up, there was a third member at the party. It was summer after all, and what hurt could come from letting himself dream a little.

————

The cloaked man pulled the carriage to a halt under a small cover of trees in the otherwise open countryside. He had ridden until there was nothing man-made in sight in any direction. Stopping at last, he grabbed the cask of water from beneath his feet and drank voraciously. It was the best taste of anything he could remember. His plan was going exactly as he had imagined, and most importantly he had escaped without notice, save for the vagrant, who was of no concern. Her words would be considered those of a raving fool. It pained him deeply to kill the boy though, but life and death had come to mean something far different to him of late. It had been quick in any case, though certainly not painless. Most of all it had been necessary, and in that regard he had always maintained a clearness of purpose and of conscience. The boy was not truly his own blood anyway, though he had been exceedingly fond of him. This time, more than any other, he had killed out of necessity. As shrewd as the boy was, he might even have agreed with the decision himself, if he'd had the chance. No difference now, it was the next twenty-four hours that presented the most danger to his plan. He was being followed, of that he was sure, but he must not let them catch up to him.

It was now completely dark. The birds in the grove, usually silent by this hour, were strangely unsettled, and he could hear the howling of wild animals far off in the distance. The man pulled from his cloak the stack of letters, finding the one from his dear friend and teacher. He read it slowly. At the bottom was the list of names. His hands shook uncontrollably, and the veins in his neck swelled. His eyes hardened before a flood of tears raced down his cheeks. He knew the names well, but the confirmation was more powerful and disturbing than he had imagined. It all made such sense now. How had he not seen it coming?

There was blood at the bottom of his boot and up his arm, now dried. It was not the boys. He hadn't had time to clean it, and now he thought of a bath. Probably the safest place for him, but he couldn't risk reentering the city. The river stream was all the way at the bottom of the ravine, but he would be able to watch the carriage from there at least. It wasn't likely his hostage would wake up anyway. He had slept for three days after the first shock himself, not to mention the days of sickness afterward. Gratefully, you only suffered the sickness once with such acuteness. After that, it was purely a matter of maintenance. Plenty of water and, of course, as many sugar cubes as you could stomach without going stark raving mad. He reached into his pocket and pulled two out, popping them into his mouth. He could feel them taking effect instantly. He had felt a cold sweat coming on, the nauseous, but now the relief of the drug was undeniably pleasurable. He looked into the back of the carriage at the man sleeping. He looked like a child, peaceful and harmless, as all men do when they slumber. He punched at the ribs.

"Hey, old man, you in there," he prodded with a fake growl. There was no response. "Sleep it off, my friend. We will have our day together soon. The future belongs to us."

CHAPTER 7

Downy's car sailed silently into the garage of his home overlooking Mission Bay. It was empty, which disappointed him mightily. It could mean but one thing: Naomi was trapped at work. He reached into his pocket to look at his messages. It read six. It was a lot, even for someone in as much demand as he had been lately. Only a very few close friends had his number now. It was the only way he could get any work done. Sure enough, Naomi was the first two.

Be home late...sorry my love. Eat without me.
N

And then a voice mail saying the same thing. Then a number he did not know appeared. It too was a text.

Your secretary is a pushover...gave me your digits...sorry, but I have to see you...Woody's at 7?...tell Naomi not to wait up...

Your dutiful student,

Sam(ara)

His pulse raced. It was worse than he thought. He put the phone down and stared into the rearview mirror. Samara must have remembered that Woody's had been his and Charlie's favorite drinking spot. Why couldn't Naomi have been at home, waiting for him tonight of all nights? It was very bad luck, and a familiar but almost forgotten feeling came over him of the exhilaration of misdeeds. It had been a long time since such an opportunity had dangled itself in front of him, one so enticing at least. Age, relationship, proximity to his wife—there were a thousand reasons he should simply decline. He laughed at the pressure he suddenly felt. He had done nothing wrong, and already he was trying to figure out how to rationalize the situation. It ended badly any way you looked at it, and so that was that. He looked at his watch. It was 6:00 p.m. In an hour she would be waiting for him. His other option was reheated Mexican food and bad TV for the whole evening. It would be easy enough to get away and go out drinking with the guys. It would give him time to explain things to Samara and put out that fire before it ever started.

He put his fingers to the keypad and muttered aloud, "This is the grown-up thing to do. Yeah, sure, exactly," he said before typing:

Samara,

See you at 7.

———

Downy realized as he pulled onto Third Street that he hadn't been to Woody's for years—however many he couldn't count. While he had been Charlie Patterson's favorite grad student and protégé, the two had become a permanent fixture there every Friday night. Woody's wasn't your typical college bar though. No one yelled. Whatever your reasons for wanting to drink in peace, or even by yourself, you could rest well assured people would respect you. It was also a primo date spot. Dark enough even in the day to feel like you were part of the wallpaper. You could blend in. The gourmet Greek coffee, still boiled, helped flush the toxins of whatever poison was your pick. He missed simple pleasures like these now more than ever. He thought of Charlie and their endless conversations in the back, darkest corner of the place, a table that was reserved for them exclusively. Any two guys that spent as much on fine scotch as they did "had earned a regular spot," the owner had said. He had once threatened to hang a plaque in their honor with their names on it. Both were shocked when a month later one appeared. Charlie had jokingly dubbed their booth "the couch," in honor of the picture of Freud just above the table. It had made the both of them laugh uncontrollably, especially when they got drunk and started talking about their fathers, which happened almost every night. Two glasses of scotch erased all need for self-analysis, thankfully. Tonight though, he had to stop thinking of his old friend. He was there to see Samara, and drinking like that was out of the question.

He remembered with sober clarity the question he had once posed to Charlie during one of their all-night orgies on philosophy: "What do we do when the ones we love die?" It was the only thing he ever truly felt lost talking about, and he was sorry as soon as he asked it. It was too heavy a remark for what was usually a light occasion, a chance to decompress from work. Charlie's response stung now.

"You must go on living. Bury the dead. They stink up the joint."

Typical Charlie. He was a hard man to bury though.

It was at that same table that Charlie had forced him to tell his stories about Roman history. Charlie had been the teacher for so long that he had never really considered himself any kind of authority. When he finished, Patterson had applauded.

"You've far outgrown my teaching, Noah," he finally admitted. "I'm serious; you know this subject better than anyone in the field, myself included. I have nothing left to teach you, I'm afraid." Then at the end of the conversation, he had produced the tape. He had secretly recorded everything Downy had said into a tiny recorder without telling him. "My dear boy, here is the first few chapters of your new book. Just have my secretary transcribe it for you, and you should be able to finish by Christmas easily. I will submit it to my publishers, and then you can cash big fat checks in perpetuity. Drinks are on you from now on though, OK?"

And that night they had both laughed hard, but early the

next morning, he was wide awake, working on chapter two of his multivolume history of Rome, beginning with the strange twins, Romulus and Remus, credited with Rome's founding and ending with Cleopatra's dramatic death in Egypt. There was still more to tell, of course—the death of Caesar; the reassessment entire of Caesar himself, who to both Downy and Charlie was no tyrant, more hero; and finally the ascension of his adopted nephew Octavian, one of the shrewdest men in all of Rome, whose reign truly began the golden age of Rome. To Downy though, the death of Caesar marked the end of something that was never recovered. For him, Caesar was the ultimate Roman. His book had begun right there in Woody's with Patterson as the ever-eager audience.

Unbelievably, it had happened exactly as Charlie predicted, checks and all, then came the documentary film, and then, of course, being made advisor to the miniseries. He had even met Naomi while on set. She was playing Cleopatra's sister, Arsinowe. Gratefully, Naomi's job had lasted only a day, since Cleopatra had had her sister killed, fearful that she too would try to take the throne. He remembered telling Naomi that she died with great majesty. He hadn't been joking, but she had cracked up anyway. In some ways he owed Charlie Patterson his whole life, and when he died suddenly, so unexpectedly, he found he could hardly breathe, much less work for months. Even Naomi couldn't help. He knew he should have been there with Charlie on the boat that day, but he'd backed out at the last second when his publisher demanded another volume of his series. It was the first and only time anyone had given him a hard deadline.

Some timing. How often had they both talked about the strange Roman conception of fate? Downy had been the first to know. It was Nazim, their boat handler, who had made the call. His sorrowful voice over the phone sounded ancient and foreign, distant. He strangely remembered the calls to prayer he could hear in the background, ringing out in seeming looped echo, so awful in their finality. He had screamed at Nazim to go find Charlie, but Nazim could only weep himself.

"Mr. Charlie has been lost overboard, and he is not with us any longer, sir. I am so terribly sorry. I have lost him. I do not know how. He is gone." At the funeral Nazim had fallen to his knees and begged Downy's forgiveness for not looking out for his dear friend more carefully. Nazim was a good man though and had done nothing wrong. It was better not to think of these things. His mood was sinking until he thought of Samara again. He remembered looking for her at the funeral, but she had been a no-show. Her mother claimed it had been simply too much to bear and that she wouldn't leave the back garden, except to sleep for a few hours in Charlie's favorite hammock. She was a piece of Charlie in so many ways, and it felt good to be near her now, even if her beauty did scare the hell out of him. Now if he could just figure out how not to sleep with her.

CHAPTER 8

"Wait up, Detective!" the voice came from across the room. Sullivan was headed for the door, manila folder under his arm. It was the bulldog-turned-softy sergeant who had been railing at him earlier. "Let me give you a lift over to impound. I can get Rita to knock half off the cost at least. We dated in high school. Well, she let me play with her boobs once anyway." Tackett seemed like an over-sized teddy bear but looked like a man who suffered from permanent hypertension. He was a bit more than overweight and far too sweaty. "Lemme get you a drink tonight and give you a real introduction to this city."

"Uhh, that's really tempting, but you know I gotta get a place still, so I need to—"

"If you think you will find a place to move into tonight or even in the next month, sport, let me tell you ya got another thing coming. This is Southern Cali, boss. Come on, I know a place you can stay temporarily until good real estate becomes available."

"OK then, I'm with you I suppose, Sergeant."

They jumped into Tackett's black SUV. SUVs virtually filled the lot, seeming like replicas lined up in perfect formation.

"You ever get in the wrong one by mistake?" Sullivan mused.

"Nah, this one is always covered in bird shit, because I'm too cheap to wash it."

"Oh, OK." He realized he might have gotten Tackett all wrong. Perhaps they were kindred spirits after all. He also realized they were leaving the lot.

"What about my car?" he said.

"Don't worry about it. We can get it tomorrow; it couldn't be in a safer place."

He leaned back, accepting that Tackett seemed to be in charge, and not just at the office.

"San Diego has a ton of classy bars, but that's not where we're headed."

"Thank goodness," he replied. "I'm starting to get the feeling this is more of a planned date than a spontaneous get-together."

Tackett drove in silence while Sullivan surveyed the cityscape. He swerved the SUV suddenly onto a side street, down a dark tree-covered driveway.

"Or maybe a professional hit by the looks of things," he muttered nervously.

He peered, squinting into the darkness, before they finally emerged onto a vast flat spot overlooking the ocean.

"Best view in town and not ten people know about it," Tackett said, pointing out over the seemingly endless ocean.

"Wow."

"I pulled your file, kid. It's impressive work you've done in Richmond. You know what though, Richmond is a pretty-small fishbowl. Out here you're swimming in a whole ocean of it."

The car finally pulled to a stop. Tackett reached into his coat pocket and pulled out a flask.

"Open the glove box," he said. Sullivan complied and found a stack of paper cups and a small plastic bottle of Coca-Cola. "Jack and Coke OK with you?"

"Sure. You really know how to make a gal feel special," he said, batting his eyelashes.

"What is it they call you, Ice Cube?"

"No, actually Ice Man is the correct pronunciation. This is after the actor who is considered decadently handsome by the way, or at least was."

"Yeah, yeah, I saw the fucking movie," Tackett said, pouring. "Look, Sullivan, if I might ask that our conversation tonight stay just between the two of us—I know that's asking a lot since we just met, but I need to know that you and I are the only two discussing this topic. If I find out you've told anyone, I won't be able to offer my help again."

"Help? Please, Sergeant, go on; this sounds juicy."

"That case you got from Tierney today, Case 1032, right?"

"Yeah?" he said, looking down at the folder in the floorboard.

"That's an old case around here. You're not the first guy to be given a chance to crack that nut. How was your meeting with Tierney by the way?"

"Fine, I guess."

"Tell me what do you think of Bob so far? Did he do that stupid routine where he asks you to analyze him?"

"Yeah, as a matter of fact, what the hell was that? He does that to everybody?"

"Drink up," Tackett said.

He slammed the Jack and Coke, remembering its taste from the night at the lake with Caroline, the true beginning of his trip in some ways.

"He seems like he does things by the book. Maybe he tries a little too hard to seem human. I don't know; I just met him really."

"I've known Bob since the academy. We went through together. Everybody called him Robby then, believe it or not. By the time he was thirty though, it was definitely Robert. He became head honcho at thirty-seven, and then he made everyone at the precinct call him chief, even me, which is funny because the job was mine actually—for forty-eight hours anyway. Then Bob dialed in one of his big favors from Sacramento. Bob has the soul of a politician, Sullivan, and to him using political favors to get what he wants is as natural as breathing for most of us. I even went home and told my wife when I got it and then, of course, had to untell her when they took it away. It's been twenty-two years, and Bob has never once said a word to me about it. That's his style. To his credit he has given me the maximum raise every year and has given me a ridiculous number of commendations. His way of paying penance or tribute or whatever, I'm sure." Tackett paused to refill their cups. "Don't get me wrong, Sullivan. I am not the type to hold grudges, but I want you to know that Bob Tierney is a man who is always looking out for himself first and often at the expense of others. "Case 1032," Tackett said, pointing, "the first guy to get that case was Danny Fleming. Fleming was a great cop and a great friend." Tackett stopped pouring into his cup and turned up the flask before he spoke. "He is the reason why I became a cop, frankly. He played a couple of years of NFL football actually, before injuring his shoulder with the Raiders. Then he joined the force, so he could stay around some action, I guess. He was a family man with two kids. He liked getting a cat down from a tree as much as busting a crook though. Everyone in San Diego loved the guy, in spite of his playing for the wrong team. He and Tierney never got along. Bob thought he was too old school, and, of course, he hates anyone who is naturally popular. It cuts into his theory that the wheels must be greased for you to win in this world. Once Tierney became the chief, he purposely gave Fleming the worst cases—1032 started out as a simple breaking and entering actually. Someone called it in anonymously. But no one could explain all the blood found at the scene, and none of it showed up in the DNA databases, then or now for that matter. Fleming only had the case for a couple of months before he disappeared."

"Disappeared?"

"Yeah, he hasn't been seen since. That was twelve years ago now. He left for work on a Monday morning and just never showed up. Never found his car or him, like the earth just fucking swallowed him."

"You think it was related to this case?"

"I'm sure of it, though I don't know exactly how."

"Have you looked through the files yourself?"

"Numerous times. There's nothing much in there. I even had some of the initial suspects followed and tapped a couple of phones. Nothing came of it."

"Then maybe you're wrong."

"That's always possible," he said, handing over the flask. "But I don't think so. Not this time. This case has become, very quietly mind you, one that Bob Tierney has a personal stake in, and that's what scares me the most. The pressure from Sacramento to squelch this before it ever becomes a big story in the press is immense. What else did Bob tell you about the case, if anything?"

"Only that it was ice cold and to take my time. I figured I was getting a demotion right out of the gate."

"Yeah, I figured as much, the son of a bitch. It's backwardass psychology. He knows a competitive guy like yourself will get all over it, so you can move on to bigger and better things. Look, Sullivan, after Fleming disappeared, the case got handed over to a guy named Nicky Jensen, Fleming's partner. Finish it," Tackett said, pointing to the flask. "It's only the fact that they disappeared four years apart that's kept this case from becoming a scandal already."

"What do you mean?"

"You are the third detective who has been given Case 1032. The other two have never been heard from again."

CHAPTER 9

Downy rounded the corner on Third, and he could feel butterflies in his stomach. He hadn't anticipated feeling so nervous, and he actually stopped walking so he could take a deep breath. *OK, just go in, you idiot. This was your big idea.* When he entered the room, it was unusually bright, the late-afternoon sun still pouring in from outside. At the bar sat Samara. She had clearly changed for the evening. She now wore a sleeveless black dress cut high at the thigh. Her shoes, black stilettos, dangled from her toes. This was all a very bad idea he suddenly realized. But it was too late. Samara smiled and rose to greet him as he walked in. She already had a drink in hand.

"I'm so glad you came," she said, hugging him tightly.

Her lips brushed just slightly against his neck when they embraced, and he almost lost it. He glanced down at her shoulder and could see the tattoo's dark ink against her skin.

He opened his mouth to speak, but Samara put her hand to it. She pointed to the bar.

"That's a double shot of their finest scotch. Drink now, and then meet me in the back," she said, gesturing to the far corner.

He watched her walk away silently and reached for the drink. As he lifted it, out of the corner of his eye, he could see the second-floor balcony, where he had sat so many times with Charlie. It was empty and dark. The scotch went down smoothly and was warm in his stomach. He looked for Samara but couldn't see well in the darkness. *What the hell was she up to?* he thought. In the corner, just out of view of the bar, he saw her leaning against one of those old-fashioned red-phone booths from downtown London. The booth was new, or at least he didn't remember it being there before. It *had* been a while since he'd been in, too long. Samara stood in silhouette, like someone right out of a movie. She used her finger to beckon him toward her.

"Man, the scotch is really good; I can see why you two spent so much time here," she said, looking around. "Get inside," she said, pointing with her head to the booth. His head was humming now from the shot, from everything.

"OK," he heard himself saying.

As he slid nervously inside, she appeared without warning, pressing against him and without a word her mouth was on his. They were trapped together in the booth, and she squeezed the door closed behind them. He had no space to move away, so instead he surrendered himself to the feeling of her lips against his, her body pressing against him. Worse was that he could sense real emotion coming from her. This had been saved up and planned for. The fear and exhilaration were impossible to disentangle. Finally, when it seemed like they'd both have to gasp for air, she stopped. They both froze. Her head slid down against his chest. She held it there for many seconds without moving. He was afraid to speak. Finally, she looked up at him; her eyes were misty and her pupils dilated.

"I hope you enjoyed that as much as I did, 'cause it's the last time it can ever happen," she said in a low voice. "Let me look at you," she said, squinting. He could almost recognize the face of the teenage girl she had been when he had last seen her. "Before we get out of this booth, I want you to know two things: one," she said, raising her finger, "I will never tell another living soul what just happened, especially not your wife. Two, if I ever decided to seduce you, there is absolutely nothing you could do but be seduced, so don't ever preach to me about principles and doing the right thing and all that. It's good for the both of us that that's not what I want. But we did have to do this, so we can say it's past us so that you know where you stand and I know where I stand."

"Where is that exactly?" he said.

Samara smiled. "On even footing. I'm not a little girl anymore, Noah. I need us to be equals." It startled him to hear her use his name. "I need to talk to you about something very important, and if there is sexual tension between us, that will be impossible. We both know you are married to a woman you love. You might even fall in love with me too. That happens. But it won't stop you from returning to her afterward. And who could blame you? I've seen her pictures; and to keep your attention for all these years, she must really be something. I've lost already. I'm not worried you'll tell her," she said, laughing playfully. "People are excellent at keeping secrets of their own. It's everybody else's they can't shut up about."

"How old are you again?" he said, staring into her eyes.

"Twenty-five next year," she said, pulling herself out of the booth and him with her.

They finally took a seat at the table. The waiter appeared immediately.

"Since we have opened one of our oldest and finest bottles of Macallan, shall I assume you will be having another glass?"

"Of course."

The waiter's expression could not betray the fact that he had seen all that had transpired; graciously he chose not to make eye contact. He was being overly polite.

"I will be right back with two Macallans, an exceptional choice."

"Thank you."

Samara looked all around. "Man, you guys knew all the best spots, didn't you? This place is so great. Look at all this stuff."

The room looked like one giant antique. At one end a giant boar's head jutted from the wall, face forever locked in a defiant grimace. An ancient, hulking jukebox still spun old 45s. Nat King Cole was crooning about his orange-colored sky as she scanned the room.

"It's like...like Sherlock Holmes study," she said wistfully.

"It's exactly like that," he said, looking around. He looked at her finally regaining some of his wits.

"What's going on, Samara? What's this all about?"

"It's just arrived," she said, looking over his shoulder. The waiter placed the drinks in front of them.

"Thanks," they said in unison.

"It's a long story, actually. What did you tell Naomi?"

"I'm out drinking with the guys."

"So you really were hoping we'd end up at a hotel together?" she said, arching her eyebrows.

His face flushed bright scarlet.

"It's OK. I'm gonna be smart enough for both of us, Professor. Here's to drinking with the boys," she said, raising her glass.

CHAPTER 10

"I'm sorry for what I said about sleeping together, OK," Samara said. "I sounded arrogant and foolish. It was obnoxious, and I'm sorry."

"Don't worry about it," he said.

"I can't believe I kissed you though," she laughed. The drinks were starting to loosen her tongue a bit. "It was a dare I made to myself a long time ago. You were my first crush. It's bittersweet to think back on those days. My dad was always happiest when you were around, most himself. You know my mother hated you a little bit. You made her jealous with the relationship you two had. But, of course, she loved you too." She paused, and her eyes suddenly glazed over with a faraway look. "I need to talk to you about my dad. You knew him better than anyone, I think. I imagine talking about him frankly and honestly might be a very hard thing for you to do with me. You know I've been in Italy for the past three years. I came home a month ago and was going through some of his things, and I found something. I wanted to ask you about it. Did my dad have any close friends you know of, or, you know, where there any other women who might have been close to him?"

"Charlie?" he asked, shaking his head in disbelief. "No, I mean if you mean in any way romantic—"

"No, Samara, I never knew your dad to pursue anyone but your m—"

"He cheated once for sure, but that time I know about," she interrupted. "He and my mother had that one out right in front of me, when I was a kid."

"Oh, I'm sorry. I didn't know."

"Of course not; it was before; it was a long time ago." She reached into the purse slung over the arm of her chair.

"I found this," she said, presenting a piece of folded paper.

"This is dad's handwriting:"

Sweets,

I love you more than I have words to express. Don't be afraid. We will see each other again soon. Right now I am trapped in an impossible situation, but soon I will be able to come to you. I love you always...

"What's really strange is that before I left for Italy this note was definitely not where I found it when I came back. I had already opened the box I found it in *before* I left, looking for a picture of him to take with me. Somebody must have put it there after. I'm absolutely sure of it."

"OK," he said, "but this is not necessarily a note to another—"

"I agree," she said. "In fact as far as I know, I am the only person he ever called Sweets. Then again, maybe I don't know everything I thought I did."

"Could your mom have accidentally put it there?"

"No. I asked her repeatedly, and she knew nothing about those boxes. She has been staying with her sister for the last few years; she's barely been home since he passed. Tell me, what impossible situation was my dad ever involved in?"

"Couldn't it just be an old note?" he said, turning it over.

"Don't you think it's strange that it's not signed? My dad always signed his name in letters. I have tons of others he has written, and he signed his name in every single one of them. I can't help think there is an intentional vagueness going on to hide something."

He scratched at his temple.

"There's something else," Samara said, lowering her gaze. "Last year I went to Egypt. I felt horrible for not being at the funeral and wanted to see Nazim. He was the last person to see dad alive, and I thought it would help me get, I don't know, closer to what happened. When I arrived they said Nazim was away, but then the strangest thing happened: they all acted like they didn't know who I was. It was as if they had never met me. My Arabic isn't perfect, but they acted as if my dad was completely unknown to them, like they had erased all memory of us. It was spooky. It frightened me. I spent a lot of time at their house as a teenager, you know? There was even a painting I did of a street in Sakkara that they kept on their wall. It had been taken down or thrown away. Nazim swore to me when I was a girl that he would treasure it always. You know how sincere a man he is. I can't believe he would take it down. Maybe what happened with dad was too much for him, I guess. But why would his family ignore me like that? They couldn't tell me when he would return either. Something very strange was going on in that house. They weren't cruel to me, just completely distant, like absolute strangers."

"That is very odd."

"I left two weeks later without any answers. I tried to see them again before I left, but they seemed reluctant to let me back in the house. They kept apologizing and said to wait until Nazim came back and he could speak with me, clear things up, but they were completely vacant. I left sobbing like a fool. I've never felt so alone. The whole city seemed hostile and dangerous to me after that. I started feeling like I was being watched."

"I can only imagine."

"Noah, have you talked to Nazim since the funeral?"

"Yeah, a couple of years ago. He still maintains our boat, and as far as I know, the payment still goes through each month. I always expected to return someday. Is it possible they simply didn't recognize you?"

"I don't know. I can't see how. I have changed, of course, but not *that* much."

"I can't imagine what's going on with them," he said earnestly.

"Look, I have been through a lot these past few years. More than I have time to tell you. I met someone and fell in love. It could have been perfect, but I sent him away; worse than that actually, I stood him up. We were supposed to get married, but I couldn't get my head straight. I had no idea why at the time, and now he hates me, of course. I started drinking too much, to forget. Finally, because my mother demanded it, I sat down to talk to someone about dad. One of mom's colleagues actually—a shrink. She said exactly what you'd expect, I'm having post-paternal longings that can only be expressed through rage and that I am transferring this distrust to all the men in my life. It's all to deal with my feelings of abandonment, that dad left without saying good-bye."

Downy thought of the picture of Freud on the back wall and looked up to the booth.

"If my dad wrote that note, who put it there?" she asked, snapping his attention back to her.

"If that letter was written to me—" She looked at him intently. "Do you think it's possible it *was* my dad?"

"I'm sure there is a logical explanation, Samara," he said, putting his hand on hers. His hand looked worn and beaten next to her smooth, brown skin.

"That's why I need you," she said. Her eyes were watering at the corners now. "There may come a time when I need you to tell me that my shrink was right about me. I will listen to you because I trust you. But I can't believe these things are just coincidences. That note was planted there. Maybe someone wanted me to see it to make a point or something. But why did my dad write it and when? Did he think my mom was a bad situation? He never acted like that."

"No, that doesn't seem right to me either," he said flatly.

"Can you think of a reason my dad might want to disa—"

"Don't, Samara; don't put yourself through that thought. Let me call Nazim and speak to him. I'm sure there is an explanation. I promise you, we will get to the bottom of this, OK?" He squeezed her hand.

"Thank you," she said. "I knew I could count on you."

CHAPTER 11

Downy peered in through the glass at the rows of assembled students. There were undoubtedly crashers, since the room was overly full; some students sat awkwardly and uncomfortably in the aisles, and some were even standing against the back wall. You could tell which of the ones standing were actually enrolled by the scowls on their faces. Oh well, he had warned them to be early if they wanted a seat. The crashers smiled pleasantly, trying to blend in in their chairs. Downy's lecture on the life of Julius Caesar was the most downloaded video of its kind on YouTube. Naomi liked to joke with him that he was almost as popular as porn. He would have been more nervous if there were only twenty people in the room, but a group this large was faceless. Except for one, of course. He scanned the room for her. She'd been bounced to the third row today, but there she sat, looking expectant, maybe even a bit nervous. It calmed him. He took a deep breath before he walked in. As he strode to the podium, the lights flickered dramatically, suddenly causing the room to yah in unison. In the darkness you could feel the tension building. Then Mozart's symphony blasted through the left speaker, then through the right, and finally in full stereo. The screen lit up dramatically, followed by a blitz of techno-laced heavy metal. Then came the shot of the bust of Caesar, probably the only one actually made during his lifetime, which morphed into the face of a real man— blood followed by skin and tissue filling in over the marble, the dark, intelligent eyes settling into their sockets. Technology could literally bring history back to life. Finally, what everyone was waiting for came, the full montage of blood, sex, and death from the miniseries. Many cheered. It had become an unexpected hit, especially with the college crowd, based much on it's very frank and accurate portrayal of the Roman sexual ethic and, of course, the body count at the end of each episode. The shows real success though had come from Downy's unique ability to connect with Caesar. Even the crankiest of history buffs were impressed by his ability to capture the essence of the man many considered the most important person in the history of the world. The floodlights at the bottom of the stage went up suddenly illuminating Downy in dramatic silhouette.

"How's that for a title? Most important man in the history of the world," he asked his students, testing his microphone as the music slowly faded out and the lights returned to normal. He paused. "Watch your back, Jay Z. Watch your back." It was just the kind of dry humor that had made him a teacher everyone wanted to take. You never quite knew when he might say something completely off the wall in the midst of trying to make a serious point. He had once claimed that Mark Antony had bedded many famous mistresses in his life and was briefly engaged to both Lady Amanda Bynes and Lady Gaga.

In a crowd of seventy-five students, only one or two hands had even gone up. Apathy. Oh well, that certainly wasn't the problem today. Downy waited for the chatter to ease. "I will keep the lights dimmed if that's OK; I'm eighty percent more handsome in low light." It was always a great start. He whispered again into his mic: "The guy in the helmet with the killer abs in the second scene was me." Everyone laughed. "Why is that funny?" he said, looking around wildly, feigning confusion. "Seriously though, we are here today to discuss the life of a man called Gaius Julius Caesar. We know very little about Caesar's abs or pecs sadly, but..."

The laughter continued. It was perhaps the thing he most loved about his job. He was a hog for the spotlight and always had been. Charlie really had pulled him from obscurity in some ways, but Downy had hardly been your average bartender, any more than he was an average professor. Even then, as now, he'd had a loyal following of customers. One of his close friends had once insisted he'd make a great cult leader. He hadn't known quite how to take the compliment. Calming the crowd, he slipped into his almost conversational tone, a tone that somehow made each individual in the room feel like they were the only person he was talking to, and continued. His students would laugh if they knew that he had really cultivated his public speaking skills mostly in bars. It was certainly where he had first charmed Charlie with his wit and, of course, his vast knowledge of history.

He looked for Samara in the low light before he began:

"It may be observed that a man's upbringing stays with him throughout his life, and that whatever else may happen to him his heart always belongs to that place that he saw first and to those who first nurtured him. If this is true, then it may be said of Julius Caesar that he was a man of the Roman streets and of the Roman people. His home, humble by Roman standards, was in a district called the *Subura*, famous for its prostitution and gambling. The young, aspiring Gaius must have learned a lot about human nature living there. You'll remember from your reading that Caesar had what we might today call the common touch. He was equally at home conversing with the average man, the lower classes, as he was the aristocratic, or as the Romans called them the optimates. Unlike the optimates, who ruled Rome and controlled the senate, Caesar owed nothing to the men of wealth of the state and held strong antiaristocratic feelings from the start, even siding with his uncle Marius in the civil war that nearly decimated Rome during his teens. Marius eventually lost the war. But, the young man Gaius, as he would have been called, was so well liked and noted for his talents by this time that many of the opposing regime's own men spoke out in his defense. Prophetically, Sulla, the champion of the senate and Caesar's bitter enemy, is reported to have warned them that the young man would one day destroy the aristocracy, even though he eventually agreed to Caesar's pardon. Charming indeed.

"Housing in the Subura would have been humble. Caesar

likely grew up in fairly modest home: a simple cot for a bed, maybe a spare writing table at best, stone floors, and perhaps an animal-skin rug. The room would have been extremely modest, six by nine, maybe smaller. A bit like Taber Hall for those of you who live there."

The class laughed, but now they were truly listening.

"His family had been wealthier in earlier generations and, according to tradition, semi-divine, being related to the goddess Venus. It's a pretty typical story, probably mostly made up to support the notion that the family came from divinity and thus could hope to see it restored. Venus was often associated with luck; ironically, this was a quality Caesar was fond of promoting about himself and was considered a necessity for becoming a great military leader. Whatever the family's true past, young Gaius Julius Caesar had his sights set on a glorious future. Caesar faced tragedy early though when he lost his father at the age of sixteen. Such was the reality of life in the first-century Rome. It's entirely possible his premature death affected Caesar's view of himself and his own mortality. A famous story places a twenty-five-year-old Julius standing at the foot of a statue of Alexander the Great, not in awe of the man but shaking his head in disgust with himself at how little he himself had achieved in comparison. It's a telling insight into his psyche and his sense of ambition. Some of *you* will undoubtedly start thinking about how to take over the world when you turn twenty-five."

He paused. You could hear a pin drop in the auditorium, and almost everyone was leaning forward in their seats. He somehow found Samara's face in the crowd again. He locked eyes with her this time. It was like a page, he realized, ripped from the endless conversations he'd had with Charlie, much of it in fact material Samara had probably heard him develop while he was still Charlie's protégé. In truth the word protégé was inaccurate. Charlie had always treated him as an equal, even when they'd first met. Downy was only a twenty-six-year-old bartender then, but he already knew more about history than most academics. His gift for storytelling was just that—a gift. His grandfather had shared with him the stories of the glorious ancient Romans; he'd also steeped him in the great Greek mythologies, told to him as bedtime stories when he was only a boy. He had absorbed every word. Somehow, he always managed to turn his own enthusiasm for a subject into a reason why everyone should listen. And listen they did.

"Gaius made his first true stab at fame when he staged a run for one of the state's most coveted positions: Pontifex Maximus. Those of you who are friends of the pope will recognize the prefix pontiff, which we still use today for the head of the church. It was a lifelong appointment, and it did something else that Caesar wanted. It put him at the center of Rome, both physically and spiritually, and gave him a permanent seat in the senate. It's fair to point out that Caesar wasn't a deeply spiritual man, certainly not by the dogmas or standards of his age. We know of at least one episode in his life when he felt compelled to taunt sages openly who claimed they could read the future by looking at the livers of a sacrificed animal. This *was not* the famous warning to beware the ides of March, by the way, which is most likely a piece of retroactive fiction. Probably someone claiming clairvoyance had warned Caesar about every other day on the calendar as well. This episode came earlier in Caesar's life when he had first achieved great power and wider fame. When the sacrificed animal in question was found to be without a heart, a bad omen, Caesar claimed, 'You can tell nothing about the future by looking at a heartless beast and that the sage might instead just ask whether Caesar willed it or not.' Caesar seems to have had a healthy contempt for the supernatural and so was a decidedly practical man for his age. He corrected the entire Roman calendar, which had been woefully inaccurate with regard to the seasons. We still use his version, the Julian calendar. We derive the name of the month of July from Julius. His nephew Augustus, who seized power after his assassination, lays claim to August. In spite of his pragmatism, it cannot be overstated how much the notion of fate or destiny still dominated the Roman imagination. The flight of birds was monitored constantly as an omen. The author Suetonius claims portents of Caesar's death were so well documented that one gets the impression predicting the future was something of a cultural obsession, like the weather."

Downy put on his best fake newscaster voice, which landed somewhere between Howard Kossel and Ron Burgundy: "News at eleven calling for dangerous afternoon assassination attempts, possible daggers, more at eleven, Bob." He had to wait for the laughter to subside on this one. "Are we not just as superstitious in some ways now, Sylvia

Brown anyone? Nostradamus? OK, I forgot you guys are high-brow, horoscopes then." He was in the groove.

"Caesar also had a scary eye for talent. Only weeks before his assassination, he put his young nephew Octavian (later Augustus) as his primary in his will, giving the barely seventeen-year-old boy the keys to Rome, effectively jilting Mark Antony in one fail swoop. No one had seen it coming, but Caesar's genius was always in outwitting his opponents, always being one step ahead."

He took a quiet breath. "That's true of every day but one," he said. The lights in the auditorium dimmed. "All of Caesar's luck ran out at once it seems. But that's for later," he said with a wave of his hands.

Then a voice interrupted. People turned in their seats, grumbling, as it was understood questions should be saved for the end. It was the strange man in the hat again. He sat closer now.

"I have read your book, Professor, but not everyone agrees with your sympathy for Caesar, you know."

"I'm sorry, excuse me?"

"You speak of this man as an almost hero, not a ruthless dictator. Surely, you don't mean to elevate him to such heights, Professor?"

"Well, many of his contemporaries, the best men of Rome, in fact, sided with him in the civil war, many of whom were friends to the aristocracy as well. There was something about Caesar that drove people to either love him deeply or hate him with equal passion. Even the people of Rome expelled his assassins and rioted at the news of his murder. You see, even after the civil war, Caesar pardoned his worst enemies and returned their estates to them. His sense of clemency was admired by most, but it absolutely drove his enemies crazy. It took away their pretext for painting him as a ruthless tyrant. In any case, I welcome the criticism, and Caesar does not need my support; his actions speak for themselves in most cases. You make a nice transition to my next point, actually. Your name is?"

"I am Taro."

"Taro, I will answer more questions at the conclusion, if we can revisit this then?" Downy smiled warmly. The man smiled back.

"I have rudely interrupted again it seems, my apologies."

"No worries, not at all; that's what we're here for Mr. Taro, to challenge ourselves, to try to find the truth in our shared history."

He went on telling the story of Caesar's early life—his daring military exploits; his being captured and ransomed by pirates, who he openly ridiculed for not liking his poems, which he read to them incessantly while captive; his outrage that they had only offered fifty talents for his ransom, claiming he was worth five times that; and his promise to return, capture, and crucify them, which he made good on. Out of the corner of his eye, he could see Samara, who now seemed focused on the man in the hat too. Downy turned toward back to the screen to pull up a slide of Campus Martius, where Roman politics had played out in the first century, and then, of course, the slide of the newly discovered Theater of Pompey, where Caesar had actually been slain. It was Charlie's discovery in fact, his last contribution to the field he so loved. He had completely forgotten that Charlie was in the picture pointing proudly at the very spot where Caesar had probably fallen, and, of course, Samara was in the audience. Downy looked up at the picture and went silent. He put the clicker on the podium in front of him.

"This final slide shows our own Professor Charles Patterson, known affectionately as the man with the Midas touch, pointing to the location of Caesar's assassination at the foot of the statue of Pompey the Great, his rival, one of the great archeological finds of our century. Caesar himself had the statue erected to honor his slain adversary. It was his style to be gracious in victory, overly so in fact. More on that later. Let it be an inspiration that there are still many great discoveries to be made by studying the past. I'm sorry," he said, "that's all we have time for today." An hour went by faster than he could believe sometimes. Few moved in their seats though, and he knew he would be staying around to answer lots of questions.

He looked for Samara, but her seat was now empty. He hoped he hadn't upset her. He turned and standing in front of him was the man in the hat.

"Hello, it's Taro, right?"

The man stepped closer, which was unfortunate. The smell of body odor hit him like a wave. Downy tried to plug his nose but to no avail.

"Yes, yes, Professor. My name is Guy actually, but friends call me Taro. I know what an incredibly busy man you must be, but I wonder if you will accept this letter of recommendation? I know it is somewhat an old custom, but where I come from such a thing is still highly valued. I would like to schedule an appointment to speak with you, once you have had a chance to read it, of course." He handed a rolled parchment to Downy.

"Thank you, thank you, please come by my office any time though; really no letter is necessary."

"How wonderful of you, Professor; still the letter may help explain some things in advance. I will schedule an appointment then."

The man's English was good enough, but he could tell it took great effort for him to put his thoughts together in what was clearly a foreign tongue for him. There was Italian in there, but Italian from the country, rustic even. He tried to place the accent, but it too was somehow indistinct.

The man bowed a half bow and turned to go. Some of the other students waiting in line watched suspiciously, snickering and laughing as he walked away, half at the smell and half at the bow. There was something overly formal in the man's demeanor, but he smiled as he left, seeming unfazed. He felt bad sometimes for older students who faced the wrath of the younger one's sense of what was cool and what wasn't. He stared at the line of students and sighed. He needed a chair. It looked like he wasn't going to be leaving anytime soon.

CHAPTER 12

The moonlight made it possible to see in both directions and most importantly up the hill to the carriage. The horses would be spooked if anyone disturbed them, so the man felt free to taste his first true air of relief. The water was very cold, but it didn't matter. He stripped off his clothing. In his state he needed something to slow down his heart, to temper the heat of his fevered mind. In the darkness he lay on his back and floated toward the center of the stream. Stars darted in and out of clouds, and the night sky looked immeasurably vast. He suddenly remembered a story told to him as a child about the boy Icarus. It was a very old story, Greek actually. The boy Icarus had flown too close to the sun after his father had fashioned for him wings made of wax. Icarus had flown higher and higher, in spite of his father's protestations, until the wax melted, and then he plummeted to his death. It was a metaphor, of course, for the dangers of acquiring abilities that were meant to be the sole province of the gods. The story had been useful to him all his life. It was the difference in a man's temperament that dictated how he would view the moral of the tale. Romantic souls tended to focus on Icarus's achievement, which was beautiful but tragic. He had flown closer to the sun than anyone and had peaked into the realm of the gods. The pragmatist saw only folly. The man swam toward the bank. *He* was no romantic. *He* would be the divine punishment then.

The man fully submerged himself in the water, swimming down as deeply as he could. The dark and the silence were peaceful, but as he cleared his mind, he thought he heard the sound of muted voices from above. Where had they come from? There had been no one only moments before. He held his breath and waited. It was definitely voices. He wasn't sure how long he could stay under but decided to test himself. He thought of the time in Egypt, his only real disaster. He had swum many miles, too far really. Finally, after what seemed like minutes had passed, the talking seemed to be getting further away; then he gulped in his last breath, deciding to push himself to the absolute limits of his endurance. In case his body grew too weak, he dove down to the deepest part of the river into the darkness, pumping his arms wildly through the silence. All he had to do was not lose consciousness. If anyone had seen him go under, they would never believe he could survive so long. He would wait longer still. But suddenly his limbs stopped responding. His head felt like it might explode. He felt himself rocketing rapidly to the surface. He finally burst through the canopy, exhaling in a mighty gasp, and then guffawed inward. His rib cage was on fire. He commanded his arms to swim, to move, but only his left arm meekly responded. Sideways now, he felt his knees scrape against the rocky bottom, and he knew that he had survived. He was in the shallows. He crawled to the water's edge and lay in the sand, breathing heavily. There seemed to be no one about. Had it all been his imagination? He turned his head to look up the hill. The horses seemed undisturbed, which was a good sign; he could see their bowed heads against the faint light of the moon. He crawled to his cloak and wrapped himself in its warmth, moaning. He remembered the teacher's recounting of the story.

"Lying there on the cold floor all alone," the teacher had said, "wrapped only in the dignity of his cloak." The man cried out in agony. Wild night animals from far away howled back in response.

CHAPTER 13

"Come on," Tackett said, "let me take you to your new digs."

He was slightly buzzed from their drinking and didn't realize Tackett wanted him to actually get out of the car.

"Goddamn Southerners can't hold your liquor," he shouted as he finally staggered out of the car. Tackett jangled with the keys on his belt as they walked toward a small, old house at the end of the driveway. It looked mostly abandoned, but it was neatly kept.

"When the budget was better, we had this as a safe house for the narcos. Then when the budget was cut, we stopped paying, but the owner has never said a word. He's older than Cootie Brown. The city records don't even list the place as existing at all."

Tackett pointed toward the couch. "There's a bed in there; just pull it out. The icebox is full of beer, but don't touch the cheese; it's mine. Or the Ritz crackers; they are also mine.

There is a stack of playboys and penthouse in the drawer, though watch out cause Rodriguez keeps them in a particular order. If they get moved, she gets furious."

"Oh," he said, "she lik—"

"She likes the articles. Don't mention you're staying here, OK. Tierney has forgotten this place even exists. You'll be safe. Look, tell me if anything unusual comes up on this case, OK? Tell me who you speak to, just so I can watch your back and keep an eye on you."

"OK, dad," he said, saluting awkwardly.

Tackett raised his head squinting at him. "Man, you sure are one goofy bastard for a supposed genius. Then again, maybe you're just a country genius. You better get some sleep," Tackett said, opening the door. "The train comes by here at about seven a.m., so don't worry about setting an alarm. Drink a bunch of water before you pass out. See you bright and early sunshine."

He was all alone at last on the couch. It wasn't bad actually. There were candles placed randomly around the room. It smelled of a woman's touch, even if it looked like a complete flophouse. He opened the refrigerator. It was full of beer, and good beer at that. There was a piece of moldy cheese wrapped in plastic in the corner, which smelled mightily bad. On top, there was a pack of Ritz crackers, only slightly stale, which he opened and proceeded to eat with reckless abandon. He finished all but two, trying to remember where Tackett had said the playboys were, before passing out on the couch covered in crumbs.

———

The blast of the train's horn caused him to think he was in Richmond, and for a few strange seconds, he thought he could smell the fall leaves. He heard a football-game marching band playing to cheers off in the distance, but then the sound all seemed to roll together into the breaking of waves, and he realized where he actually was. California. He had slept at least. His head felt tender though, and if he moved too fast, he knew he might cause a real headache. Suddenly the coffee maker kicked on with a beep, but there was no water, so it only hissed. He was too tired to bother. He sat up, running his hands through his hair. He wasn't a Richmond cop anymore; he had to remember that. San Diego had certainly been eventful so far. It technically wasn't illegal for Tierney to lie to him, but it sure was a helluva way to start a job. He walked to the window and peered out across the street. It was empty. A child rode by on a bicycle and waived across at someone he could not see. He looked on the table and saw the folder for Case 1032. He sat down and opened it. It was not much to go on. He had already called and left messages with anyone even remotely connected to the case. It was a short list of names. It was a long way from the crime. Probably no one remembered anything accurately after so much time. He stared at the pictures of the scene of the break in and, of course, the apparent struggle, blood literally splashed all over. Whose blood was it? No body was ever found, and it hadn't matched anyone in the database. During the follow up investigation by Detective Jensen, they hadn't even considered there could be any connection between the two events—the disappearance of Fleming and the apparent murder without a body. Why would they? Sullivan wanted a look at the scene, even if it had changed completely. Maybe there was something about *where* the crime took place that was significant. Maybe the homeowner could remember something valuable. He suddenly remembered that his car was still at impound. *Shit.* He was going to be late for sure. Just then the front door flew open.

"Rise and shine, valentine!" It was Rodriguez. "Time to get your hung ass up, homey," she said, handing him a coffee and donut.

He realized he wasn't wearing pants, only his shamrock-covered underwear. Rodriguez looked down.

"Those are cute, but the chief hates the Irish, so put on some pants." He looked down and laughed.

"Not that you care," he said without thinking.

"No, no, I appreciate good equipment," she said, walking around the room, apparently unfazed by the remark. "This place needs a cleaning. Beer?" she said, opening the fridge.

"Isn't it a little early?"

"Suit yourself," she said, cracking the lid off the countertop. "I gotta get into character. Wanna hear a joke?" she said after downing some of the beer.

"Sure."

"What do you call a hooker with fresh breath?"

"I don't know."

"A cop."

She threw his pants at him. "Get dressed. You're gonna

make us both late. The only thing I hate more than being late is fucking late people."

"Me too," he said, but Rodriguez was finishing her beer all in one drink, ignoring him. She slammed it on the table and pulled out a tube of fire-engine red lipstick and started to apply. Then she let out a giant burp. Sullivan put his hand over his face in protest.

"Oh yeah," she said, "sorry you're a southern boy, right? I suppose I must ufh forgotten my mannahs, Rhett. Please do forgive a silly little peach like me for upsettin your delicate sensibilities."

He laughed in spite of himself and finally pulled on his pants. It was their fifth consecutive day in the rotation. Eventually, he realized he would have to unpack all his stuff. Eventually.

CHAPTER 14

Downy awoke to the caress of his wife Naomi's hand against his forehead.

"Who won last night? You or the bar."

He suddenly remembered that he had lied to her about where he was. He hated the feeling. Butterflies filled his stomach, and he decided pretending a bit of a hangover wasn't such a bad idea.

"Ahhhhhh!" he said, rolling over. "It was a tie I think."

Naomi stretched herself and got out of the bed. He loved the view, and the kiss from the night before had him especially charged. As Naomi tried to walk away, he grabbed her by the boxer shorts, pulling them down before she could escape. She always slept in his boxers. It was for him. He loved how she looked in them.

"Ah, ah, ah," she said, pointing her finger at him, "I have the luncheon with Max and Cynthia today. No time for shenanigans." Downy could never keep up with her schedule. It was too bad.

"Your loss," he said.

Naomi laughed, reaching down between his legs, giving him a squeeze. "Save it," she said with a kiss. "Rain check."

"Damn right," he said.

He stared up at the ceiling fan as it twirled, and he could hear the birds chirping away outside the window. He thought of Samara's conversation about Nazim. He also thought of how easily he had let her kiss him. And what had she meant about the principles of a man and a woman exactly? He wasn't too self-righteous to recognize the truth when he heard it. He needed to let Naomi know about Samara as soon as possible. There was simply no way he could keep meeting with her alone without arousing suspicion.

"Hey!" he yelled, "you won't believe who showed up to my class yesterday."

"Who's that?"

"Charlie's daughter, Samara."

Naomi suddenly appeared back in the doorway.

"You're kidding?"

"No, I'm not," he said. "She has been overseas and just got back to town. She wanted to surprise me, I guess. Remember, I told you her mom called and said she might be headed back to the states for school? I'd forgotten almost."

"Oh yeah," she said. "Poor girl, how is she doing?" Questions like this he hated. Naomi would see her soon enough, and it was dumb not to tell the truth. It would seem suspicious after the fact.

"She's grown-up now, that's for sure. You know the last time I saw her she was about twelve, I think. She's really beautiful," he said. "Reminds me of both Charlie in the eyes and her mom, of course."

"Oh, another beautiful girl in your life, eh, Professor?" she said half mockingly.

"Yeah, but—"

"I know, I know. I was just kidding."

Even though she was in a hurry, he now had her attention to a different degree. He shouldn't have used the word "beautiful."

"She actually wants to meet about something. I told her to come over whenever she wants."

"What's it about, any idea?"

"Not really, I get the sense it's not school related though. You know she missed the funeral, and maybe it's something to do with that."

Naomi pulled her straight black hair up into her headband and twisted it into a perfect knot.

"Maybe you two should meet alone then; I don't want her to feel awkward, and it'll give you time to catch up."

He marveled silently at his wife's confidence, her willingness to accommodate, and her perfect profile.

"Grab a coffee with her, and then we can have her over for dinner or something."

"Yeah, we'll see."

He thought of Samara's lips against his and the pressing of her body, the way she had almost collapsed into him.

"I love you," he said suddenly.

"I know you do, but I'm so late," she said, rushing to collect her things.

At thirty-four she was an absolute picture of beauty and confidence. He leaned over the edge of the bed like a boy and rolled off into the standing position, whispering into her ear.

"I still can't believe your own sister had you whacked," he said, thinking back to her time on set as Cleopatra's unfortunate sister.

"Then again, stealing the throne of Egypt wouldn't be hard with an ass like this."

Naomi laughed, chasing him back to bed. "Go back to sleep. You're still drunk."

He lunged for her again, but she was gone.

He took her advice and dozed off again, but his first dream was of Nazim. The family had seemingly turned their backs on Samara. Why? In his dream there was black smoke off in the distance, and Nazim was whispering something to him, something terrible, frightening. He was weeping. He woke up with a start and threw on his pants. He would call immediately. It was evening already in Cairo, and he wanted some answers.

CHAPTER 15

The phone rang and rang before he finally gave in and switched to Nazim's cell. The only time he wouldn't answer was if he was at the helm of his boat. It was off-season for travel in Egypt, not to mention late evening, so he expected Nazim's voice to pick up instantly. The line went directly to voice mail instead. It was Nazim's same generic message he had had for all the years he had known him.

"Nazim, it's Noah. Please give me a ring as soon as you can." He hated leaving messages. He realized he had absolutely nothing to do for the rest of the whole day. He thought of the backlog of messages at school and considered the unthinkable. Going in on a Saturday. The office would be quiet; he could get a ton of work finished in no time. He suddenly realized Samara was going to be in his class for the whole semester. What had he been thinking letting her kiss him? Oh well, he could get used to it if he had to he supposed. It would certainly keep him on his toes. It was funny that so many people asked him about the lure of female students in his classes. The truth was nineteen-year-olds weren't nearly as attractive as one might believe. For him at least the notion of having a romantic or sexual relationship with someone who was trying to also get a grade from you was the very definition of unethical, and frankly not very sexy. The power dynamics were insulting to both. How could a student ever know whether she was simply being used for her body and, for that matter, a teacher for a potential "A"? How could any teacher be objective when sex was involved? Gratefully, he found he had little intellectually in common with his students anyway. He certainly knew of some professors who were willing to take advantage of the situation, but the aftermath was always a catastrophe.

"Thank God for the teacher's union," one professor had confessed to him. He had held his tongue but never felt the same about the guy again.

He felt a ping of hypocrisy over Samara though but then reminded himself that what had happened was certainly no love affair. And now that he knew what was going on in her head he felt even more paternal toward her. He realized that feeling had a dangerous quality as well. It was only a kiss, but my god it had been electric. Her vulnerability only made things worse. He tried to remind himself that the word *help* had all sorts of connotations when it came to relationships between men and women. He needed to be careful going forward, for everyone's sake.

As he drove toward the campus, he stretched his arms in the air and let out a loud yelp. It was his relief yelp. They hadn't slept together. He yowled into the wind, "No sex for me, please. Thank you!" and laughed.

"I'll be smart enough for the both of us," she had said. *What if she had had a room key in her pocket*, Downy thought. *Seriously? Jesus.* He'd be smarter than that he hoped.

The campus was certainly easy to navigate on weekends, so his trip took only minutes. He paused at the top of the stairs, thinking he heard someone. Who would it be on a Saturday? His office was situated on the western corner of campus, the "suite" as the other professors called it. There was plenty of envy over the space, not to mention the personal assistant who came with it. He listened again, but the sound was gone. When he opened the door, the room smelled musty and a pungent gust of body odor hit him in the face. *There must have been a janitor at work*, he thought. On the shelf there was the bobblehead of Julius Caesar and Mark Antony that Charlie had given him after the publication of his first book. Their heads still wobbled. He touched them, and they both stopped. The guy had dusted them too he supposed. *Thorough if not overly motivated*, he thought, but the goddamn smell was certainly lingering. He sat down at his desk, propping up his feet and looking at the blinking light of his message machine. Still two messages, though his secretary was supposed to have returned all his calls with the usual "we'll get back to you." He almost never did. It was one of the great things about being so in demand. You didn't have to talk to anyone you didn't want to.

He punched the button: "Uh, hello there, Professor Downy. I'm calling from the precinct; uh...actually, this is

Detective Sullivan calling from...uh...sorry SDPD. Just needed to ask you a few questions and hopefully set up a time to get together. Shouldn't take long, and I'm completely flexible timewise."

He grimaced. It was that again. Of course, they would want to see the house.

He grabbed his cell, pulling up Naomi's number and typed.

Guess what? Need to let the cops into the house again.
Ahhhrghhhhh...

This made the fourth time in so many years that police had come to their home. It had started to become annoying, because he and his wife hadn't even lived in the house when the crime had taken place. Every few years they were reminded of it by another visit from the police. They never gave details, of course, but it had been bad enough that they were still trying to find clues apparently. It had helped tremendously with the price of the house though, which was undoubtedly worth a million or more. He and Naomi had made an offer that very day because of the outrageously gorgeous views of the ocean, even when they were still barely in the pink because of his first book. The offer was accepted immediately, even though they'd way underbid. He had guaranteed Naomi there would be ghosts, but that hadn't panned out. He wondered why the police were still interested, since everything had been redone and painted since they moved in. Whatever had happened, there couldn't possibly be a trace left now. He hit callback, and the same voice from the message answered the phone almost immediately.

"Detective Sullivan here."

"Just returning your call, Detective. Hey, I can leave you guys a key at the house, if you want to come in. It's all been looked at a few times now—any idea how much longer this will be going on? You know, this makes the fourth time you guys have looked."

Sullivan shuffled the phone. "I'm super sorry for the inconvenience. This is an old case, and we're just trying to tie up a few loose ends. If it's all the same, I was hoping to ask you a few questions as well."

"OK," he said hesitantly, "but you know this all happened befo—"

"Yes, yes, I know; I read through the file, and, of course, you weren't the occupants of the house then, but I am brand new to the case. And I'm just trying to orient myself to the timeline. I'd really appreciate it. You tell me when and where, and I'll come to you, OK? Take fifteen minutes of your time at the most."

"Sure," he said finally giving up. "Come by my office on Monday, say, ten o'clock?"

"That's perfect. Thank you very much, Professor Downy. See you on Monday at ten."

A silver lining, he now had an official excuse to skip class. Samara would wonder why if he didn't show, but he hoped to speak to her soon anyway. He wondered why Nazim wasn't returning his call. He usually called back very quickly. He still represented huge income for Nazim's family, not to mention their genuine friendship. What could be going on over there? It wasn't yet time to worry, but it would be soon. He threw open the windows. The pungent smell was still wafting around the room, and as he looked around the office, he could see dust almost everywhere. The janitor had done a shit job on everything but the bobble heads apparently. Standing there in the silence, he knew he wasn't going to be able to get any work done. Fuck it, he would head over to Woody's and toast to an old friend. He flicked Mark Antony one final time on his way out the door. Antony looked like he was trying to tell Caesar something important, but Caesar wasn't listening.

CHAPTER 16

The man climbed the slope of the grassy hill slowly. The time underwater had completely drained him, and his muscles still burned. Finally, reaching the covered carriage, he peered in anxiously. His prisoner was out cold. Whoever had come past the water must have moved on unaware. In the dark almost no one would recognize him anyway, but the daylight was another matter. It could just as easily have been a gang of thieves. The roads were no place to be in this part of the world in any case. Any sane man knew that. It would be daybreak in less than an hour, and he realized he was too tired to move again. He would camp here for the morning. He could find the ruins easily when his energy returned. He was technically way ahead of schedule anyway. He wouldn't need to be at the pond until three more moons had passed. It was too difficult keeping up with the days of the week, so the movement of the moon and stars would have to suffice. It was an ancient means of measuring but incredibly accurate. What good was a clock in a place like this anyhow? Half of the zodiac was clearly visible in the night sky, so he knew dawn was near. The ruins were barely a day's ride, even at a slow pace. He had to give credit to the members of the network. They had made the inherent difficulties of navigation easy to overcome, even for someone like him with limited language skills. He was never lost. They had been thorough. Men of science had always appealed to him for this reason, but certainly, they were weak in other ways. Who was more self-centered, more pointlessly arrogant, than the man of science? There was at least a sense of one's place in the grand scheme in the religious man, and even if he himself could never sense the real presence of a god, he preferred the man of some belief over the fool who could imagine nothing bigger, nothing grander, than himself. Religious men knew how to die well at least. Men of science died like little squealing pigs. He'd seen it himself. He'd spared almost any man who showed poise at the moment of death, no matter how much of an enemy they had been. It was an internal rule he'd always obeyed. He reached into his pocket for the sugar cubes and took two—one for now and one for later just in case he slept too long. A gentle wave of euphoria overtook him.

In the moonlight he could see down his leg. Blood had dried around the cuts from the rocks. It stung. Otherwise, he was clean. He thought of the boy, his corpse now at the bottom of the river. He had died probably never realizing exactly what had happened, which was for the best. Choices had to be made. The worst kind of killing was that of a youth though. Older men had had time to accumulate plenty of sins, for which death was almost always a justice served. He knew he had to stay focused on his goal no matter the body count. If he was successful, all wrongs could be justified, and all could be set right again. He looked into the back once more and could see the prisoner's lips moving, but his eyes were closed, his mouth agape. It would be wise to chain him just in case. The man pulled the shackle from the bag in the back and slid it up the ankle, locking it securely in place. He doubled the chain around the center axle and fastened the smaller lock. With the clicking of it in place, his prisoner let out a low moan. From here on out, he had to prepare himself for when he woke up. That would come soon. Then the hysteria. He would make sure not to let his face be visible this time and hope the memory of the shock wouldn't be too fresh. The boy had insisted it was the only way to convince his uncle. It had backfired, as he knew it would. Once they reached the ruins, he could safely lock his prisoner in a cell. The second wave of the sugar cube erased the need for further thought, and the man fell asleep almost in the sitting up position, eyes flickering behind their lids, a half smile across his lips. He dreamed he was Icarus flying through the clouds, higher and higher. He heard a voice in the dream. It was his first lieutenant shouting that the way had been cleared. He was back on the battlefield then, where he truly belonged. He should never have returned home in the first place; perhaps none of this would have happened if he'd stayed with his men. Fate was impartial though, wasn't she, and without much effort could sway events one way or the other.

CHAPTER 17

The scurry and bustle of Monday mornings in San Diego was less hectic than he had expected, and he had inadvertently shown up to work early. He made sure everyone saw him as he passed their desks. Who could say when it might happen again? Finally, he sat down at his chair drinking a large coffee from Donut Haven. It had turned out to be a great spot to review the files, since no one spoke a word of English in the place. They smiled fluently though, and he genuinely appreciated the silence. Then, just to drive home the stereotype, they had insisted on taking his picture with one of those ancient Polaroid cameras, which the woman running the place had then dutifully added to the wall. It was a motley crew of faces. They were the expressions of people who still insisted coffee should never cost more than ninety-nine cents. Sullivan looked at his watch. It was still two hours before his meeting, though he would need to leave early since he really didn't know his way around the campus.

"You know there's a Starbucks a block away from us if you need something with taste."

He looked over his shoulder. It was Tierney. Tierney looked too fresh for the morning; his shave was immaculate, and his clothing starched to within an inch of its life. He sat down in the seat opposite Sullivan.

"Detective, I wanted to update you on some protocols you may not be used to. It is imperative here that I know where to find you and that if asked I can speak with authority about what you have and have not done when it comes to police work. Your laptop is connected to the main feed here," he said, pointing to endless rows of computers and people with headsets clicking away at them. "Please make sure to orient yourself to the software and log all of your appointments, OK? Technically those are Homeland Security folks over there, but I managed to carve out a little of the budget for us as well. I know where you come from being a wolf and hunting alone is the norm. It's the opposite here. Methodical is the word. It's the only word."

Sullivan held up the laptop, turning it in all directions like a cavemen analyzing something utterly foreign and perplexing to him. He put his teeth to it for a taste and then sniffed it. Tierney rose to leave in disgust, but Sullivan stopped him. "I synced my phone with this yesterday from home; I hope you don't mind. My appointments calendar is updated. It's a little too easy to hack into your shit, to be honest. I cleared out some bugs for you guys as well. Is there an actual IT guy, or is everybody over there taking orders for value meals?"

Tierney walked away without speaking. Sullivan chewed absent-mindedly at his pen. So Tierney was keeping him on a truly tight leash. Perhaps he was worried about his lack of full disclosure on the case after all. *Nah*, Sullivan thought, *he just wanted to be the first to know if there was a break in the case. He was snooping.* Tackett was probably shooting straight on Tierney. He looked two desks down where the chief's son sat typing away at his computer.

"Hey, Sheppard," Sullivan yelled. "You know the fastest way to San Diego College?"

"Yeah," he said without looking up, "MapQuest it."

"Thanks," Sullivan said, "you're the best."

CHAPTER 18

Downy had almost forgotten about his appointment until Janine buzzed him. "Should I bring in any refreshments, boss?" she said.

"No, it's not a social visit, or at least I don't think it is."

He had been awake since early morning staring at his cell. Nothing still from Nazim. It was getting very worrisome. His class would begin in ten minutes. He thought of his grad student up there nervously walking everyone through the discussion. He felt a little disgusted with himself for not being there. It would have been nice to see Samara again too. He thought of texting to warn her, but that seemed too... well...too something. Downy needed to keep what happened at school and outside of school separate. Why in hell did the cop need to speak to him anyway? You had to give credit to the police though, for their commitment. The first visit had been many years ago now. How long, almost ten? His cell started buzzing on the desk. It was a 202 area code. Thank God, it was Nazim. Then his secretary buzzed.

"Professor, there is a Detective Sullivan here to see you."

He looked at the phone with dismay. He would let Nazim talk to his answering machine then. Why did everything have to happen at once? It was one of life's great mysteries. Still he was relieved to know he was calling.

"Send him right in, Janine."

Sullivan walked in the office with a big grin.

"Hello, Professor, thank you so much for your time today. I'm Detective Nick Sullivan."

Downy rose for a handshake, and the two men sat back down quickly.

Sullivan surveyed the room, looking at the pictures on the wall. He rose again and walked to a picture of Downy with his wife on set of the miniseries.

"Wow, man, this is some picture! Is that your wife?"

"Yeah," he said with a nod, "it is."

"So, she's like a princess or something?"

"It was for a miniseries; she had a small role."

"She makes Elizabeth Taylor look like a dog. Cleopatra, right?"

"Right, well her sister actually, the one Cleopatra executed."

"No shit?"

"No shit," Downy said, smiling wide.

"Congratulations. I should get married someday, probably," he said with an emotionless laugh.

"I'll spare you the pep talk, but it's pretty great. Marry the right person though."

"Good advice, thanks."

Sullivan continued to stand and looked at all the pictures in the room with a sense of genuine marvel. "Man, it's some life you got here. Egypt, Rome, I had you professor types pegged as a bunch of goateed hippies, but you got the world by the *cajones*."

He laughed. It always made him uncomfortable when people flattered him so completely. Sullivan finally returned to his chair and opened a folder in his lap.

"Hey, could I get you a coffee or tea or water?" Downy said.

"A coffee would be just great."

"Janine, could you bring coffee for two, please?"

"Cream? Sugar?"

"Black is fine."

"Two black coffees, please, Janine. It's Greek-boiled coffee, imported from one of my favorite restaurants right here in town."

"Nice."

"Yeah, really good stuff. If you like it, it's from a place called Woody's over on Third. Nice place to drink it too."

"I'll check it out," Sullivan said gratefully.

"So what part of the South are you from, Detective?"

Downy knew accents almost instantly. He wanted to guess South Carolina, but the cadence seemed too flat.

"All over really. I spent most of my time in Charleston but ended up in Richmond."

"How long have you been here?"

"About a year," he said, lying. He couldn't bear the thought of a whole "welcome to town" discussion.

"I grew up in the South as well, Kentucky actually."

"No shit," Sullivan said, looking genuinely surprised.

"I went to college in England for a while and lost most of my accent."

Janine tiptoed into the room and offered each man his coffee.

Janine looked back at Downy on her way out the door and fluttered her hand in front of her face like she might faint. It took him a second to catch her meaning.

He smiled at her. He had to admit the cop was awfully good looking.

"This is really great," Sullivan said, putting his cup back to the plate. "Let me get down to tacks here," he said, returning to his folder with a smile. "Could you remind me when it was that you moved into the house on 381 Latimer Street?"

"Oh, man, that was in 2005, I think. Maybe 2006."

"How did you guys find out about the property?"

"Well it was empty when we bought it, but it was a friend of mine who lived nearby that told me about it originally."

"And what was the friend's name?"

"It was Charlie Patterson and his wife Sarah who told us about it."

"Would you mind if I contacted them?"

"I'm sorry, but Charlie is deceased."

"Oh, gosh. I'm very sorry."

"And his wife, Sarah?"

"She lives out of state now, but it was just a house near them is all. That's how they knew about it."

"Oh, OK. I know we've just about pestered the hell out of you guys with this investigation," Sullivan said, changing his demeanor. "Let me level with you that this case is about as cold as they get. I'm grasping at straws, to say the very least. I'm still kind of the new guy, and my boss is taking it out on me."

Downy laughed. "My first classes when I became a professor were Saturday mornings at seven a.m."

"Ouch," Sullivan said, laughing.

"Hey, as long as you're here, could I ask you what it was that happened at our place? I never had the nerve to ask the other detectives, but I'd like to know, my wife too."

"Fair enough. Thing is, it's a bit of a mystery even to us, obviously. There was an assault there we believe, probably a fatal one. There was blood, mountains of it actually, but there was never a body. DNA came back with only one blood type, one victim. Sorry, I hope this isn't too shocking to hear," Sullivan said, catching himself. "I know you live there."

"No, no," Downy answered. "I asked. Go on, please."

"We might have a missing person who could be connected, but that's about it. I'm just being asked to reexamine the case with fresh eyes."

"The house is available during the day, so feel free to come by. It's been redone for a long time now though, painted."

"Sure, I understand. We so appreciate your patience, really. The first detective you met with, Fleming was his name. Do you remember anything about what he looked at when he was at your place? Anything seem to interest him particularly?"

"I think he spent most of his time in the large, front room next to our bay window. I excused myself both times as I recall, but the second guy looked in that area too, for a while actually. I figured it was kind of better not to know, at the time."

"Yeah, I can see why."

"I can show you where later, if you want?"

"I don't think that's necessary. Just one more thing: anything unusual about the detective when he interviewed you? Either of them, actually? Were they behaving normally? Anything stand out as odd to you?"

"No, not that I can recall, but gosh it's been a really long time."

"Yeah, it has."

Downy was surprised by how nervous he felt talking to the police, especially when they started asking about each other. He was careful to express that he wanted to be forthcoming. The detective leaned back in his chair.

"I grew up in a college town. I never considered it though," he said, looking around the wall again at all the pictures of Downy's life. "I'll bet there are some cool things I missed out on, but you know what, I like how things have turned out anyway."

"Great. Being happy is so important," Downy said. "Oh, I didn't mean I was happy exactly. Are you?" he said, looking at him suspiciously.

"I'm sorry," Sullivan said, coming to his senses. "You meant to compliment me, and I got very philosophical and dark, didn't I? I'll bet the girls love you here, huh," he said, smiling a toothy grin, trying to change the subject.

There it was; everybody went there eventually. Downy smiled demurely, "A lot fewer than before."

He laughed with him. "Come on, you're about my age. You're still in the fight."

He raised his ring finger and pointed, "I don't have to fight anymore. They're not as interesting as you might think either, though. Of course, they are forever young."

"Yeah, I hear you. You know, there is just one last thing I wanted to ask you about. In Detective Jensen's notes, he mentioned possibly collecting a blood sample from you. Did he ever ask you for one? I think I'm misreading his notes actually. Probably I am."

"From me? No, he never did."

Sullivan paused.

"He had written 'get blood from the professor'?" he said, holding up the page and pointing to each word of the detective's hand-scrawled notes. "It's weird though; he put a question mark at the end. Maybe he was only considering it, but even that seems...well...I mean you didn't even live there yet."

"No, as I said, we never really discussed the case with them."

"Right, not with Fleming either?"

"No, not that I recall."

"Another professor he meant perhaps?" Sullivan sighed and closed the folder. "Professor Downy, I can't thank you enough. Maybe our paths will cross again sometime under better circumstances."

"The pleasure has been mine," Downy said, finally rising from his chair to shake hands.

"I'll see myself out."

"So you won't be needing keys to get in then, to the house?"

"No," he said, smiling, "I have gotten everything I needed. Thank you."

Downy sat for a few moments staring at the wall in front of him. He looked at the pictures and had to agree life had been pretty good to him. He snatched his cell phone off the desk. It was time to figure out what the hell was going on in Cairo.

CHAPTER 19

Sullivan got on his cell as soon as he was in the parking lot. He hit the name Tackett and waited patiently. It was always an incredible feeling when there was a break in a case. He had to tell someone. Tackett seemed like he had his best interests at heart, even if he was being a bit overly protective. It couldn't hurt to share some at least of what he had found.

"Tackett here," he said, picking up.

"Sergeant, this is Sullivan. Could we meet? I think the uh...house...would be best."

"Uh, yeah, yeah," Tackett said with noticeable surprise. "Everything OK?"

"Yeah, sure," Sullivan said. "I just want to have a quick chat, probably best had there."

"OK, give me ten minutes. I'm on the other side of town. I get to serve a warrant on a lawyer. It's my absolute favorite part of the job, so give me a few minutes to savor it, OK? I'll be right there."

"OK, see ya in twenty then."

"Don't go anywhere else. Just drive straight there, OK? I'm coming as soon as I can."

"Fine. Fine," Sullivan said, clearly annoyed. "I won't move a muscle." He passed a small cluster of girls walking together as he arrived at his car. They all giggled and looked impossibly young.

"Nice suit, man," one of them chided.

Sullivan flashed his badge. "Are you girls parked legally? Do you have your decals up in their proper positions?" he said with mock authority.

They laughed more. "You can arrest me," one of them said, fluttering her eyelashes.

Being overdressed on a college campus was a major giveaway apparently. He opened the door to his car and in one swooping move grabbed the yellow parking ticket from his windshield. Then, as if he were dancing with an invisible partner, he turned to pivot toward the car next to him. He placed the ticket on the windshield, slapping it down under the wiper blade. He then reversed the move back toward his own car and rolled in through the window. He started the engine and a black cloud of exhaust burst out of his tailpipe. He revved the engine like everything depended on it and squealed out of the parking lot. *Yes*, he thought, *college could have been a good place for him.*

———

Downy wanted to talk to Naomi immediately. She would definitely want to hear that the cop had seemed more interested in the other detectives than he had been in the crime. What a strange interview it had been for all that. There was something guarded about the detective though. And why did they want to speak to the Pattersons? It bothered him, but Nazim's message was the most important thing on his mind at the moment. He hit the voice-mail button. The phone rang only once before a voice answered. The voice was Nazim's.

"Hello, Mr. Downy. This is Nazim Celedana returning your call. I presume you must be looking for a boat, and I am just your man. You may call me anytime, and we can discuss what you're looking for, and further I can tell you what range of accommodations I can provide. My craft is very large and can hold up to twenty-five crew, fully serviced."

It was another generic response. *He must not have listened to his message and must have him mixed up with a new client,* Downy thought.

He ignored the rest of the message and hit the Redial button and waited. But surely, Nazim recognized his number? *Weird.*

He felt a surge of nervous anticipation as the phone rang.

"Yes, hello. This is Nazim."

"Nazim, it's Noah, Noah Downy calling. Thank God! Is everything OK over there?"

"I don't follow you, sir. Have we met? I am sorry I do not recog—"

"Nazim, this is Noah calling, Charlie's partner, Professor Downy." Downy's throat tightened as he spoke, and his voice went up noticeably in pitch.

"Ohhhh, so sorry, sir. Yes, Charlie Patterson's friend. How are you today, sir? I mean Professor Downy; I hope all is well."

There was something off in his voice though.

"Sir, I believe you sent a messenger to my home recently, and there was a bit of a mix up; my family did not know why she had come. One thousand apologies if she was upset by us. I just feel terrible. Charlie has told me all about you but didn't mention you were looking for a boat, so my family was confused. They said she seemed very distressed, the girl."

Downy sat up stiffly in his chair. What the hell was he talking about?

"Nazim, how could Charlie tell you?"

"Sir, I am very sorry if we have met, and I have forgotten. I am getting on in years now, and some names and even faces escape me."

"Nazim, are you sick? Are you OK?"

"No, sir, I am sorry. I just do not recall our having ever spoken before. Charlie is a dear friend though, and anything you want, I can assure you I can provide."

"It was Samara at your house, Nazim. You remember Samara?"

"I cannot, I'm afraid. Perhaps you have me confused."

"So you do know Charlie, but not Samara? I'm sorry, but could I speak to your wife? Can you put Diba Jan on the phone, Nazim?"

"I am so utterly confused right now, my friend. My wife is at home, sir. I am at my office. Have you and she met before?"

He was speechless and sat motionless for many seconds.

"Sir, perhaps I should call Charlie, and you can speak with him to refresh my memory."

"Nazim, Charlie is dead. Why would you say that?"

"No, sir, that cannot be. I only just saw him, only two weeks ago. Has something happened? Sir?"

"Yes, Nazim, he died on your boat five years ago, goddamnit. What the hell is wrong with you?"

"Sir, there is a terrible confusion here. No one has died on my boat. Let me call Charlie and get back to you immediately. Charlie, he is fine. I know it. I would have heard. I will call after I—"

Downy threw his cell across the office, hitting the wall. Janine rang immediately.

"Professor, is everything OK in there?"

He could barely speak, "Fine, Janine. Cell-phone trouble."

He darted to pick it up. The line was dead. It was for the best as he was about to lose control anyway. Was his friend losing his mind? Had Charlie's death caused him to go insane, or was it something else? It seemed like the only rational explanation. It was just as Samara said. He was polite like always but seemed genuinely confused. It frightened him how much it sounded like true mental illness. He didn't have Nazim's home number in his phone, so he buzzed Janine to get it for him.

"Yes, sir," she responded.

"Janine, do you ever have one of those days when it seems like the whole world has gone crazy?"

"Every Monday through Friday, sir. Without fail."

He dialed Naomi. She answered in a low tone: "Hey you, what's up?"

"You coming home round five?"

"Yeah, sure," she said.

"Good, it's been a weird day."

"Everything OK?"

"Nothing bad, just odd. Tell you about it later."

He was lying. It was bad. He couldn't imagine things being worse. Like Samara, he felt both anger and sorrow. *And what now to do about her?* he wondered. What could he say to Samara?

"Going home early again, Janine."

"I hope you're not still sick," she buzzed back.

"Chad will have my classes again. Could you send him an e-mail to confirm?"

"Done."

He looked at his desk. The letter that the student had given him caught his eye. It was a thick, almost antique gauge of paper with a wax seal in the center. Downy had never seen anything quite like it. He opened it:

Dear Professor Downy,

I write to you on behalf of Monsieur Guy Taro. I have been acquainted with Mr. Taro now for some eleven years...

Downy skipped to the bottom of the page. The signature looked formal and at the bottom was a stamped seal, which read "Sacred Order of the Gracchi Brotherhood."

Jesus, he thought, *some reference.* He didn't have the energy to read on, so he tossed the paper aside. It would have to wait. He had far more important matters to tend to.

CHAPTER 20

Sullivan pulled into the parking space behind the house and put the car in park. *How many more years would it run?* he wondered. He had been planning to have it painted before he left Richmond, but everything had happened so fast. The paint had worn down from candy apple red to faded, scarlet rust. He pushed the eight-track tape of Elvis Presley's '68 come-back special into the slot. He would have kept the car for the stereo alone. It was his meditation music. *Why would Jensen have wanted to take a sample of Professor Downy's blood?* he wondered. Jensen would have known the odds of a match were astronomical, unless he knew something else, of course—unless there was some missing piece of information, tying the professor to the blood at the scene. The fact that an anonymous caller had initially reported the crime lingered in Sullivan's mind. It bothered him in the same way being lied to bothered him. This brought him to the other thing: Professor Downy was definitely lying. He wasn't sure on which point, but his instincts were never wrong. Exactly what kind of killer would move into a house where he had committed a gruesome murder? This case was giving him a severe headache. He leaned his head back and cupped his hands over his eyes, letting out a loud exhale. As he opened them, he saw the same kid on the bike from the other day. He was across the street talking to a man wearing one of those horrible, floppy tourist hats that made everyone look like they were on a goddamn safari. It looked like an important lesson he was giving to the boy. He wondered if one of the cold beers in the refrigerator might help untangle things in his mind, so he hopped out and made his way to the front door, jangling with his keys. As he put his key in the lock, he felt a tug at his waist and jumped back.

"Damn kid, you just about gave me a heart attack." It was the same little boy from across the street. He was pointing.

"The man across the street said you better run. The police house will go *boom*."

It took him a second to process what the boy had said. He grabbed the boy into his arms as quickly as he could and ran. He made it to the grass, a seemingly safe distance and stopped.

"Which man? Where is the man?" he said in his calmest voice.

Then, a thunderous boom ripped through the silence. Shards of wood and debris flew in every direction. Sullivan covered the boy's head as the pieces fell all around them. Smoke billowed into the sky in great black plumes. When he finally looked up, he couldn't believe his eyes. There was a crater at least six feet deep where the living room of the house had been. *Jesus*, he thought, *what if someone was in there?* He ran as close as he could without endangering the boy to look, but there was clearly nothing left of whatever or whoever was inside. Only smoke and crackling debris waved in the wind.

"Where did the man go?"

"I don't know," the boy said barely able to speak through his tears, shaking his head.

Sullivan tried his best to embrace him and comfort him, but the boy was shaking violently with fear, with shock. A car skidded to a stop just behind them, and Tackett came running from his vehicle.

"Goddamnit! Are you OK? Jesus, I thought you were in there."

"Where's Rodriguez?" Sullivan shot back.

"Wait!" he said, grabbing his cell. He pushed the button and waited. The expression on his face was one of complete anguish.

"Please answer, please answer. Damn you! Answer, Rodriguez."

Tackett cupped the phone around his ear as he walked away from the blaze. She wasn't answering. Sullivan noticed the black police SUV he had seen Rodriguez in across the street. His heart sank.

"Thank God!" Tackett said, suddenly erupting.

"Is that you, Rodriguez? Oh, thank Christ in heav...where the hell are you?" he yelled into the phone. "She's OK. She's not here," he said, finally looking up at Sullivan. "She's getting a goddamn coffee at Starbucks. Get over here. The safe house just got bombed. It's fucking gonzo." Tackett sat on the curb where Sullivan was still consoling the young boy. Tackett bent down and let out a loud exhale, rubbing his face with his hands.

A small crowd was beginning to form on the other side of the street. They were pointing, many holding their hands over their mouths in disbelief.

"This is not going to play well at the station. It's my responsibility in any case. Goddamnit that was a close call."

Squad cars and fire trucks were now making their way down the side street.

"There was a man talking to the boy. I saw him actually, but he was wearing a hat that covered his face. Five ten maybe, tanned, somewhere in his forties or fifties, maybe older—I thought he was a fucking tourist."

"Meet me at the station, and you can talk me through it. After I talk to Tierney, of course, and if I still have a job."

"Who else knew about this place?"

"Me, Rodriguez, a couple of other guys, but they never even used it."

"So, it was being watched?"

Tackett nodded silently. Paramedics swarmed Sullivan and the boy.

"I need him at the station as soon as you can. He's the only one who can ID our perp," Sullivan said, imploringly to the medics.

"As soon as he's cleared, sir."

Sullivan's right ear ached with a piercing ring. He realized his car was probably toast as well. He walked toward the house and through the smoke ignoring the firefighters. Sure enough there sat his El Camino, covered in debris but very much intact. The blast had been centered on the front room of the house, just where he had slept, so his car had been spared. He cleared the shards of wood off the hood and opened the door, which fell off its hinge and onto the ground with a rusty groan. He dragged it to the side and in one giant heave threw it into the back. Everything else was amazingly intact. He sat down at the wheel and turned the ignition. Old reliable. Elvis was still singing, "We can't go on together with suspicious minds." As he pulled the car on the road, he could see in the floorboard a half-burned page of Miss November still simmering.

Rodriguez was going to be furious.

CHAPTER 21

Rodriguez and Sullivan sat outside Tierney's office like sullen school children waiting to see the principal. It wasn't like in the movies though; no chairs were flying. Tierney's office was almost morbidly quiet, and they could see the back of Tackett's head through the blinds. Every few minutes he simply nodded or shook his head. It worried Sullivan. Anger would have been better. He thought of Tackett's comment about Tierney. It wasn't his style to lose it and move on. There would be real consequences. Rodriguez sat rubbing her hands together, looking like a young boxer nervously waiting for a fight.

"What's going down in there?" he said to break the tension. "That's the calmest ass tearing I've ever heard."

"Yeah, this ain't good," she said. "Motherfuckers. I was in there not twenty minutes before; my ass would be grass right now."

"Who'd do a thing like this?"

"That's a great question. We all have enemies around here, but none of them this motivated or this sophisticated. You're on 1032, right?" she said without looking up.

Sullivan nodded.

"There ya go. That case is fucking cursed, my friend. Maybe you should go back East man, seriously. I never saw anything like it."

"Not my style. Now I'm in it for the long haul, I'm afraid. A man has to have principles," he said, shrugging. "And if you don't like those, I have others."

Rodriguez forced a laugh.

Just then the door opened, and Tackett walked out silently.

"Call you later," he said, walking past without stopping to speak. "You two get in here," came Tierney's voice. "Close the door. Where to begin? First, I'm glad you're both alive. Second, what the hell were you thinking keeping a secret like that from a superior? By rights, I could send you both packing for insubordination right now. Your sergeant there saw fit to explain that neither of you knew that I was unaware of this little secret of yours. That's happy horseshit, and you know it. That's why he's suspended, indefinitely."

"Sir, if I—" Rodriguez and Sullivan both erupted at the same moment.

"Save it," Tierney said unemotionally, raising his hand. "I went through the academy with Tackett. He's a good man, but his decision to put personal loyalty above professionalism is why he has spent his whole career as a sergeant. He lied to me, and I can't have that. There are things bigger than friendship, believe it or not.

"As I just explained to you," Tierney said, pointing at Sullivan, "I can't support you if I don't know what the hell you're up to. You have now put me in a position to either lie to my superiors or give this department another black eye, not to mention a week's worth of free shit for the press to sling at our expense. Are either of you up to the task of making that call? Huh? Wanna go outside and explain what happened at our secret flophouse." Tierney looked genuinely anguished, and his voice was now almost a whisper.

"You put everyone's ass on the line when you lie. You'll both answer to Sheppard now. He's your acting sergeant until further notice. If you lie to him, I can assure you you'll be finished in law enforcement for good."

"Permission to speak frankly, sir."

"If it's about my son, I'd suggest you mind your fucking good southern manners, Detective Sullivan."

"No, sir. It's about honesty. Don't you think I might have been told about Case 1032, the truth that is? My ass has certainly been hanging in the wind; wouldn't you say?"

"You have as much information as any other detective would get on that case. I didn't want to contaminate your thinking by pretending the case is something that it may or may not be. Let me tell you something else. Danny Fleming had himself a little *chica* south of the border and a cocaine habit, so he may or may not have disappeared because of this case. I knew him well. He was a pretty depressed guy when his NFL days ended. Maybe only being a cop wasn't good enough for him in the end." Tierney paused. "You remember the Sherlock Holmes fella' I was telling you about, Detective?"

"Yes, he was a figment—"

"Holmes says it is a capital mistake to make prejudgments about a case. You let the evidence guide you, and you follow wherever it leads, when you start telling yourself goddamn fairytales before you've even seen the evidence. You'd both benefit from reading a book once in a while."

Sullivan and Rodriguez bowed their heads.

"The kid should be processed by now. Go find out what if anything he remembers about this tourist of yours."

"Yes, sir."

"And one last thing: Joe Tackett is not an active member of this department. If he attempts to call or contact you, he is to be ignored. Sharing information with him about this case is out of the question. Understood? "Yes, yes, sir" are the words you're looking for."

"Yes, sir."

Rodriguez and Sullivan walked out silently. They waited until they were at the end of the hall before Rodriguez spoke.

"Goddamn, I hate that prick sometimes."

"Let's go talk to this kid."

"Yep." Sullivan was looking at his phone.

"What the hell you doing," she said annoyed that he wasn't paying attention.

"Downloading the Cliff's notes of this fucking Sherlock Holmes ass hole."

"Ah man, you're too much."

"By the way," he said, "the house wasn't a complete loss." He handed her the half-burned picture of Miss November from his pocket. All that remained was from the waist down.

"Rachel Arias," she said without flinching. "Very nice equipment. Likes sunsets, wine, and curling up with a good book. Turn offs: jealous men and cigarette smoke. She's still pretty hot, even without a face, wouldn't you say?"

"Yes, I would," he said, arching his eyebrows. "Yes, I would."

CHAPTER 22

Downy propped his feet on his desk. It was Thursday already, and he had no courses to teach and a clear schedule, which was ideal. He had much to do. He still needed to get ahold of Diba Jan. He was certain she would have answers but maybe not ones he wanted to hear. His buzzer rang.

"Professor?"

"I'm here, Janine."

"There is a Mr. Tannehill here to see you. Says it's an important matter. I have him waiting in the lobby. He seems a bit...well..."

"You mean Professor Tannehill?" There was a long pause on the other end.

"Yes, sir."

Downy could tell Janine was flustered. Tannehill had been Charlie's friend really, a professor of Physics from Oxford no less and a bona fide nut job. The academic community had largely written him off after he had attempted to publish work that was apparently all, or largely, based on junk science. He and Charlie had seen him have a full meltdown at a conference in Prague some years ago. It had effectively ended his career. *What on earth could he want now?* he wondered, and why would he come to him? They'd barely even spoken to one another.

"Janine, you can send him in. Buzz me in ten minutes for an important call, just in case."

"OK."

He looked at the phone and thought of Diba Jan. Tannehill limped into the room, favoring his left leg. The man looked positively ill. His hair had gone snow white since the last time he'd seen him, not to mention eyes that glared with what Downy could only call an unnatural zeal. His face was beet red.

"Please, Professor, don't get up on my account." Downy did love the British accent, especially in men of Tannehill's age. It was an older England he came from.

"Professor, I haven't seen you in years. Please sit down."

"I'm sure I am no less easy on the eyes than ever," he said almost apologetically. "To quote my father, if I'd known I was going to live this long, I might have taken better care of myself."

Downy laughed sympathetically.

"You on the other hand don't look a day older than what I can remember. You must have been barely a boy though, when Charlie plucked you out of that grimy bar and made you a household name. And look at you now."

He remembered immediately why no one could stand Tannehill. His brusque manner put everyone off, though Charlie had always seen fit to put a positive spin on his rude behavior. Tannehill seemed to notice that the comment had stung a bit.

"I've read your books, Professor, and you are quite deserving of the mantle. If I didn't know better, I'd say you and old Caesar were drinking buddies, maybe Antony too. An amazing imagination you have."

There it was again. He wasn't a historian then; he was good at making stuff up. "Thank you."

"I'm sure you must be trying to understand why I am here." He didn't give Downy a chance to respond before continuing. "I know my reputation precedes me wherever I go, but please understand these commonplace insults have no effect whatsoever. I am quite beyond all that now, I assure you. I have no need for the approval of so-called twenty-first-century academia. I will perhaps build my own university one day, where my ideas can be better understood and appreciated, if *time* permits."

Downy nodded and smiled politely. He had no idea how to respond. "Could I offer you a coffee or glass of water?" he said, trying to change the subject.

"Oh yes, water would be lovely."

He rose pouring from the cooler in the corner. He handed the glass to Tannehill who finished it as if it was the last water he would ever get. He watched him gulp away in stunned silence.

"Perhaps one more would be OK. I have traveled a long

distance to be here, and I'm afraid I have underestimated my thirst."

"Sure," he said, getting up again, pouring him a second. The fervor with which he drank suggested something more like madness. Streams of water ran down the sides of his mouth, and he started to choke a little, coughing erratically.

"This mortal coil, eh?" he said.

Downy looked at his intercom, praying that Janine would ring early.

"I am here on a social visit only, Professor Downy; call it a courtesy call; and to tell you what you must already perceive to be true."

"Charles Patterson," Tannehill said, leaning forward with a wide-eyed stare.

Downy sat back in his chair. His pulse quickened.

"I believe one Samara Patterson has visited you of late. I'm certain she has told you of her own suspicions."

He had Downy's complete attention now.

"The poor girl, Samara. So beautiful. Her fate is most upsetting of all to me. I can assure you it is not of my doing."

"I don't follow. Is Samara in some kind of danger?"

"Samara believes her father's death was something else entirely, and about that at least she is quite right."

"Do you have some information about Charlie's death?"

"Oh, I don't know what happened exactly, but he's gone, in a purely physical sense, here at least."

Tannehill looked nonchalantly at his fingernails. "I have no information that a man of your intellect would accept, I'm afraid."

Downy's buzzer rang. "Professor, I'm so sorry to bother you, but you have a very important call on line two."

"Janine, tell them I'll call back."

"Yes, sir."

"Do you know that in almost every single office I have visited over the past eleven years, a sudden, urgent call has come through for the person I'm speaking with? It's OK; I would think me a madman myself if I didn't know better; I'm quite used to being thought unworthy of attention, in these hallowed halls anyway."

Downy smiled sympathetically.

"Do you know how the universe is arranged, Professor? It's just like your computer there, except infinitely more vast, of course. Eternities of code spreading out in all directions. Just numbers really. If you have a correct name and address, well you can call almost anyone."

It was odd; at times Tannehill seemed like he was talking in riddles, pure nonsense, but at other moments he seemed absolutely lucid and clear.

"I'm sorry my knowledge of physics is limited, Dr. Tannehill."

"I wonder, Professor Downy; have you ever read Dicken's *Christmas Carol*?"

"Sure, a long time ago."

"I feel just like the ghost of Christmas past sitting here in your office. You will be visited by three ghosts," he said, putting on a spooky voice. "Actually there's no such thing as ghosts, but for you it will certainly seem so. Old dear friends, long gone, now ghosts." Tannehill looked around the room at the pictures on the wall.

"My dear friend Charlie," he said, looking at the shot of them all on set together in Rome, almost mumbling. "He was kind to me through it all, you know? The only one." Tannehill reached into his pocket, pulling out what looked like a sugar cube, putting it to his tongue. Forgive an old man and his need for sugar. I am in the advanced stages of the illness."

"I'm not sure quite what to say, unless you know something important," Downy said.

"Say nothing. I thank you for your hospitality, and if you talk to Samara Lee Patterson, as I'm sure you will, you need not trouble her with the wild apparitions of this old has been. I wish the best to the both of you. Before I leave though, I have something I want to give you. It's a gift, I suppose." The old man reached into the satchel at his feet and pulled out a piece of rolled cloth. "I imagine you may be able to appreciate the value of such a thing more than most." He sat the object on the desk as he stood up, grimacing in some pain. "It's this hip of mine, and the other and on and on. Old age takes from us far more than it gives. You needn't worry about it though, Professor; you are young yet."

Downy leaned forward toward the cloth.

"Ahh...I would prefer if you open it later. I know you will do your due diligence to verify its authenticity."

The old man hobbled out the door, limping without a word. He could hear him asking Janine for another water, which he drank as before. Downy watched through the blind as Janine's expression morphed from curiosity to disgust. He finally walked into the lobby once he had gone. Janine looked at him perplexed.

"What the hell was that all about?"

"I wish I knew," he said. "I wish I knew."

CHAPTER 23

The carriage pulled to a stop at the peak of the hill. Below the man could see the ravine where the ruins stood. How long had they been there? No one knew for sure. Perhaps long before the Greeks even, he supposed. Gods had built them for certain, not mortal hands. Titans. The architecture was impossible. Everything was built to the scale of giants it seemed. Strange lights reflected out from the interior as if the gods still lived there. Flowers of unknown origin, not native, bloomed suddenly and then disappeared. They could be seen growing and wilting again in only a few minutes of time. Men and women of the most beautiful physiques were often reported to be wandering the edges of the ruins. He had been told the stories as a child of these ephemeral creatures leading unwary travelers into the ruins, never to be seen or heard from again. Some thought it an ancient madhouse, or an asylum, and few dared tread there. The pond was just beyond the wall. A ghastly odor emanated from its depths. It was the unmistakable smell of death.

The day was a beautiful one though, with a soft, cool wind, which blew against his face. The hills were almost silent. Even nature retreated from the place it seemed. It reminded him of his boyhood, traipsing across the meadows pretending to be heroes from the past: Hercules fighting in the Trojan war alongside brave Achilles, holding him as he fell in battle, killed by an arrow to the back of his foot, where the goddess had held him as she dipped his body into the ocean, making him forever immortal. As he approached he could see the dark surface of the water. He turned his face away so as not to get lost in the strange visions that shone in its depths. It was a picture of chaos in the pond—inky, primordial chaos. Some said it was full of snakes, but he could see none. He had made it. There would be no stopping him now. He tried to put the feeling in perspective but found he could not. His blood surged with the victory. There was simply no other feeling like it. He wondered if the gods would speak to him once it was finished. That wasn't too crazy to believe was it? A kiss from Venus, perhaps? Perhaps she would take him as her lover. He looked back into the carriage and saw his captive still sleeping. He would be awake soon. He would be free. His color had returned, though, and he was completely still; his expression was light, almost pleasant. It looked like his eyes might flutter open any second, but it would all seem a dream to him anyway. Once he returned home, his mind would return as well. It would be an unrecorded episode. "Barely a ripple on the surface of an unimaginably large ocean," the teacher had said.

The man circled the courtyard before pulling the carriage to a stop. He popped two more sugar cubes into his mouth and waited. The usual rush didn't overtake him. He was already in such an elevated state and needed to slow down. How could he experience more pleasure than this? He laughed. He was a god then. He would not need to take any more cubes in any case. There were several left in his pocket, but he would eat them only at the very end, all at once, just for fun. That should test his godly powers. The sleeping man opened his eyes with a soft whine, but they fluttered back shut. He whinnied just like a child waking from a long afternoon nap.

The man got down from the carriage and pulled his cloak back over his head. He needed to move his prisoner to one of the gated cells just to be cautious. Walking around to the back, he grabbed the man's sleeping body and heaved it over his shoulder in one swift jerk. He struggled down the staircase, stopping at the bottom only to wipe great streams of sweat from his brow. He lay the man's body as carefully as he could manage onto the floor, but it hit with a dull thud.

"We always hurt the one's we love my dear," he said with a laugh into the man's sleeping ear.

He now lay on his back against the cold floor. The room smelled of amber and incense. There were bones of slaughtered sacrifices in the corner in a great pile. They were nearly opaque now, otherworldly. He had certainly never seen such creatures in his travels. The sound of a woman's quiet laughter echoed through the halls. A sudden wind blew past, and a man's voice sounded off a "No!" He had to ignore these things. They meant nothing. They were a distraction, probably intentional, but couldn't hurt him. He was merely among jealous peers now, a feeling he knew all too well.

He rolled the man's body into the cell and clanked the gate shut behind him. OK, so he wasn't completely a god yet. His heart pounded in his chest. He rather liked the feeling, but he could not yet move himself. What a spectacle was before him. Something or someone was chained to the wall in the next cell. He looked in. It looked like a gladiator, a hulk of a man completely stripped nude. Great lashes bled from his back. He wanted to ask the man if he was OK, but he was interrupted by a voice.

"Don't speak to me. You must never speak to me." The man had read his very thoughts it seemed. A neat trick. He could nearly do it himself though.

"I need nothing," came the voice again. "Go away."

Fine, he thought.

The man walked back to the top of the staircase and then through the courtyard, resting finally at the edge of the pond. The valley walls seemed to sway with the wild grasses that grew there. *What great struggle had taken place here?* he wondered. That he would like to see, but it was too late for any more adventures. It was time to assert his place once more. He laughed at how grandiose his thinking had become. He thought of the Vestals. They would be consumed in the very morass they had created. Poetic. Beautiful. He had nothing to write with, or he would have written some lines of verse to commemorate the occasion. He missed writing actually, but of these things, it would be for others to write. He had chosen someone perfect for the task in fact. He had his life back now and soon so would his dear companion. They were prisoners no more.

CHAPTER 24

Downy stood at the window overlooking Mission Bay. He was relieved to be home finally. He went to the liquor cabinet and pulled a bottle of scotch from the shelf, pouring a little longer than usual. He looked at the spot just in front of the bay window where he had seen the detectives and tried to imagine what might have taken place there. That someone might choose a spot of such beauty as a place to kill someone was unimaginable. But a true killer probably cared little about beauty did they? The detective had said "mountains of blood." *What could have happened?* Downy couldn't get the image from *The Shining* from his mind, of the blood flowing like a river through the corridors of the Overlook Hotel. The two twin sisters. Ghosts. Downy drained his glass. He was a writer after all, just like Nicholson had been in the film. Maybe it was time to get out his typewriter and retire to the grand hall of the Overlook Hotel.

He threw his bag down and opened the doors to the bay.

The scotch tasted smooth and warm going down, and he laid his head back, letting out a long exhale. He might have slept but instead got up and walked back to the kitchen to pour another glass. Reaching into his bag, he put the strange gift that Tannehill had given him on the table. It was still wrapped in a fine piece of linen, which was tied with a purple ribbon at the center. He could see what looked like a seal of some sort, but the writing was too small to read. He pulled at it, unwrapping it carefully so as not to break the seal, hardly knowing what to expect. He saw the gold immediately. Holding it in the light, he could see it was a laurel, covered in gold leaves, clearly made to be worn on the head. A tiny string of what looked like black pearl or amethyst hung from the back by a clasp, which connected to a smaller amulet. On the amulet was an insignia. He had only seen it once before: the first-century Roman sword, in the collection at school, one of the few in the world of its kind. He turned it with his fingers. There was also a Latin script written on the amulet, which he immediately recognized as Roman. It read as follows:

C. Caesari,
Romam primain animis.

He paused for a moment and translated.

For Gaius Julius Caesar. First in the hearts of Rome.

He could see a piece of paper sticking out from the linen.

The writing was a scrawl, undoubtedly from Tannehill's unsteady hand:

This is exactly what it appears to be. It is stolen, for the record. Have its age tested at once.

Professor Jacob Tannehill

He shook his head. Poor man. It was a clever prop, probably fabricated by a talented artist in fact, but it was clearly too clean and far too unblemished to be a true relic. But the insignia interested him. Why would someone take the trouble to copy that particular feature unless they were truly trying to pass it off as real? It could be a serious forgery, and Downy felt an obligation to look into it. Tannehill, in his state, might have even paid for it. He plopped down into his chair, putting the laurel on his head like an old hat. It nearly fit. He grabbed for his phone and dialed the school. Janine answered at his office.

"Hey, you're still there."

"Sure, ever the busy bee."

"Could you do me a favor and phone the archives and let them know I'm coming by to check out one of their pieces?"

"Sure. Only one piece?"

"Yep, just give them our budget number."

"Done."

"Thanks, Janine. You're the best."

"That's what you keep saying."

Looking back at his bag, he could also see the letter of

recommendation from that rather strange student. *What was his name again? Tero, Taro?* It was poking out of his bag. He leaned forward pulling it out and sat on the floor with his glass. He unrolled the pages and began to read:

Greetings Distinguished Professor Downy,

I apologize that I must write to you, but in my advancing years, travel has become something of a difficulty for me. I write to you today on behalf of Monsieur Guy Taro. Monsieur Taro came to our brotherhood, the Brotherhood of the Gracchi, under what I can only call vague circumstances. Let me take a moment to explain that this is not unusual in the brotherhood. Many men who choose to renounce the material world and the pursuits of the flesh in favor of a purely spiritual life never share with us what their lives were like before they arrived. It is a policy going back nearly two thousand years in our order to never force a man to make an accounting of his past. Having said this, I must confess that our order must at times protect its interests, both in the name of safety and of continuing good relations with the community. In any case, our inquiries, which were quite thorough, revealed nothing of concern either legally or personally; therefore, we welcomed Monsieur Taro into our community with open arms. That was nearly eleven years ago. It has turned out to be a most prosperous decision on our part.

I must be frank and tell you that I believe Mr. Taro to have suffered some great misfortune or tragedy in his past. In the years I have known him, only a spare, few details have given any glimmer of the true nature of what this tragedy may have been. One gets the impression that his loss was of a deeply personal nature, some great indignity perhaps. Of his origins I can tell you only that a man who did not wish to be identified delivered him to us late one night. He came to us a broken soul, nearly mute and completely disoriented, probably intoxicated, having been rescued by the stranger from a local tavern near us, where he was found unconscious. We thought him possibly mentally ill when he arrived. I have never seen one so pitiable in his demeanor in my long years, and let me assure you I have seen many a broken man. His recovery, while slow, was nevertheless steady, and after only a year's time, he was a fully functioning, though silent, member of the brotherhood. Allow me to stop for a moment to tell you on this point that Mr. Taro is without question one of the most industrious and motivated men I have ever come to know. Even before he began to speak, he worked with great diligence and energy, as all who live among us must. Our order operates under what I must call a rather strict standard of both spiritual and physical obligation, but Mr. Taro took to our Spartan ways immediately, without complaint. It is common for us to work sixteen-hour days in our vineyards or on construction projects in our surrounding communities. Mr. Taro has clearly had much experience in this regard, as his understanding of how to get things done as a manager of men is only eclipsed by his individual ability at doing them. He is a natural leader and a man of few but choice words. He is also a deeply learned man. We have many scholars of renown among us, but rarely do such men appear in our midst under such circumstances. In fact, a great part of our work here at the monastery involves the translation of ancient texts, and in this regard Monsieur Taro excels to a degree that is difficult to measure. His mastery of classical Greek and Latin is unparalleled. In his time with us, he has decoded texts that our most prodigious scholars have struggled with for many years. Furthermore, his elocution of the Latin tongue offers rarely seen insights into the true nature of that language as it might actually have been spoken in antiquity. For this reason and many others, I suspect he comes from a very distinguished background, though on this point he has only spoken of his people rarely and always with a note of melancholy.

I must finish by telling you that when Mr. Taro indicated his desire to leave the order some months ago; he also made known his wish to bestow upon us an endowment. It would be a breach of his trust to divulge details, but let me say that his gift to us was truly astonishing in its scope, so much so that the continued preservation of our lifestyle will be guaranteed for many generations to come. I must tell you on a personal note it was a great shock to us all that he made the decision to leave the monastery. Each of our members may leave whenever they wish, of course, but it is unusual since we had only recently passed his ten-year confirmation, a time when our brethren may freely depart without explanation, should they choose to move on. His reasons are his own, and I shall not speculate on them, not in light of his incredible contributions nor his impeccable character.

Monsieur Taro has asked, as is his way, very little of me in writing to you on his behalf. I do so with great enthusiasm. His interest, if I understand correctly, is to be allowed a chance to both receive and share knowledge with you. I know how busy a man of your talents must be. I would consider it a gravely missed opportunity though, for someone like yourself, who is so deeply interested in classical studies, to miss out on the opportunity to converse with Monsieur Guy Taro. His knowledge of the classical period is second to none I have ever encountered. Your interests and his converge in every respect I would say. Our order has benefitted tremendously from his presence, and it is with something of a heavy heart that I present him to you, knowing we are losing such a man. We had come to believe that he would in fact be staying with us, as most in our order do, until the end of his days, but we wish him God's own speed, and all the blessings life has to bestow nevertheless.

Professor Downy, thank you for your consideration in this matter, and should you ever need to speak with me in person, I can be reached by telephone at our front office number, which is enclosed. If you should ever find yourself

in the Parnassus region of Greece, consider yourself a
welcome guest with us. It would be my honor to receive a
man of your talents and prestige as a brother.

With great respect,
Vigo Alfonse Gracchi
Head Prior of the Brotherhood of the Gracchi

π

Downy lay the letter on the rug. Some reference indeed. He thought of the man's overly polite demeanor and general awkwardness in class, which made more sense now. He was a goddamned monk.

He looked at his phone, which had fallen from his bag as well; two messages blinked. The first was a text from Samara:

I hope I haven't spooked you. You doing ok? Your stunt double,
Chad, is a barrel of monkeys...whole class seems highly disap-
pointed...just sayin.

Sam

The second was a voice mail. It was Nazim's number. So he had called back. Downy never had his ringer turned on because he could never remember to turn it off when class was in session. If his phone rang even once, he could look forward to an entire semester of listening to his students horrible ring tones, not to mention their incessant texting. He pushed the speaker button:

Professor Downy, I apologize for our last conversation. I have left a message with Mr. Charlie, and his hotel assures me he has been there all this week without incident. I know the owner personally. I hope you are not angry, and I would like to set up a conference call for the three of us as soon as I hear from him. I also indicated to the front desk person that Charlie might simply call you directly. I hope it will help calm your fears for his safety. I hope all is well and look forward to clearing up this matter soon. Thank you very much, sir.

He poured much more scotch into his glass. He thought back to the funeral. Nazim had been distraught over Charlie's loss; it was true. Could it have pushed him over the edge though? This far over the edge? He had fallen to his knees in fact, in private, when he and Downy had been alone with Charlie's wife, Sarah, at the funeral. It did seem extreme, but he had always assumed it was a cultural nuance. Intense and visible grief in Middle Eastern countries was always treated more as an expression of the extent of one's love and respect for the deceased. The suffering of the bereaved should be equal to the loss. Wailing, even self-flagellation wasn't considered taboo. The ancient Egyptians had practically made a fine art of suffering in fact. Professional wailers could be bought if there weren't sufficient family members or loved ones who could provide the necessary intensity at a sendoff. But this level of denial made no sense. There was something else though that had always bothered him. Nazim seemed excessively puzzled by how Charlie could have fallen overboard. He could only say, "We lost him. I do not know how." He had pressed him for more details, but Nazim only hung his head repeating, "I do not know how." The boat had been full of Charlie's grad students as well, and yet no one could quite explain how it had happened. Charlie was there one moment and simply gone the next. Nazim clearly felt it was his fault nevertheless. "I have lost my friend, I have lost him," he had said over and over again, banging his fists against his temples. He had wept so violently he had torn his shirt. Downy needed to talk to Diba Jan, Nazim's wife, but it seemed that she too was somehow involved in this horrible charade. Why else would she turn Samara away and pretend not to know her? There was something truly amiss, possibly criminal going on. He could feel it. There was some unknown pressure at work here, something causing his friends to act in such a strange way. He felt their very lives might be in danger. Why else would Nazim deny him?

The light on his phone lit up, and he looked. It was Naomi:

Late at work again!!! Sorry...thinking I'll be home round 8.

He tossed his phone down against the table. *Shit*. He really did need to talk. He picked up his phone again and dashed off a text to Samara:

Coffee at 6:30?...Woody's...then dinner with me and Naomi at 8:30? She'll come late from work...

He hit Send and walked out on the deck overlooking the bay. It was time to get Naomi and Samara in the same room, for everyone's sake. Why did he get butterflies in his stomach every time he texted with Samara? He already knew the answer. He remembered her message and typed again:

Chad will be a great man one day...wait and see...I shall return in any case...

He watched the sun fade to a soft orange. The ocean looked endless and glistened. He needed to get back in the classroom. The last few days had been completely frenzied. He always wondered if anyone understood how much his love for his job had to do with his need for escape. It was ironic, the notion of escaping in front of a packed room of absolute strangers, but that's exactly how it felt to him.

His phone lit again.

See you in 30 min...I promise no traps...no phone booths...
Sam

He was eager to share what had happened to him, even though he knew Samara wouldn't be happy to hear it. He typed again:

Coffee at Woody's with Samara in 30 and then meet for dinner at 8:30...? Short notice I know, but let's do it...
Me

He hit Send and went to the shower to get ready. It had been another stressful day, and he needed to wash it off before his evening began. It had nothing to do with his meeting with Samara he told himself. Of course, not; he just needed to freshen up, and his wife was coming for God's sakes. What could be safer than that?

CHAPTER 25

Sullivan watched through the double-sided glass of the mirror as Rodriguez took a crack at the boy. She sat very close to him, exuding almost maternal warmth. He had already said more to her in five minutes than he had to him in an hour. The boy claimed the man in the hat had given him a five-dollar bill to deliver a message to his friend across the street and that they were "playing a game." It annoyed him a little. He was usually very good at talking to children. This wasn't the usual case though, and the boy was clearly still in shock. His face was too closely associated with that shock probably. His phone buzzed in his pocket. It was a number he didn't recognize.

"Hey, it's me. I'm calling from a safe line." It was Tackett.

"Tierney will be watching for calls between us. Meet me at Aero Club at seven for a drink."

"OK, sure."

Since it was going to be a social visit, this clearly didn't fall into Tierney's warning against involving Tackett in the case. He still needed to talk to him about the professor, about the strange clue.

"See ya then—"

He looked at his watch. The big briefing was in only five minutes. He sat alone in the dark room just for a moment thinking of the professor. He had genuinely liked the guy. What was it that he could be lying about? Was it the blood sample? What were the odds it was another professor Detective Jensen had written about in his notes? Or was it something else entirely?

Rodriguez broke his concentration opening the door. "Come on, we're gonna be late."

"Yep, on my way." He grabbed his stuff, dashing out the door, trying to catch up to her.

"So I heard you guys can get married now, out here anyway."

"What?"

"Congratulations, I think it's aweso—"

"I'm already married stupid," she said, pointing to her ring. Man, you are just all kinds of awkward, aren't you?"

"Oh, I didn't know you could already—"

"And stop yelling."

The pair walked into the conference room, which was already full. Tierney was at the head of the room, going over papers of some kind with one of the suits from downstairs. Legal. You could tell by the grimace on his face.

"Everybody get situated, please," he said. "Nine blocks from here at 242 A Street at approximately eleven forty-seven a.m., a safe house, formerly managed by this department, was hit with explosives, which were most likely detonated remotely. Complicating this situation, members of this department have continued using this residence for departmental purposes, in spite of the fact that we stopped paying rent on it more than eight years ago. We are still attempting to contact the owner, who now lives out of state apparently. One of your peers has been put on suspension pending investigation of his role in the illegal continuation of police activity at this location. In his place Detective Sheppard has been promoted to acting sergeant. Let me remind everyone that this is an internal matter and is not to be discussed outside the doors of this station. There is reason to believe that the suspect in this case has had contact with the department before. We have developed a sketch from testimony given by two eyewitnesses. One eye witness was a seven-year-old male who was paid by our suspect to deliver a message to one of our own detectives in the vicinity only moments before the blast occurred. That detective, Detective Sullivan, also made a partial ID but was at such proximity not to be able to elaborate with any concrete facial details." Tierney was now reading directly from his notes.

"Both witnesses place our perp as a forty-five- to fifty-five-year-old male, slim or slender of build, five ten. He was dressed to blend in as a tourist, with a safari-style hat, tan in color. He also has a long, prominent scar running across his neckline. There is some reason to believe that he was sending a message of some sort to this department, rather than trying to incur loss of life. Detective Rodriguez along with Detective

Sullivan had also been in or near the house before the incident. They were most likely observed by the perpetrator. This further corroborates our suspicion that the perpetrator or perpetrators wanted to destroy the residence only."

There was mumbling across the room.

Tierney interjected more loudly to squelch it.

"The bomb squad is still analyzing materials from the scene for leads on who might have put it together and whether we are dealing with domestic or international style terrorism. Make no mistake; the person or people we are dealing with are very dangerous, and they must be caught before their already criminal actions escalate further. Their capture is priority number one for this department. Please know all overtime requests related to this case will be honored. Thank you. You are dismissed."

Jesus, Sullivan thought, *they made it sound like he and Rodriguez had been on a date.* The other officers looked at the two of them and snickered. Sullivan could feel their eyes all over him. Rodriguez walked out alone and quickly. Still no mention of Case 1032 though. Tackett had it right; Tierney really was an angler.

Tierney suddenly approached him. "Now, Detective, I get to go talk to the press. You should watch it later on Channel 6, how they abuse me and how I just have to grin and eat every bite of shit they serve up."

Tierney didn't give him a chance to respond, walking away without a word. It looked like all their conversations were going to be like this: quick and one sided. Oh well, it was a start. Sullivan was feeling thirsty but knew he wasn't meeting Tackett for another two hours. Maybe he would get there early and sample the wares. He walked past Sheppard's desk on his way. Sheppard looked up.

"It's going to be a real pleasure working under your direction, Sergeant Sheppard, sir."

"Come on, let's be civil," Sheppard said, sounding disappointed.

"I'll bet dear old dad was your football coach in high school, and you started every game, huh?" he said, leaning on the edge of Sheppard's desk.

"Barely a week on the force and already banging another man's wife in a secret flophouse. I'll give it another two weeks tops before formal charges are filed."

"Wait, I thought Rodriguez wa—"

Sullivan furrowed his brow.

"And I started because I could play. First team All-Conference."

"Nooo, shit! I was only joking, but you really are daddy's little superstar."

"Look, bring me your reports and copies of all your casework by noon tomorrow, and get your fucking ears checked for God's sakes; you're yelling. I want to review with you in person at the end of each week. I know all about Case 1032 and don't want to see you make a mess of it. I would be interested in anything fresh you find though. Who knows? Maybe we can even help out each other?"

"Why, Shep, I feel like we're old pals now. Stop with the sincerity, please; you're breaking my heart."

Sheppard waved his hand dejectedly and turned away. He

felt a bit bad. He had been too harsh, a little. A beer would no doubt help ease his conscience, so he dashed past his desk picking up his things, map questing Aero Club on his way out the door.

When he arrived to his car, he'd forgotten that the door was still off. It did little to damage the appearance frankly. A yellow ticket flapped in the wind. He pulled it out. It was a citation for "illegal operation of a wrecked vehicle." On the ticket someone had drawn a picture of him with the caption "Ice Man" written above it. There was also a likeness of Rodriguez on her knees. She was servicing him. Above her was written: "Investigating prostitution." *God, cops were such assholes*, he mused, like a gang of shitty middle school kids. A few cars down a group of them were laughing and pointing. He grabbed the ticket, throwing it in the air nonchalantly. Not having to open the door was actually an improvement. One less thing. He popped out the eight-track tape of Elvis and replaced it with Frank Sinatra, speeding away in a plume of black smoke, with his middle finger extended for all to see.

CHAPTER 26

This time when Downy walked in, Samara was already at a table with someone. A younger guy. She saw him, and they both stood up.

Samara erupted, "Uncle Noah!" and threw her arms around him. "This is Mitch. He's in our class. We were studying actually, sort of, and we just bumped into each other," she said, making her eyes big and round.

"Man, I had no idea you guys were related, but that's awesome."

"Yeah, hi, Mitch," Downy said, squinting a bit.

"It's OK. I sit pretty far in the back," he said, picking up on Downy's unease, "but I love your class so far. I hope you're back in time for the second half of that Caesar presentation though. All my roommates made me watch the miniseries, and it's practically why I signed up."

"Yeah, I'll be back for sure."

"Hey, can I ask you a question about Caesar?"

"Sure."

"Why do you think he sent his guards away? I mean he wouldn't have been assassinated if they had been there, right."

"Yeah," Downy said, "the senate promised him by decree that he was safe in their midst."

"Oh, OK, oh wow. So they tricked him?"

"Caesar wanted to show his faith in their word, I think."

"That was dumb," Mitch said abruptly.

"Yes, it sort of was," he said, smiling sympathetically, and then he looked at Samara who looked unimpressed as well but was laughing anyway.

"Have a great dinner. Thanks, Samara," Mitch said, winking at her.

It made him uneasy. Why was he winking? Samara sat down and rolled her eyes.

"Small town, huh? Imagine me just bumping into the guy. His frat meets here once a week for some damn whiskey social or something. He was coming back for his hat."

"No worries," he said, trying to seem at ease.

"I'm two beers in already. Sorry, talking to frat boys stresses me out. I always feel like they're trying to sell me something. Just coffee would be nice, if it's OK with you?"

"Yeah, sure...Uncle Noah?" he said with a grin.

"I didn't really know what else to say, sorry. I hope you aren't missing class on account of me because of last time."

He laughed.

"No, no. I was worried you might think so. I've been up to my ass in admin stuff these last few days. Seriously, things that never come up, and all at once."

"I can't wait to see Naomi. Seriously."

"Yeah, she'll get here as soon as she can."

The waiter came, the same one as last time. He smiled warmly, "It's so nice to see you both again." They nodded. He thought they were a couple then. Great. It actually felt oddly exhilarating, and if they had been carrying on an affair, he knew this would be just the place to do it.

Tonight a piano player sat in the far corner, their regular guy. He was playing something by Dean Martin but very slowly.

"Two stubby Greeks, one with a shot of espresso on top," he said.

"Coming right up. Hope you will be joining us for dinner?"

"Yes, actually we'll need room for a third."

"The pescador tonight is straight from Coronado, came in this morning. It's the chef's signature dish in a calico and mango butter reduction."

"Great." Downy said.

"I could live here," Samara said, laughing.

"I used to," he said, laughing back. "I wanted us to have some time to chat before Naomi comes."

"OK," Samara said, "until our third arrives." She tilted her head a bit to the side, arching an eyebrow.

He hadn't considered the way he had said it. It did sound

rather impersonal. He chose not to react. "What?" he said, finally shrugging.

Samara was dressed in faded blue jeans and a black shoulder cut sweater. Somehow, she looked even more elegant than before. Her hair was pulled up off her shoulder in a simple clip. He tried not to stare for too long before speaking. The waiter put down their coffees.

"So, I wanted to tell you I talked to Nazim, well sort of."

She leaned forward with a serious look on her face.

"And?"

"I'm deeply concerned about his well-being, to be honest. He refused to acknowledge that he and I knew each other at all; though very strangely, he claims to know your dad still."

"What, what do you mean?"

"I don't know quite how to explain it, but he seems to believe your dad is still alive, though he claims he doesn't know you either, so I think everything he's saying has to be put in context. And well, he seems very ill or perhaps under some sort of pressure to lie."

Samara's face drew back in a daze. She had been holding her coffee cup, and her hand began to shake uncontrollably.

"Just wait, OK?" he said, trying to keep her calm. "I know what you must be thinking, but I'm afraid there may actually be a dementia of some kind or even something else; I'm not sure what yet. It would explain almost everything."

Samara's eyes watered. "You don't think this, coupled with the note I found, means anything?" she said incredulously.

"The note, I can't explain. Not yet. It's way too soon to know anything until I speak to Diba Jan."

"She ignored me, Noah. You're wasting your time. I'm telling you all of them did. What are we going to do?" she said looking at him imploringly.

"We are going to keep our heads. I need to contact my publisher. He has known Nazim's family forever. He grew up in Cairo. He knew your dad well too. I think it's safest if we let him reach out to them first."

He wanted to tell her that Nazim had also said he would conference call with Charlie, but he felt it would upset her too much. Sadly, he knew he was never going to answer that call anyway. He looked up at the second floor toward his and Charlie's old booth. He had the strangest sensation, like Charlie was back somehow. He had forgotten how much he enjoyed the sound of his old friend's voice. It had been the first thing between them, his manner of speech; how he made you feel you deserved the world and everything in it, and that it was only as easy as reaching out to take it. He had treated Downy like he was a genius, so he had always tried his best to act like one. Charlie was, of course, the fiercely intelligent one, but like Downy he had an edge to him. In truth, it was probably why they became such fast friends. The almost twenty-year age difference hadn't mattered at all. Charlie was the wise old owl and Downy the young prodigy. Both seemed to love the roles they had cast themselves in.

Samara's head was down. She stared into her coffee blankly. "Have you ever heard of a place called the pond?" she said suddenly, looking up at him.

"No, it doesn't ring a bell."

"I looked through my dad's travel logs, and every year he

went there it says, with friends, but he never says which pond or even what friends. You guys ever travel to a place to fish or something, part of a dig? My mother wasn't very suspicious about it either when I told her. He traveled so much after all."

"Seems perfectly explainable. I'm sure if you ask around with some of his other friends."

"He had none, Noah, none except for you."

"What?"

"Yeah, you were enough for him. He could be a deeply solitary person you know, almost secretive. That's why it doesn't seem like a thing he would do, not without you along, or somebody he liked at least. Who would he have gone with instead?"

He couldn't believe it. Charlie was instantly the life of any room he walked into. Downy had always assumed he had a wide group of friends.

"I never thought...I mean...I always figured there were lots of other people he was close to."

"His work, really. Sometimes my mom. That's why having you around was so nice. He really came out of his shell, but then you always left. My mother and I felt sort of second rate. It sounds awful, I know. It sounds like I'm being critical, but I just mean that you brought out something special in him."

"It must have been doubly hard when I moved, huh, for such a young girl, I mean?"

"Yeah, it was." Tears streaked down her cheeks uncontrollably. She seemed even more beautiful, fragile. He wanted to touch her face but dared not.

He saw the waiter coming, and he handed her a tissue quickly. It was too late. The waiter poured more coffee silently. "I'll come back and check on you soon," he said sympathetically, turning quickly to avoid eye contact with them and speaking in almost a whisper.

"They'll think you're breaking my heart," Samara said, laughing through her tears. "How much power there is in a woman's tears," she said, wiping her face with the tissue. "Grown men flee like frightened children."

"We're gonna get through this, OK?" he said, trying to sound confident, but Samara looked unconvinced.

"I'm gonna need a drink before your wife gets here, OK? That scotch from the other night would be just perfect."

"Sure."

"We'll switch back to coffee when she gets here, OK. Just for the sake of appearances."

Downy laughed, but his heart was troubled. He looked up to the booth over her shoulder. The framed picture of Freud was still there along with their plaque for being "The World Champions of Scotch."

Samara stood up. "I have to go fix myself; Naomi can't see me like this. I'll be right back."

"Yeah, of course."

The waiter came over immediately.

"Could we have two Macallans if a bottle is open?"

"Yes, sir, of course."

"Excuse me, could you do me a favor? Deliver a third glass to the booth upstairs, the one with Mr. Freud presiding."

"Of course, I will, sir. For Mr. Patterson, then?"

"Yes, that's right. You remember him?"

"I'd been working here only a few months when he passed away. I was still a busboy. It would be my pleasure, sir, and it's on the house."

"Thank you," Downy said. "Thank you."

Sullivan could see the blinking neon sign of the Aero Club all the way from the interstate. In spite of it being a major So Cal city, San Diego had somehow managed to avoid the urban sprawl of cities like LA. The Aero Club was tucked right beneath the overpass but still near enough to the airport to have earned the name. Inside though it was simply a square bar in the middle of an old room, it reminded him of a thousand bars in the South, minus the rednecks, of course. He scanned as he walked in. Tackett raised a hand from the back booth next to the jukebox.

"I already ordered two more Jack and Cokes, one for me and another for me," he said, yelling above the music.

It was a little too early for "Don't Stop Believin'," but already there were small groups of people getting rowdy together—the after-work crowd trying to shake off the day.

"You're early. What are you a cop or something?" Sullivan shouted over the roar. Tackett seemed a bit unsteady on his feet. "Are you drunk already?" he said accusingly. "Goddamn, let me catch up."

"I lost my job. It's a moral fucking imperative that I get drunk." Tackett suddenly became sober sounding, though clearly he had been at it for a while.

"You just got suspended; you didn't get fired."

"Never mind Robby fucking Tierney's sorry ass. What did you find out?"

"Well, the kid gave us—"

"Not about that, about 1032? You said you needed to chat, so chat."

The waitress came by with two cups of coffee.

"Hey, where's my Jack and Coke?"

"You drink too much kid, and my tank is already full, sorry."

"OK, coffee it is," Sullivan said disappointedly.

"Now tell me what the hell you've found out already."

"A couple of very interesting things. Each on their own maybe seems like nothing, but—"

"Go on."

"Well, I was reading Detective Jensen's notes on the case. He was a very organized guy it turns out. He seemed to have reason to think this professor Noah Downy, who is a big shot over at the university, might be connected to the case, which at first made no sense to me."

"Yeah, I remember the name; we ruled him out, right?"

"Yeah, he was the guy who bought the house after the crime. Weird right, but Jensen's notes on the case ended officially in May 2006, with an entry where he seemed at least to be considering getting a blood sample from Downy. Now I have to believe there was a specific reason he wanted it, which leads me to the second thing. I met with Downy this morning, and he wasn't entirely telling the truth in our interview."

"About what? How do you know?"

He leaned back, flashing a wide, toothy grin. "I just know."

"Oh shit, are you kidding me? Look, man, you can't ever pull that telepathy shit out here, not with real suspects, especially not with a goddamn college professor."

"I figured you would say that. My superpowers are so rarely appreciated. That's why I saved the best for last. Get this, your friend Danny Fleming was a terrible note taker, and he wrote almost everything on scraps of paper. His case files looked like a fucking third grader's Trapper Keeper. But that's good news for us because on September 5th he visited Downy or was planning to at the college. I know because he wrote the address and directions to Downy's school office on this." He reached into his pocket, producing a tiny piece of weathered newspaper. "Top right corner, look at the date. Probably he picked it up on his way."

"Jesus, the day he—"

"Yep, the day Fleming went missing. Everybody else who looked at the case assumed he was just taking down info probably—name, address, standard shit—but this proves it was *after* he had been to the house already to meet Downy and after he looked at the crime scene again. It was his last chance before the Downys moved in. This would have been their second meeting then, but Downy says they never discussed the case, and he never mentioned a second meeting at the college or anywhere else, which means either Fleming never made it or that Downy *was* his last meeting." He paused.

Tackett had his hands on his head, trying to fully absorb what had been said.

"If I tell you one more cool thing, will you buy me the Jack and Coke you promised?"

"There's more?"

"Of course there's more. You think I'd call you with only that? I asked the good professor about the house, how he and his wife had acquired it, and it turns out it came as a referral from a friend, a friend now deceased. The widow is out of state he claims. I asked his secretary before I left, a real cutey by the way, and she says he died in a boating accident a few years back and that they were superclose friends. If you count our missing detectives, that's four people who have gone missing or died around the professor in a pretty short time. The friend's name is Patterson, Charles Patterson, though I haven't had a chance yet to run a background on him."

"Shit."

"You're welcome."

"Shhhh—" Tackett said, "it's not that loud in here."

Sullivan pushed his finger against his ear, grimacing.

"So you think Jensen knew something more on our professor?" Tackett asked, looking into his drink with a scowl.

"Well, he probably never connected the date on the newspaper. I can't say for sure. It was thrown in with some other notes, kind of randomly. Then again, none of our detectives knew they were working for posterity's sake, did they? As you said, everybody and their mother have looked at that file. I don't think anyone else caught it, which means Jensen was probably operating on a different hunch, something more concrete; the same one Fleming must have uncovered. I mean why would Fleming want to talk to Professor Downy twice if he hadn't found something? He'd already been to the house. That Monday morning, when he disappeared, he wanted to talk to Downy again. There had to be another reason. I'm hoping Jensen found the same thing. Something led them both to him. It best explains why he would want the blood sample."

"But why would he want the professor's blood, unless he believed it was his at the scene?"

"I know, I know. It's a problem. I'm still working on that."

"Maybe asking for blood was a bluff on Jensen's part, trying to flush him out."

"Maybe it worked a little too well."

The waitress arrived with more coffee.

"Thank you, finally," he said, rolling his eyes at Tackett. "Downright uncivilized to sit in a bar and drink coffee, wouldn't you say?"

The waitress was pretty, young, and her tiny shirt was clearly struggling under the weight of her chest. She smiled a beaming smile at Sullivan.

"I agree completely," she said. Tackett groaned.

"Seriously though, any guesses on who would want to blow up the house?"

Tackett looked across the bar outside to where the planes passed over on their way to landing. "It's this case," he said, putting his finger on the scrap of newspaper.

"But why take the trouble and then warn us?"

"Bomb-squad results will help. If it was set to a timer, it was probably dumb luck. Maybe he wanted someone else dead. Maybe he wanted to get rid of something in the house; what, I have no idea. Either way my cheese is gone."

"Yeah and my hearing," Sullivan said, grimacing again. Tackett smiled.

"Come to my place tonight. You can sleep in the garage; there's a pullout from my divorce. I'll set you up at El Cortez later. It's an old joint, but it's pretty cheap and rents by the month, cuts a special deal for cops."

"I need some new clothes—in the house all my clothes blew up."

"Sorry."

"They were shitty clothes. Can she stay in the garage too?" he said, pointing at the waitress as she walked back toward them.

"Eh?"

"Hey, I'm Nick, Nick Sullivan, and I'm new in town," he said, extending his hand and then holding on for a bit too long. "You know any good places to shop around here? I need a whole new wardrobe."

"What for?" the girl said, smiling.

"For dancing."

"What?"

"Tonight, with you. You're going to take me dancing."

"Where you wanna go?" she said playfully.

"Take me somewhere really loud and sweaty with stupidly expensive drinks."

The girl laughed out loud.

"OK. I'm off at eight."

Tackett shook his head in disbelief.

"Do me one more favor," Sullivan said. "Make sure when we leave, they take good care of my dear old dad here. He doesn't get to leave the home very often, and I want him to have some fun, you know before...well...you know."

Tackett grabbed his jacket, yelling, "I'm outta here."

"Hey, wait!" he shouted, "How do I find your house?"

"I'm texting it to you right now. Keys under the front mat."

"That's really your dad?"

"Nah," he said, "my uncle."

"Yeah?" she said, grinning.

"Make the next one a Jack and Coke, OK. A double. I like to be nice and tight when I'm tryin' on clothes."

"Coming up." The girl twirled herself flirtatiously back toward the bar.

He stared off into the distance at the planes landing overhead. He raised his glass. "To San Diego!" he said. But he was really thinking about the guy in the hat. He could almost see his face if he had just known to pay closer attention. Whoever he was, he was bold and dangerous. He was going to catch the son of a bitch one way or another.

CHAPTER 28

Downy awakened startled and looked across at Naomi while she slept. Her leg was twisted around the blanket. It was all he could do not to wake her and demand more of what she'd given him last night. Their evening had turned into quite a party. Everyone had had a little too much to drink. Of course, he and Samara had quite a head start, which probably helped set the tone. He marveled at how well the two girls had gotten along. It had been too much though when Naomi had insisted on showing Samara the vintage phone booth in the back. They were like two long lost college girlfriends, giggling and laughing their way through the night. It was nice not to have to think about the situation with Nazim for a change.

Naomi's job was sometimes a stressful one and in the end corporate, so it was always a fun release for her to get out. She had missed out on college unfortunately and seemed fascinated by Samara's life. He had decided to keep the situation under wraps about Nazim for at least another day or two. He hoped he could simply resolve it before he had to tell her, but more and more he feared that was wishful thinking. And what had the strange old Dr. Tannehill meant when he said "dear friends now ghosts?" Why was he so concerned about Samara?

Samara was now downstairs in their guest room asleep. Naomi had absolutely insisted that she not try to drive home, both of them had. The two girls had ended up in the backseat singing along together like teenagers, while he drove. Gratefully, he had drunk only coffee for the last two hours of dinner and was buzzed by caffeine much more than scotch. To say that his position as Samara's professor was seriously compromised was an understatement, but that was already true wasn't it?

He had been surprised how insistent Naomi had been that they make love when they arrived home. Usually, when a guest was in the house, sex was strictly off limits, but the scotch had undoubtedly fixed that. Samara was a safe distance away in any case, downstairs, and undoubtedly exhausted herself. In her drunkenness Naomi was in the mood and, as usual when she drank, loose of tongue.

"Professah Noah Downy," she had said in her hilarious mock southern accent, "who is always surrounded by tha' most beautiful gurls, always right at the pretty lil' center of everyone's tenshun—attention." "I'll give you some attention, boy," she had said loquaciously.

She had lunged at him with a kiss before they'd even made it upstairs. And they hadn't even made it to the bed, so the bathroom counter had to do. He tried to *shoosh* her several times for fear of the noise, but Naomi was even more vocal than usual.

And then she had made the strangest remark of the evening, after he tried to quiet her again, "Oh, she'd be doing it if she could, so who cares what she hears."

Then she had spoken in French, so he couldn't understand a word. It was a trick she loved to play on him when she wanted to say the unsayable right in front of him. It was also extremely sexy. He wasn't sure she was actually feeling suspicious, but as he lay there, he knew that her sixth sense must have been on overdrive. Women could always tell. She hadn't been angry about it at least, and it certainly hadn't affected her treatment of Samara. Oh well, maybe Naomi wanted her to hear it.

"God, last night was fun." Her voice came out low and sonorous. She had been watching him think silently the whole time. "Penny for your thoughts, Professor."

"Hey," he said groggily, "how's your head?"

"It'll get better, but I need pancakes stat. Do you think she heard us?" she said whispering.

He looked at the clock. It was 10:47 a.m. Samara was sleeping it off too it seemed. He hadn't heard a peep.

"Nah, not me anyway," he said, laughing.

"Ahhhh," she said, laughing back, "I'm not sorry. She looks at you like you are the most fascinating thing God ever created, ya know."

"Does she? No," he said, protesting.

"Make me pancakes, OK? Don't forget the blueberries,"

she said, rolling her eyes and falling over into the blankets face down.

Against the white of the sheets, her body looked soft, her skin a light butterscotch. He rubbed his hand across the nape of her neck with his finger, and then he got up and walked to the bathroom to clear his face in the mirror. All their clothes from the night before were strewn wildly about the room. He put on his pants and a shirt and made his way down the hallway. There was still no sound in the house. He went downstairs as quietly as he could but couldn't see into Samara's room, which was still dark and silent. Pancakes for three then. He walked back upstairs trying to be quiet and stood in the front room overlooking the bay. Birds chirped away, and he could hear the whinge of crickets, which reminded him so much of home. He walked into the kitchen to start the pancakes, but his attention was distracted by a piece of paper on the counter. She had gone already then. He picked it up, eyes scanning the page while he rubbed his eyes.

If you want her back, ask your publisher for directions to the pond.
Call the police, and you will never see her again.
Come alone.
G.

His hand began to tremble, and his pulse raced. *Holy Jesus.* He ran downstairs as fast as he could and threw open the door. The bed was empty, though the sheets looked like she had slept there. He knocked at the bathroom door franticly. No answer.

"Samara? Are you in there?"

He pushed open the door, but the lights were out, and it was empty. He looked back at the bed to the sheet hanging down the side and could see a long smear of what looked like blood. It was not yet completely dry. He bent down holding it in his hand, which was now shaking violently. He sprinted up the stairs as fast as he could, his heart racing.

"Naomi!" he shouted. "Get up! I need you to come down here right now. Naomi!" He ran to their room and could hear the shower. "Naomi!"

"What is it?" she said, emerging from the shower, still dripping with water and towel.

"Put on a robe. Something has happened to Samara."

Naomi could sense the fear in her husband's face immediately and ran silently to get her robe as the two of them hurried downstairs.

"Look at this!" he said, shoving the note at Naomi, who read it with a disturbed look.

"What the hell does this mean? Where is she?"

"She's not in the room. And then there's this," he said, pulling her along down the stairs.

"Stop pulling me. I'm coming! I'm coming!"

He pointed to the sheet.

"Is this, Oh Jesus—"

"What the hell do you think?"

"It looks like blood. Oh Jesus, it's blood."

The two of them walked almost unconsciously out of the

house to the front driveway, looking back at every step. There was no sign of anyone.

"What do we do?" she said.

He reached for his phone. He pulled up Samara's number and started dialing frantically.

"We can check at her dorm."

"We have to call the police now," Naomi said, holding the note.

He stared at the house, not answering her for a moment. "OK, but not yet. I have some things I need to tell you first, OK?"

"What things?"

"Come inside and hurry. It's important."

Naomi frowned as they walked. "What the hell is happening, Noah?"

They stopped on the porch step together, never making it to the door.

"It's about Charlie," he began. "Something very strange is going on."

CHAPTER 29

Sullivan awakened to the smell of brewing coffee and coughing. The girl, he couldn't remember her name right off, was next to him on the tiny pull out, smooshed against the wall of Tackett's garage.

"I can't believe I went on a date to your garage," she said groggily.

"It's not even my garage," he said, licking his lips. "Sorry to disappoint."

"Man, you never stop," she said, rolling over.

Her breasts looked even better in the morning light. She kissed him softly. The ringing noise in his ears had finally calmed.

"Nice to meet ya, stranger."

She slid off the edge of the tiny cot into her jeans, which were impossibly tight. "I'll let myself out."

He lay staring at the ceiling, marveling at a girl who could leave like that. He thought of the professor and his wife, their seemingly perfect life. Maybe it wasn't so perfect after all. He heard Tackett and the girl laughing in the room above him and jumped up pulling on his own pants, the only pair he now owned. The night hadn't exactly gone as planned. They had only made it to Tina's truck, where she had offered him a joint. As she handed it over, she asked him, "So what you do, Nick, you know, for a livin'?"

"You don't want to know," he said.

"That's silly; of course, I do."

He looked at the joint in his hand. "I'm a cop."

"Holy shit," she said, cracking up, smoke billowing out of the tinted windows of the truck, coughing.

"Are you kidding?"

"Scout's honor," he said, flashing his badge without making eye contact. He stared at the joint in his hand. He would need the help sleeping after all that had happened. He'd had two doubles already and his hands were still shaking.

"Are you like gonna arrest me?"

"That depends," he said.

"Depends on what?"

"How good this is," he answered, pulling the joint to his nose for a sniff and then taking a hit.

"Ahhh, goddamn!" the girl laughed. "This is gonna be a fun night. What do I have to do to get handcuffed?" she said suddenly looking serious.

"Drive north on Interstate Five," he said, looking at his phone. "Go left on Via de la Valle and make two rights."

"Whatever you say, Officer. Whatever you say."

He replayed the images of the night silently with a sly grin on his face, running his hands through his hair. Tackett came to the top of the stairs yelling, "There's exactly one cup of coffee left. Ya got thirty seconds before it's gone." Sullivan appeared, yawning deeply at the top of the stairs.

"Before you say a word, that Tina seems nice, so keep it on the up and up. I like drinking at that club, and if you fuck it up for me—"

"I don't think you need to worry about Tina," he said, laughing. "If anyone got used last night, I'm pretty sure it was me."

"You know Tierney is going to be so pleased we're living together."

"Fuck Bob. I'm done as police, but I want to solve this case before I really quit."

"You're not serious."

"I am. Especially about catching this guy. It may be the only way left for me to really spit in Bob's face, metaphorically speaking, of course."

"Metaphorically, right."

"Let's talk about your theory for a minute," Tackett said grimacing.

"I don't have a theory, actually. I didn't mean to give you that impression. I just know when I'm being lied to."

"Do you really think a college professor is a good candidate as an explosives enthusiast?"

"I doubt it. Ten to one he hired someone to do the job. Maybe he thinks we have the evidence on him and was just trying to get rid of it. It would explain why he warned us beforehand, with the kid; maybe he'd given explicit instructions not to kill anyone."

"Suddenly he's grown a conscience after murdering two detectives?"

Sullivan slurped at his coffee. "This is really, really shitty, you know?" he said, wincing as he drank.

"It's been in my fridge for over a year I think, no shit."

"Fuck, I'm going to die, aren't I?" he said, spitting dramatically into the sink.

They both laughed.

"Let's see, you met with him at ten a.m. right? And before noon the house went up. That's quick."

"Maybe he is involved with someone else like I said. Someone he could call right away. Should we tap him?"

"Based on? No chance with Tierney with as little as you have. I'd tell him nothing by the way."

"Now I'm answering to Sheppard."

"Ahhh—daddy's little tick turd. He's a sight better than Bob in some ways and worse in others. Good thing is I'm a civilian now. Maybe I need to investigate the possibility of higher education as a building block to my future."

"What you need is a goddamn decorator," he said, looking around the empty room in disgust. Hang a picture on the wall, for God's sake. Here, I'm sending you one right now. Keep me posted on what you find, and I'll let you know what the professor is up to, if anything."

"Be careful, OK."

"Of course. I'm gonna check in with Rodriguez, see if the

bomb squad has come up with anything." He walked to the stairs. "I'll just let myself out through the garage."

Tackett looked down at his phone. It was a picture from the night before; Tina was flashing the camera, already in her underwear and shirtless.

Ah, to be young again, he thought. *And to have a face like the son of a bitch wouldn't hurt either.*

CHAPTER 30

"What if they're telling the truth? What if they hurt her?" Downy said, looking frightened.

"You're not suggesting we don't contact the police? How did they get in to the house?"

They had checked every door. Everything was locked.

"The blood on the sheet, my God; they must have kept her quiet, walked her out with a—"

He couldn't finish the sentence.

"The garage?"

"It's the only way."

He pulled at the garage door, but nothing happened. It was stuck solidly in place. He yanked at it with all his strength. It moved only a few inches and then sprung back into place.

"No way, not without us hearing, and how would they get it back down?"

He grabbed his phone again, dialing Taber Hall, where all

the freshmen students were forced to spend their first year. "Hi, this is Professor Noah Downy calling from the history department. I am checking in on a friend's daughter who is staying there; we're having a hard time locating her. If you could have an RA check if she is in her room, it would really be really appreciated?"

"I'm sorry, sir. Your name was?"

"Professor Noah Downy. I'm looking for Samara Patterson, a student from my class," he said, shuffling the phone awkwardly. "Her family is having a hard time getting in touch. I'm a friend of theirs, and we just want to make sure she is OK."

He could feel in his heart that it was a wasted call. She wasn't there, and she wasn't OK.

"I'm ringing her room right now, sir."

He paced.

"There's no answer, sir. Let me send Lisa, our RA, over there; she's on the laundry floor, and it will just take her a couple of minutes. We can stay on the line, OK."

"Yes, yes, thank you."

He sat down and huddled next to Naomi, who kept looking around as if she thought they were being watched. She stared back at the note. It was a strange kind of handwriting, somehow too angular and rigid. She was sure someone foreign to English had written it.

"Sir, Lisa is actually at her door now, but there's no answer."

"Can she go inside to look, just to be sure?"

"Usually not, but I know you professor and under these circumstances."

He could hear the woman telling the RA to "just go inside and see if she is there, that's all."

"Sir, are you still there?"

"Yes, I'm here."

"Her room is empty, Lisa says."

"OK, thank you."

"Professor, should I contact campus security?"

He realized the call was going to alert the authorities and set off a chain of events that would quickly be out of his control. Just what the note said not to do.

"No, ma'am, I don't think that's necessary yet, but thank you for your help. We still have a couple of places left to look. If you should see her, could you have her call immediately? She has my number; I am a friend of her family."

"I've seen her; she's the really pretty, dark-haired girl, right?"

"Yes, that's right."

"I will tell her, sir."

"Thank you."

Downy gripped the phone. Naomi looked up at him from the note.

"The writing is definitely foreign; it's English, but the letter shape is Greek or maybe Arabic. This has to be connected to Nazim. Maybe they are being held too, blackmailed somehow." It made some sense. But who?

"We need to call the police, Noah."

"We will. The cop I talked to the other day. I can ask him what we should do."

His phone beeped. He looked down.

"It's Samara!" he said excitedly. "It's a text."

She breathes only because you haven't made that call.
Come alone.
G.

"Jesus!" he screamed, showing the screen to Naomi. "I need to call Clellon, maybe he knows something."

"Come inside, it scares me standing out here alone," she said, looking nervously in every direction.

"Let's go to Woody's and use the phone there. I don't feel safe on this line anymore. How else could they know?" he said, throwing his hands in the air.

"They're watching us right now—"

"Yeah. OK, let's go."

They jumped into the car as fast as they could and sped off. On their back patio at that very moment sat a man in a hat, a cheap tourist's hat, the kind that makes everyone look like they're on safari. He propped his feet up on the balcony and turned up a bottle of Downy's finest scotch for a good long drink.

"Here's to—to getting things right the second time," he said.

CHAPTER 31

The man awoke, eyes fluttering, and could feel the beating of his heart against his throat. The ground was cold and hard, and his face had been pressed against it for some time. He knew he had been sleeping a long while from the lack of pain in his legs, which had become a feeling so common to him in old age. His eyes were clear now though, and if not for his confusion, he would swear he'd had the best sleep of his life. The smell in the room was an odd mix of something burning and something sweet. Smoke, nearly translucent, billowed sideways from the corner of the room, and he moved his body up to the sitting position. Where the hell was he? Cast iron bars told him he was not in friendly territory. He remembered the cutthroats from his youth who had taken him. Being a prisoner didn't frighten him then, but not knowing the nature of the threat did. He was still alive, so there was a good chance someone was planning to ransom him. If it were only revenge, he would be dead already. Who on earth would think they could get away with such a thing? He wanted to meet them.

A voice, barely a whisper, echoed from the corner of the room. "Hello my friend."

He tried to speak in response, but when he opened his mouth, only a croak came out, followed by a violent fit of coughing.

"There's wine over there," the voice said again, coming out low and deep. His fit lessening, he reached for it, swallowing wildly. The thirst was overwhelming. He had been asleep for a long time indeed. His stomach was empty, and pangs of hunger sent waves of nausea through his entire body.

"You can't eat yet. You'll get sick."

"Who are you?" the man finally managed to say, though he still could not see to whom he spoke. Through the smoke a dark figure appeared, cloaked so that he could not see.

"I'm here to watch over you, my friend."

"My friends rarely lock me up. Are you sure we're friends?"

"Absolutely sure. I'm your only friend, in fact. I brought you here to save you." The cloaked man's voice was raw and deep.

The image of his nephew suddenly returned and with it their strange early-morning meeting. His begging him to come with him, and then his last memories were of some trick, a deception. He hadn't anticipated being betrayed by the boy.

"You are with my nephew then?"

"No, not anymore, I'm afraid. He is with the gods this night."

"Dead then?"

"More or less."

"You speak in riddles and hide your face. If you plan to ransom me, let me tell you that you'll be the richest man in the world for the short time you live."

"I really do love you sometimes, you know. It's rare to get a glimpse of—"

The man was confused by the response. In the darkness he could hear the cloaked stranger now weeping.

"Do we know one another? I admit your voice is familiar, but unless I can see you—"

"You don't want that."

He had seen the cloaked face already hadn't he, but now remembered the sight had somehow horrified him. What had scared him so? A wave of unexpected terror overtook the man, and without warning he began to vomit violently onto the floor. The man in the hood came closer.

"It will pass. I have fresh food coming for you in a few hours."

The man dry heaved a few final gasps and sat up again. "Why am I so sick?"

"It's the medicine I have given you. I assure you without it you'd be much worse off. I put a fresh change of clothing over there, when you feel up to changing."

The man looked into the corner and recognized his own cloak and undergarments. "How have you come by my things? Where is my wife?"

"They're all safe; you needn't worry about them."

"Where are we?"

"Not far from home, not really."

"There will be a great riot over my disappearance, you know? Even now the whole city will be in a frenzy."

"Yes, I'd love to see it in fact, but that's a part of this adventure we'll both have to forgo I'm afraid."

"So should I just lay here and be content?"

"That would be wise. Later we can talk, but right now the less you know the safer you will be. I have but a little time left I'm afraid, but you have much, much more."

The cloaked man coughed suddenly, shaking his whole body violently.

"You're ill too?" the man asked.

"Terminally," he said with a sarcastic laugh. "But I'm not afraid. I know you aren't a vengeful man, but you may one day feel a need for revenge. It's up to you really. Maybe you will forgive everyone instead, as you so often do."

"Free me now, and I will leave you with a day's head start."

The cloaked man laughed now, a laugh so familiar that it quieted his building rage.

"Are you from Bithynia? I have heard you laugh before, haven't I?"

"Perhaps you have," he said. His hooded face leaned in closer. "Do you remember the girls in Bithynia? What a night that was."

So they did know one another, he thought silently.

"I have no doubt that if I tried to kill you, which I don't want to do by the way, you would charm me out of it somehow, and have no doubt that if you hunted me, I'd be a most happy prey."

The man raised his chin just a little and stepped forward so that his lips were almost visible from under the cloak. In the light he could make out a large scar which ran across the man's throat.

"Are you mad?"

"Not yet, though the thought has occurred to me of late."

"Then I will spare you, my friend, if you will only let me go. That is a promise."

"Thank you for that kindness, but it's unnecessary."

"It is I who has spared you."

And as he spoke the mysterious stranger pulled the hood of the cloak away from his face. His captive sat stone-faced on the floor, suddenly speechless. His eyes glazed over, and his pupils enlarged at the sight.

With barely a whimper, he spoke, "You!" before slumping again on his side, falling into deep unconsciousness.

CHAPTER 32

Downy and Naomi walked hurriedly into Woody's. The place was empty, and the morning crew could still be heard cleaning up from the night before. They raced toward the back. He hit his contacts button for Clellon his agent in London. From a real phone, he could barely remember how to dial overseas, so he simply hit zero for the operator. He figured you could still make a collect call. Naomi sat nervously at the table. The night they had spent before now seemed like a cruel dream. He couldn't help but think the worst from the bloodstain.

The phone rang on and on, but finally a voice picked up.

"Dear boy, a collect call, you must be lost in the jungle again. Is everything OK?"

"Clellon, thank God you answered! I'm calling about Samara Patterson; she's been taken I think by people connected to Charlie somehow, to Nazim. They said I should call you and ask about the pond? Can you please tell me what the hell is going on? What are they talking about?"

There was a long silence on the other end of the line.

"Clellon? Are you still there?"

"I am, Noah," came the voice hesitantly. "I'm sorry, I'm a bit in shock. This is very bad news."

"Where the hell is this pond, and why does Nazim think Charlie is still alive?"

Another long pause ensued.

"Dear god, m'boy, I have no idea what to say."

"Clellon, what do you know about all this; please fucking just say something?"

"Noah, is Naomi with you?"

"Yes, she is."

He looked out of the glass pane of the booth and could see Naomi, who was now talking with someone near the bar. They were looking at something together.

"You must get her out of there immediately, get her far away from you."

He looked again but couldn't see the man's face. She turned and seemed to look in his direction but then suddenly ran out of the bar, the man following closely behind.

"Hold on!" he said, throwing the receiver down.

He chased after her, but as he ran he could see papers strewn about the floor where she had stood. He stopped to pick them up. He held in his hand a picture. It was of he and Samara in the phone booth locked in a passionate kiss. He continued running franticly out the door, but as he emerged someone knocked him to the ground. Then a swarm of men were upon him. It took him a moment to realize who they were.

"You have the right to remain silent, douchebag," one of them said.

It was the detective from his office.

"Looks like I'm going to have to pass on that coffee too," he said, struggling to get the cuffs on. "Too bad, I love a good cup of coffee."

"What's happening here?"

"You're under arrest for the murder of Samara Lee Patterson and two fucking cops, you son of a bitch."

Naomi stood in the wings, crying uncontrollably as they pried the picture of he and Samara from Downy's shaking hands.

"Naomi!" he shouted imploringly. "This is a mistake. I have to talk to Clellon. She's still alive!"

"You'll get your phone call, asshole. Calling the Pope won't save your ass though."

"Samara can't be dead; the kidnappers said she was at the pond."

"Yeah, we found her there already. Did you guys go for a little midnight swim, Professor? Kidnappers, huh? That's original."

It was like a bad dream. He stopped talking, realizing no one was paying attention. The staff of the bar stood looking on in confusion at the melee. Police cars were lined up around the block, and as they brought him to his feet, he could see into Woody's to the second-floor balcony. Smoke wafted down from above, and a hazy figure stood in silhouette. He could swear it was...but his mind was now too far gone to reason.

"Char...Charlie?" he muttered, before being led away.

PART II

CHAPTER 1

Bob Tierney held what was perhaps the most triumphant press conference of his career after the arrest of Professor Noah Downy, announcing that the case against him was as airtight as they come, with mountains of physical evidence, not to mention motive and a soon-to-be-found murder weapon, which had been taken from the college's ancient-weaponry collection. Accolades rained down from every quarter on behalf of the two vanished policemen and, of course, the beautiful college student Samara Lee Patterson, whose lifeless and partially mutilated body was discovered by teens skinny-dipping in a nearby pond on the night of her disappearance. In a rare move, Tierney also announced the reinstatement of Sergeant Joe Tackett, divulging that Tackett's suspension had all along only been a clever ruse to lure the killer into a false sense of security, since the department had long suspected he was closely watching them. Noticeably absent from the hat tips was any mention of Nick Sullivan, who now sat idly outside the interrogation room, drinking an almost cold coffee from Donut Haven.

"Cheer up, kid. I told you my days are numbered here."

He looked up to see Tackett with a wide grin on his face.

"You'll be sergeant in no time and good riddance to this place I say. I'll leave the bottle of Jack in my desk for you when I go."

"I'm not leadership material."

"Have it your way, kid."

"You should let the pros handle this interrogation, you know. This guy is a cold, calculating SOB. They'll write whole books about the fact that he used a goddamn Roman sword to slice up that pretty little coed."

"He's asked to speak with me actually. I'd rather not be here at all."

"I know the feeling, man. It's the hunt that drives guys like us, and now look at you—blue as hell. There'll be other cases."

"It was good work you did," Sullivan said, suddenly coming back to life.

"Not really. We still don't know who sent the photos. Probably someone tired of seeing him get away with it for all these years. They'll come forward I'm sure. I'm still looking into it."

"Any word from the university?"

"Oh, the teacher's union is quiet on this one actually, though as usual the goddamn academics are lining up from here to Fresno to support the bastard. I spoke to his school dean, and he says Downy wouldn't hurt anyone. Typical."

"Yeah, no one ever believes anyone they know is capable of this kind of shit."

"Why do you think he wants to see you?"

"I don't know. We bonded a bit, I guess, when I interviewed him."

"Well, enjoy. Maybe you'll get an honorable mention in the book. Hey, speaking of your fame, I was talking to Sheppard, he and I were wondering, can I ask you a question?"

"Shoot."

"The Redneck Killer? How did you find him? Really? I know you ain't no supernatural phenom; that's a crock. You never said in your big TV interview about any lie detecting."

He paused, looking despondent.

"Milk."

"Come again?"

"Margie Wells had been buying one gallon of milk at Cut-Rate Supermarket since I was a kid, without fail. Her son, who had a rape charge on him from a few years earlier, was supposedly out of state, or so she claimed. On the day I ran into her at the market, she bought two gallons. Found him in her basement that night with one of the girl's underwear."

"No shit?"

"No shit."

Rodriguez opened the door to the interrogation room and yelled, "Next."

"That guy is awfully cute and nice for a goddamn butcher man. Tell you what, none of my teachers were like that."

Sullivan raised his eyebrows in seeming agreement.

"None of your teachers used first-century cutlery to disembowel college girls either, did they?"

"Fucking A right. Douche says he will only talk to you, so get in there."

"Yeah, so I heard."

He walked into the room silently. Noah Downy looked up from his cup of tea, still playing absent-mindedly with the tiny piece of paper at the end of the bag. All the color was gone from his youngish face, and his eyes blazed hot with red. He'd been in the room now for nearly forty-eight hours but had steadfastly refused a lawyer.

"Hey, man, the last time I saw you, I told you I wanted to meet under better circumstances. *This* sure ain't it," he said, sitting down.

"I didn't kill Samara or those cops. The other detective said you have a kind of sixth sense. What's it telling you?"

"Look, man, the teachers' union is sending over a lawyer for you, and if you want to avoid the chair, I'd say my sixth sense says do it."

"Where's my wife?"

"She's here, but she doesn't want to speak to you just yet."

"I wasn't having sex with Samara. That picture was just a childish mistake."

"Oh yeah, how about this?" he said, throwing the pictures of Samara's body onto the table.

Downy threw his hand over his mouth. Tears raced down his cheeks.

"She was like a fucking daughter to me," he said bitterly,

pushing the pictures away. Sullivan threw down the picture from the phone booth.

"You always slip the tongue like that to your daughters?"

"I don't have any children, but I—"

"Probably best."

"Please put those away," Downy said grimacing. "You have absolutely no idea how it feels to see her like this. She was family to me."

"Is that why you dumped her in the water?"

"My wife is only angry about the picture. I could explain it to her if I had the chance."

"Yeah, she was ready to talk actually until her drug screen came back positive for Darvocet, fifty milligrams, which we also found in Samara's system. You put it in their drinks, I presume?" You're lucky she isn't dead too with a dose like that plus the booze. But, hey, at this point who's counting? Is that so you could talk to them? Explain things?"

"My wife takes those when we travel; she hates flying."

"Yeah, but she said she didn't take them that Friday night, and you're really the only one with access to her drugs besides her, or so she says."

"She lying too; she in on this Middle Eastern kidnapping conspiracy, boss?"

Downy looked up again from his tea. "Why would I do a thing like this?"

"You can tell me or not, man; it makes no difference really. That weapon you used is some medieval shit though, I gotta admit; I didn't necessarily have you pegged as the type."

"The sword is part of a collection; I never used it for anything but research."

"Yeah, but the university says you checked it out just last week, rather unexpectedly. Some timing."

Downy went silent.

"Hey, maybe you don't need a lawyer after all. I mean you got an explanation for pretty much everything. Those cops do have families though, man; don't you think they deserve some closure? Tell me where their bodies are, and you might even get some leniency."

"Can I ask you to do one thing Detective?" he said, ignoring the comment altogether.

"I don't know. I'm a pretty busy man, cleaning up after all your messes."

"You have to contact my agent, Clellon Holmes, in London, Wingate Publishing, and ask him about Charlie Patterson, about the pond; that's where they said she was being kept. They said she was still alive. I don't know why they killed her or why they would want to."

"Yeah right, Patterson; that's the dead guy you claim you saw when we arrested you. Somehow he's involved in his daughter's murder too?"

"You know, I thought you were an awfully good cop when we met before. If you really do have a sixth sense, you'll be able to tell that Clellon is lying. He knows something about all this." Downy leaned in in exasperation. "You can see for yourself, on my cell phone, where they messaged me, for Christ's sake. Don't you cops check evidence at least?"

"Yeah, we checked it already. That's pretty clever, texting

us from your office computer like that. The IT geeks are still trying to figure out how you managed that trick, but I bet you got a lackey is all. Same one who tried to get rid of these pics for you by torching my first and only residence in California. Rude, man. Rude."

Downy looked stricken.

"Still, hard to figure. You looked happy as hell to me, man, but I guess for some people nothing is ever enough."

"Clellon Holmes. Please. Do it for a fellow Southerner who has no other hope of clearing his name."

Sullivan frowned.

"The number is in my phone. Just call him, I beg you. If you still think I'm full of shit after, you can just let me rot in jail or fry or whatever..."

"That's it then. You ain't talkin?"

"Samara kissed me, not the other way around. She thought her dad may have been involved with someone or possibly even still ali...never mind," he said, bowing his head in seeming defeat.

Sullivan grabbed the pictures before turning to leave.

"That's not what she was wearing," Downy muttered almost imperceptibly.

"What's that?" he said, turning back around.

"The night she disappeared, Samara wasn't wearing that outfit. She had on a black sweater with the shoulders cut out."

Sullivan nodded and walked out without a word.

"How did it go?" Tierney said, suddenly appearing from nowhere, the way he always seemed to.

"Mum's the word. Any news on that murder weapon?"

"They're dredging the pond still. Look, Sullivan, you get high marks for initiative on this case. If you can learn to be more disciplined, you could go a long way around here."

"Thanks, Bob. So clever of you to use Tackett as bait like that."

"Don't ever fucking call me Bob, ever you little shit."

Sullivan walked away without a word, already thinking about Tina from the Aero Club.

Surely, she could help him decompress. He really did get down as hell after a case was solved. The chase was over. The boss was full of shit.

Tackett saw him on his way out. "Any luck?"

"Negative."

"Where you headed?"

"To the Aero Club."

"Got it on the brain already, eh?"

He laughed. "See you tonight, OK? Make coffee for three, not the shit from the fridge either."

Sullivan walked past the evidence room on his way out. There was only the late-shift person still working. He paused momentarily but then walked on. Screw the bastard. He was tired of police work, tired of pretty dead girls and bad professors.

CHAPTER 2

Noah Downy raised his head from the pillow and for a moment imagined he was still in his own bed. He thought first of his wife, but then the horrific images of Samara's mutilated body intruded. Then he thought of the smoking man on the balcony. It couldn't have been Charlie. He had a sick feeling in his stomach and writhed in agony. He heard a voice calling from down the hall. It was impossible from his holding cell to tell if it was night or day, but his body clock said it was probably early morning.

"Got a visitor here for Professor Frankenstein."

Downy's heart leaped at the thought that Naomi had finally come, and he burst up out of the bed. The officer appeared at his cell door.

"Come on, Professor Frankenstein, you got at least one admirer left on the outside. Me, I'm just glad I didn't fuck my life up and go to college. You academic types got some evil shit in your blood."

He walked silently into the room, which looked just like the ones he had seen in the movies. It was surreal to be on the wrong side of the glass. The barrier in front of him had an ancient-looking phone, which he picked up almost instinctually. He nearly didn't recognize the man in front of him without his hat, though he could already smell the body odor just being near the glass.

"Mr. Taro?"

"Professor Downy, sir, my deepest sympathies for your present circumstances. I only wanted to come show my support for you at such an awful time." The man leaned in toward the glass. "I too have been accused of butchery that was not of my doing. It is a horrid feeling to be impugned so."

Downy thought for a moment before he spoke. The man's English was much better than he'd remembered.

"I read your letter, Mr. Taro."

"The man who wrote it honors me with his words. He is a brother to me in fact."

"Why are you here, Mr. Taro? I mean, I know originally what you came for, but now?"

"I have been on a mission of sorts I suppose, a mission of recovery."

"Well, how can I help you?" Downy said, looking perplexed.

"That you'd even be considering such a thing at a time like this is a sure sign of your character and, of course, your innocence. As you may have read in the letter, I am a man of some means. I wonder if you'd let me help you, financially?"

He sat back in his chair, looking the man over for the first time. A distinct scar ran vertically across his neckline. His black, piercing eyes struck Downy even in his present state. He recognized the keen look of intelligence described in the letter.

"I want you to know that I don't believe a word of anything said against you. You will be out of here when you say the word."

"That's incredibly generous."

"No, it is just. For a man such as myself, perhaps no notion is more meaningful or more important."

"I read in your letter that you suffered some misfortune yourself."

"Yes, more than any man ought to have to endure, but I have learned that perhaps I am special in that regard, that is to say, what I can endure. Is it your wife, the very beautiful woman in the gallery who weeps so?"

"She's still here?"

"Yes, she refuses to leave. I think your captors have spun quite a story about you. You would only need to speak to her, of course, to make their silly narrative evaporate completely. I wonder, could I pass along some message to her on your behalf?"

He closed his eyes trying to squelch the bitterness he felt welling up again. He tried to calm himself with images from their past, of their laughter, their beach in Tahiti all alone and so happy, so far from all this madness. And now he couldn't even speak to her. He swallowed hard against his pride before speaking.

"Yes, Mr. Taro, you could. Tell her I love her and that she

should go to her mother's until this is settled, until I am free, and that I will see her soon and explain my mistakes."

Taro nodded warmly. "She will hear these words but must already know that you are incapable of this crime. And, Professor Downy, I insist that you call me Taro from now on."

"That's it; time's up," a man's voice came as the sliding door behind him opened abruptly.

"Until we speak again, take heart. The truth is on our side, not theirs. Their power is an illusion; don't forget."

Taro locked eyes with him and put his hand to the glass in a gesture of solidarity. Then the guard unceremoniously scooped Downy up. They ambled their way down the hall. Back in his cell, he thought of Taro's words. It was true what the monsignor had said about him in his recommendation. Even his manner of speech had a classical touch, but the speech was strangely antiquated. No one used the word *gallery* anymore. Still, for the first time since this nightmare had all began, he felt like someone was actually on his side. It was too dangerous to involve Naomi any further though, that much he felt sure of. In fact, he liked the idea of her at the police station where she was probably safest. Clellon had asked first about her. Why? What kind of danger was she in, were they all in? He looked at the chains across his legs and had to laugh for the first time: the very idea that a man had to be put in chains.

CHAPTER 3

The Aero Club was already jumping when Sullivan walked in, and on a barstool sat Tina. She was dressed up, clearly not working, and in a skirt, which fit much like the jeans he had first seen her in. She had on a pair of pink high heels, which she dangled mindlessly from her painted toes. Sullivan had to laugh at the look. Her shirt hung off the shoulder on one side. It was all eighties, which, of course, she wasn't old enough to remember, but she made it look damn good again.

"Hey, stranger," she said, smiling warmly as he walked in. "You look beat, man. Everything OK?"

"Oh yeah, just another long day at the office, locking up potheads and sexual deviants."

She laughed so hard her beer nearly came up. "You might be the funniest cop who ever lived. You know that?"

"Yeah, but it's my huge penis that makes everybody swoon."

"Well," she said, "now "huge." That's a stretch."

He really liked this girl. No matter what he threw out, she gave it back. A woman who could hold her own like that attracted him on an almost primal level.

"Let's get out of here and get some real drinks."

"Yeah, where do you get 'real' drinks, Detective?"

"Woody's up by the college. I heard even the coffee is great."

"OK, but I ain't drinking coffee. Your uncle's brew almost cost me a trip to the emergency room."

"He's not really my uncle."

"I know, dumbass; still my stomach hurt for hours. It's the last time I drink anything to be polite."

"Come on, let me make it up to you."

"OK, but unless you get that door fixed; I'm driving," she said, pointing out to his wreck of a car.

It was illegally parked in a handicapped zone. He kept forgetting about the missing door.

"You should probably move it, you know."

"Nah, I'm the law. Come to think of it, handicapped people get all the breaks anyway."

"Oh, you're going to hell for that one," she said, "We'll take my truck."

"Hold on. Let me go get my Elvis tape."

"I don't have a cassette player, man."

"It's an eight track, actually. Shit, I'm getting old, aren't I?"

"No, you're just sentimental. It's OK."

Tina drove like she made love, the truck swerving all over the place. She cranked her car stereo, which blasted a song from the nineties that he couldn't recall the name of but vaguely remembered.

"I gotta be honest. College bars kinda bore me," she said, looking at him sideways as she drove.

"Yeah, me too, but this one is kinda nice actually. I'm not the college type either. Don't worry; you'll be popular anywhere in that skirt."

"Thanks, man. You're not getting out of it this time though; I'm not going on another date that ends in a garage, OK? I got class and manners," she said, laughing, "and if you want to get my panties off again, you're gonna pay for it." Tina pointed to the glove box. "There's more green in there," she said, "if you want some."

"Oh, no thanks," he said, smiling.

He had been right to come see her. He was in a better mood already.

———

The man who leaned over the balcony blew smoke rings across the top of the bar as the pair walked in. He paid them no mind. Woody's was bustling with the first round of drinkers of the evening—the early crowd. The man pulled his hat down over his eyes moving quietly back to his seat on the balcony to enjoy his scotch, unnoticed. Nick Sullivan and Tina went straight to the bar where they ordered a highball and a coffee.

"Do you have any of the Greek stuff?"

"It's all we serve. We start boiling it every morning at six."

"Great. Throw in a shot of George Dickel too, if you don't mind. I'll split the difference," he said, smiling.

"Poor man's speedball coming up."

"Wow, this place is actually better than I thought," Tina said, looking around. "It's just, you know, a bit quiet for my taste."

"Yeah, I know what you mean, but not everything in life needs to make a racket."

"OK, if you say so. I guess I'm not complicated is all."

"That's a quality worth holding on to," he said, smiling.

A table of what looked like fraternity boys suddenly erupted into raucous laughter. It broke the illusion that they were in a classy place.

"Then there are those guys," she said, pointing, clearly annoyed.

"Do you think they realize yet why they spend so much time with each other and not with the girls?" Sullivan looked momentarily perplexed.

Tina put her fist to her mouth and rolled her tongue against the inside of her cheek in a lewd gesture.

The boys rose to leave but saw her as they were walking out, one of them leering, clearly drunk, slurred, "Damn, look at that those," pointing to her ample chest.

"Hey buddy," she said loudly. "You like tits? These you will never touch," she said, laughing. "Not you or anybody else in your little choir boys' club." She now had the entire group's attention.

Sullivan groaned as he turned slowly from the bar. The last thing he needed was a brawl.

"I wouldn't let you fuck me with his tiny prick," she said, pointing to one of the frat boy's brothers, who now looked down embarrassingly at his crotch. "Look at that," she said, laughing, "You could at least put a roll of quarters in there or something, give a girl some hope."

The brothers now roared in protest. The biggest one pointed at Sullivan and said, "You need to calm that bitch down, bro."

Sullivan, barely turning to look, spoke emotionlessly, "Bitch, calm down."

Everyone laughed, except the drunkest one who was still swaying in angry protest, but out the door they roared.

He shook his head. "They're just young and stupid. Give 'em a break."

"No," she said, throwing her arms in the air in exasperation, "they're just fucking brave in their little packs. I'm sorry." "See, I told you this place was a bad idea." She looked like she might cry. It was the first break in her rough exterior, and he found he actually liked it.

"Hey," he said, standing up suddenly. "Let's eat some dinner, OK? Let's make this a real date," he said, putting his arms around her waist.

"Oh, look at you changing the subject," but she wasn't expecting him to come on so sincerely, and she could only mutter without protest, "OK, sure."

"Could we get a table for dinner?" he said, yelling at the bartender.

"Yeah, sure, man. Anywhere you want," he said, pointing to the empty tables.

"See we can sit anywhere we want; this place isn't so bad."

As they grabbed their drinks to walk away, he could see a lone man standing on the balcony above. He was wearing one of those goddamn tourist hats and for a moment Sullivan's chest fluttered. Then he could see the man was totally different looking: tall, more like six feet two, light skin, spectacles. Clearly, he belonged in this place. He would never be able to ignore that style of hat ever again, he realized.

"I'm gonna just freshen up a bit, OK?" Tina said.

"Of course," he said, rising from his chair as she left.

Tina had never seen a man do such a thing, and her face involuntarily flushed, which thankfully was obscured by the darkness. She hated being embarrassed in front of men. He could tell how much she liked him anyway. He liked her too, so that was fine. He looked around the room again and finally to the phone booth where he knew the photographs of the professor and the dead girl had been taken.

He waived for the waiter who appeared quickly.

"Yes, sir?"

"Do you work nights here all week, if you don't mind me asking?"

"Yeah, I do...weekends mostly."

"I don't want to hold you up, but can I ask if you know Professor Noah Downy? Someone told me he comes in here a lot."

"I do, sir."

He could tell by his response that he wasn't going to get any information voluntarily.

"I'm not looking to pile on, you know. I'm actually trying to help the guy out. I guess you heard he was arrested?"

"I did; it's a terrible shock. Can't believe that guy could ever do what they said."

"Yeah? I think he was in here just last week right, with his wife and another girl, real pretty girl? Did you wait on them by chance?"

"I did, sir. They all seemed very happy if you ask me, very happy."

"Did they get drunk?"

"Yeah, but not too much. They walked out of here just fine. The professor always has about a two-drink limit, always the best stuff though, but he drank coffee most of the night as I recall. We try to keep an eye out for our customers you know driving and stuff."

"That's good of you. Look, I just want to ask if you can remember anything about the girl, the one with black hair, real young, almost Middle Eastern looking. Can you remember what she was wearing by chance? I know it's a long shot."

"No, actually everybody noticed her," the waiter said, arching his eyebrows. "She had on one of those cut out at the shoulder sweaters. Black. Just some jeans I think, but she looked very chic. Very beautiful girl. We couldn't believe it when we heard that she was dead."

"Yeah, it's too bad. Hey, you sure about how drunk they were?" he said, looking intently at him to emphasize the point. The waiter seemed to concentrate before speaking.

"Professor Downy was the least drunk, for sure, but the

girls said good-bye as they left, and they didn't seem too sloshed to me. Look, I've got to get to some other tables; I can talk more after my shift."

Sullivan caught himself, "I'm so sorry, man; thanks so much. You've been a big help, really."

Tina reappeared, pulling out her chair and looking freshly made up with her hair now pulled to the side to match her outfit. She looked even younger and prettier.

"So what do we eat here?" she said, smiling. "They got burgers?" she said giddily.

"Do they ever!" he said, shaking his head and handing the menu to her. "Get anything you want, OK?"

"Seriously?"

"Yep, but I'm gonna have to leave for a bit, actually, kind of right now."

"What, what do you mean?"

"Hey, what's the best hotel in this town?"

She tapped at the table, looking clearly annoyed. "The Roosevelt, I guess."

He pulled his phone from his pocket and typed away. He handed the phone to her.

"Tell them we want their honeymoon suite if it's available, and if not, then something with a great view."

"What? Hey where the fu—"

"I'll be right back, I promise."

Tina held the phone in confusion before someone picked up.

"Good evening, Roosevelt Hotel. How may I assist you?"

"Yeah, I guess we need a room. How much is a room?"

"That depends on your needs, ma'am," came a very polite voice.

"O fuck it," she said. "Do you have a honeymoon suite?"

"Yes, we do, ma'am. And it's the best view in town if you ask me, truly breathtaking."

"How much is that?"

"That's three thousand two hundred fifty dollars for a single-night stay, ma'am."

Sullivan reappeared, taking his seat, hurriedly picking up his jacket.

"Yeah, it's a three-thousand-dollar room," she said, frowning.

"Great, get it," he said. "Here's my credit card. Go on and book it."

The waiter arrived again with pen in hand.

"Can we get our food to go actually? Something's come up."

"Um, sure...but you haven't ordered yet."

"Yeah, bring us a sampler platter, little bits of everything good, cheeseburgers," he said, pointing to Tina, "steak, fish, and french fries—everything."

"Yeah, OK. Drinks?"

"Yeah, two large vanilla milkshakes, throw bourbon in mine. You?"

"Me too," she said as she put down the phone. "Dude, what is the deal? I knew you wouldn't end up taking me on a date."

"It's police business; it just came up, and I realized something very important about a case. I might be wrong, but I have to check it out tonight."

"This all happened while I was in the fucking bathroom? Great. So who is gonna eat all this goddamned food."

"You are. That's your job tonight to eat as much of this food as possible, watch a dirty movie, and wait for me," he said.

"At exactly three a.m., I will return to the Roosevelt Hotel, where you will be sleeping in what I hope is one of the best beds in this town, maybe worldwide, if price is any indicator. Then your job is to show me anything neat I might have missed about you last time." He put his hand on hers fluttering his eyelashes, but then she pulled away.

"You seem full of shit to me, man, but what the hell, I got nothing better going on tonight. Hey, you don't show up, and I'll run up a tab on your ass you'll never forget."

"See you at three a.m.," he said. "This is going to be a fun night. Eat up. Save me my shake. Don't drink it. Promise?"

"Hey, how are you leaving? I drove you here."

"My ride's here already, actually," and he left out the door without a word.

Tackett's car pulled around the corner at the top of the hill, and he rolled down his window, yelling out to Sullivan. "That better not be Tina you're blowing off in there."

"Yeah, it is," he said, "but she's cool. We're gonna meet later."

"What is this emergency that pulls me away from my drunken self-loathing at such an hour?"

"We need to talk about the case," he said, jumping into the car.

"Ex post facto, my man. Nothing left to discuss."

"Wrong."

"Come again?"

"Look, sometimes when you pull at a single thread, you unravel an entire rug, and this is one crazy-ass rug, man."

"I forgot my poetry translator at home, Detective. Could you say that in stupid for us slow city folk?"

"I showed Downy the picture of Samara's corpse in interrogation, and he said she was wearing different clothes from the ones he remembered. She was found in a T-shirt and light-colored jeans, right? So on a hunch I go to Woody's," he said, pointing back over his shoulder, "where they ate that night to see if anyone remembered what she had on, maybe their waiter, a bartender. Pretty girl, you know. People remember pretty girls. So the waiter does, and the guy knows Downy too."

Tackett looked at him sideways, seeming unconvinced.

"He confirms that she was wearing the same black sweater and dark jeans that Downy claimed she was."

"Yeah, but they went back to Downy's house. What does it matter what she wore to dinner? She coulda just changed there for bed, the way most people do. What are you getting at?"

"Why would she change into jeans for bed? Think about it. No, no. Not if he gave her the drugs in the drinks. There were still fifty milligrams of Darvocet in both their systems. They had at least two or three drinks each. Two tiny girls, they should have been toast by then. Yet, the waiter says they left in a seminormal state, not clearly drunk. They weren't drugged until later; I'm sure of it. Those kids found the body at two thirty a.m. They left Woody's around one a.m. according to Downy's wife."

"Did you see her, by the way?"

"Jesus, I know. Smoking. Anyway, that's not enough time to get the girl home, drug her, then murder her, change her clothes, and then dump the body. The extra step doesn't make any sense anyway. It takes twenty minutes at least to even get to that lake, and don't forget his wife said they had sex when they got home. The fact that both girls had almost the same amount of Darvocet in their systems suggests they were drugged at the same time. If he was planning all along to kill her, as this supposed sword theory suggests, why was he in such a hurry to do it? Once his wife was out cold, he should have had plenty of time, and yet in our version he barely has time to do any of it with any margin of error whatsoever. Look, he at least had help. Or?"

"Goddamn you, Sullivan."

"What?"

"I knew this wasn't finished somehow. Case 1032 is cursed, fuckin' always has been."

Tackett gunned the car as they pulled onto the interstate.

"So what's our next move?"

"We have to get to the station to Downy's phone. He claims his agent knows more than he's telling. I wanna talk to the guy and see what's what."

"OK, but this stays quiet. Do you understand? Tierney

finds out what we're up to, and I'll lose my goddamn pension."

"We can't have that."

"Screw you, Sullivan. You're a royal pain in the nuts. You know that?"

"I've been called worse by better men," he said, staring straight ahead with a goofy grin.

Tackett shook his head in disgust. He pulled his flask out of his coat pocket and drove the two silently back to the station.

CHAPTER 4

The man stared silently into the black of the pond. He dipped his fingertips in for a moment and then pulled them away suddenly, as if the water were scalding. The place both fascinated and terrified him. He could understand why so many claimed they saw serpents in the water's depths, the way the water undulated. The teacher had called it black energy. *How many more times could he make it through safely?* he wondered. The last trip would be the hardest, of course, but he couldn't think about that now. Killing a good man was fundamentally against his nature, but his nature was changing lately wasn't it?

Low clouds hovered over the pond, partially obscuring the sun. You could taste the moisture almost. There was a large marble statue only a few feet away of Poseidon holding his trident, scowling in concentration, aiming at something unseen in the water. He wondered who'd put it there. In the ruined corridors that surrounded the pond, there were statues of many kinds, at least one of which seemed to move of its own accord. He had never seen it move, but its position was changed each time he returned. There was the flowering vine that died right in front of his eyes and, of course, the childish laughter that seemed to emanate from nowhere. Other sounds of exultation, fear, horror, the roar of an invisible crowd lay hidden somewhere in the water's depths. Nothing much made sense, but he'd grown accustomed to the feeling. The cubes helped, but they always wore off and that meant there were moments of unbearable anxiety and fear. He sensed that many were trapped in this place somehow, though, of course, he could not explain who they were or how they had gotten here.

Something on the far side of the pond surfaced suddenly, breaking the water's inky silence. Bubbles appeared all around, and the man moved around the perimeter to get a closer look. The thing moved slowly toward him until he could clearly make out the shape. It was the sword. *Goddamnit*, he thought; it had come through with him. How could he not have noticed? It was a problem potentially. Without the sword there was still a chance they could find him. So far his plan had been flawless, and this was a very unfortunate oversight. What were the odds it would cost him? Slim. But he hated tempting fate. The sword floated, as everything did, inexplicably on the glassy surface, but he could not reach it.

Now he had to weigh his options. Leaving his captive was

dangerous, but in all likelihood, he was safest right where he was. The bigger issue was an unforeseen calamity on the other side of the pond. The book had warned of it explicitly. Each time he went through, he was leaving little remnants, clues, of his presence, and he felt somehow his luck must be running thin, whatever was left of it anyway. Then again only days ago it seemed his luck had run out completely. Maybe he had a clean slate now. He looked down the staircase into the darkness and sighed. Why did every move of his life have to be so full of risk? He looked across to the crumbling rocks and saw a young fawn walking unevenly over the crags. He stared at it for a long while to make sure it was real. Many things that passed through were simply illusions, mirages. It was headed for the pond, probably mistaking it for water. It stopped suddenly and then peered across at him, putting its head low so as not to be seen. Then, like a flickering flame, it simply vanished. Some marble from the statue of Poseidon cracked off and fell to the ground. The statue creaked, seeming to turn on its base.

"You move too slowly," the man spat to the lifeless statue. "You're never gonna catch a wild animal like that."

Poseidon's expression was frozen in concentration, and the man thought he looked even more severe than before. It was probably his imagination. There was no reason to wait for events to take shape he realized; he could shape them, as he always had. Sitting and waiting was simply not in his nature. He'd go back. There was no other way. He pulled two tiny sugar cubes from his pocket and plopped them in his mouth. He owed it to the teacher to show him something beautiful, something amazing, and already he was beginning to like the professor very much. The professor was going to teach the whole world all about him in fact; he just didn't know it yet.

CHAPTER 5

Sullivan and Tackett cruised into the station, which fortunately was all but abandoned, save for the night watch.

"Remember, you don't check anything out; just get the digits and then we go."

"Yeah, of course," he said. "I'll be right back," he said, jumping out.

Tackett sat in the lot, tapping his finger against the steering wheel, absent-mindedly humming a tune from Sullivan's Frank Sinatra collection. He closed his eyes for a moment when he felt the cold steel behind his neck and then a calm voice from the rear. He jerked forward, lurching, but a hand wrapped around his mouth, pulling him back hard against the headrest.

"Move again, and you're dead. It's a big gun you feel there and will leave an awfully large hole. Drive quickly, but not too quickly."

"What do you want?"

"Never mind that now."

"Look, killing me won't solve anything," Tackett said, slowly pulling the car into gear.

"Yes, you're quite inconsequential. It's true, but I need you nevertheless. Now drive." The man pressed the gun into Tackett's temple to emphasize the point.

"OK, OK."

He pulled the car out of the lot, looking into the rearview for Sullivan, hoping he might emerge in time to see them, but then had to pull onto the road, finally disappearing completely from sight.

———————

Sullivan leaned against the desk of the night clerk. "Hey'a, Tim," he said buoyantly.

"It's Mark, actually."

"Mark, yeah, that's right; sorry, bud. Hey, man, I logged in some evidence earlier on the Downy case, wondering if you could let me just double-check something."

"Um, you know what policy says. Once it goes in, nothing goes out, and Chief Tierney even made a special trip down earlier to—"

"Yeah, yeah," he said, "he knows I'm here actually. It's probably nuthin', but I just need to confirm something. You can follow me down if you want."

"Yeah, OK," Mark said hesitantly. "I will have to, actually. Sorry, man, it's nothing personal."

"I'll be sure to tell Bob what a good job you're doing."

"Thanks," he said, jangling his keys for the evidence room as they walked.

He opened the door and watched from a few feet as Sullivan pulled out the basket, shuffling for the cell phone.

"Hey, can I ask you something?" Mark said, smiling nervously.

"Yeah, shoot, man."

"Rodriguez. You uh...you, you know...hittin' that?"

Jesus, Sullivan thought. He looked Mark up and down, realizing he was no more than twenty at best.

"Nah, man. I got a girlfriend."

"Really?"

"Yep, we're getting hitched later tonight actually."

"No shit?"

"No, not really," he said flatly.

"I'm sorry, dude; I didn't mean—"

Sullivan scribbled down the digits on his notepad and looked up at the kid.

"You want to hear a rumor that's true though, Mark?"

"Yeah, sure."

"I heard Tierney cross-dresses on the weekends."

The kid burst into nervous laughter. "No shit, man. Rodriguez saw him at a lesbian bar two weeks ago, was calling himself Tina Bubbles, sumthin' like that. Keep it on the down low, OK? Have a good night, kid."

Sullivan sauntered out of the station into the night and saw before him an empty parking lot. *What the fuck?* he thought. He reached into his pocket for his cell and saw a message from Tackett:

Rodriguez needed back up across town...take the truck parked at the end...key is under the left back tire.
Sorry...

He walked, shaking his head, to the SUV parked at the end and reached under the tire for the key and then let himself in. Scrolling through his phone, he looked up the London time zone of eight hours and realized it was morning there already. He could call then. He dialed the digits carefully from the paper and waited while it rang. A voice picked up with a distinct British accent. It was a woman's voice.

"Hallo, this is Wingate Publishing. How may I help you?"

"Yes, I'm looking for Clellon Holmes; I believe he works there. This is...well, I'm calling from the San Diego Police Department actually."

"Oh, OK, sir. Mr. Holmes is out on vacation at the moment, I'm afraid. Could I take a message for you?"

"Yes, this is rather an urgent matter actually. Is there some way he can be reached?"

"He's abroad. I can send him a message though, if it's urgent."

"I see. It's crucial he return my call as soon as possible. One of his clients is in well...some real trouble here. Maybe you know him, Noah Downy?"

"Of course, I hope it's nothing—"

"I can't say too much more, but it would really help if he called. It would help Noah."

"Let me send a message immediately, sir. Should he call you at this number?"

"Yes."

"I'm sure if he knew he...he will do anything to help Mr. Downy. Oh dear, I hope it's nothing too serious."

He couldn't help but think of Money Penny from James Bond.

"Please make certain he knows it's urgent."

"I will, sir. Yes, I will."

He held the phone in his hands and looked at the clock. It was 11:57 p.m., and he thought of Tina, who should by now be lying in a bed with one helluva view, stomach full. He would have to find some way to bill the department. He popped the glove compartment, and sure enough there was a flask inside. He unscrewed the lid and took a shot. Jack, but he had no chaser. He leaned his head back and started to daydream. He thought of Tina's skirt and those crazy sexy high heels. She was waiting for him hopefully right now. He realized the many dangers of a younger woman, but there was something about Tina that he couldn't shake. She was unusually strong, and well, he liked her. What was she, twenty-three maybe? It was Richmond all over again. He hadn't even thought of the place with all that had been going on. It felt far away and long ago somehow. He took another deep pull from the flask and let himself doze for a moment. His phone vibrated. It was an unknown number; it had to be London. He punched at the green accept button.

"Yeah, this is Sullivan."

"Yes, uh hallo, this is Clellon Holmes calling. I received a message from my secretary that you needed to speak with me urgently."

"Yes, thanks for returning my call so quickly. This is Detective Sullivan calling from the United States, San Diego, actually, and I was wondering if you could answer a few questions for me regarding Professor Noah Downy."

"Yes, of course. I hope everything is OK."

"No, as a matter of fact, Professor Downy is in a great deal of trouble here. He's been arrested for the capital murders of two police and a young woman by the name of Samara Patterson."

There was a long pause.

"Oh good gracious no, you cahn't be serious. That poor girl."

"I'm afraid I am. I spoke to him earlier today, and he says you might have some information that can help him."

"You know her then, Samara Patterson, sir?"

"Yes, of course. Her father was a client here. This is such devastating news. She has passed away then?"

"Yes, I'm sorry to say. Professor Downy wanted me to ask you about a couple of things. Specifically, have you ever heard of a place called the pond?"

"I know lots of ponds I suppose, but none in particular, no."

"Yeah, OK. What about a man by the name of Nazim, who I believe resides in Cairo? Downy claims this Nazim has been behaving strangely regarding Charlie Patterson, in particular he believes that Patterson isn't deceased, or at least that's what he's claiming."

"Dear lord, what sort of madness is this? Charlie has been dead more than five years now. Nazim was his boat handler and guide, but I don't know anything about this frankly."

Both men took a breath.

"Is Noah OK? Forgive me, but I'm just deeply concerned. He's such a good man; he cahn't be responsible for this. I'm just sure of it."

"Yeah, there is a good bit of evidence he is, unfortunately, but I'm sure the two of you can talk at some point. He's claiming he's been framed, and it's a pretty unbelievable story he's telling frankly. So just to clarify, Downy says he called you two nights ago and you made some comments that were suspicious. He's claiming you must be somehow involved."

"I haven't spoken to Noah in months. He hasn't written anything for us in a couple of years. We usually only chat when he's actually working. He's a top client though, and this is all coming as a terrible shock."

"Sure, I understand. I think that's all for now. Look if you can stay available for the next few days, it might be necessary to—"

"Of course, of course. You have my number, anything you need."

"Thank you, and I'm sorry to interrupt your vacation."

"It's no problem. Please tell Noah and his poor wife, well, I will try and phone myself."

"Sure I will pass along your well wishes."

He hit End and stared at the phone. Superpowers were

neutralized over the phone, weren't they? The guy sounded genuinely shocked and befuddled though. Oh well, he had done his due diligence. It was on to Tina now.

———

Sullivan pulled his SUV into the waiting attendant and dropped his key to him without stopping.

"Have this car waiting for me in exactly this spot in three hours, and I'll make it worth your while."

The kid nodded an emphatic affirmative as he tossed him his keys. "It'll be here waiting, mister?"

"Cranston, Lamont Cranston," he said, realizing the kid couldn't possibly remember such a reference, as he disappeared into the lobby of the hotel.

Running to the front desk, he found his room number from the attendant and got on the elevator. It was one of those glass cylinders, clear all around, and he could see all the way down as he climbed to the top floor. He pressed his face against the glass and rested. The honeymoon suite. He was going to need all his energy. He slid in his keycard and opened the door expectantly to a stunning 365 view of the skyline. The master bed was placed just under a smaller dome of clear glass, where the room's master suite and bed lay. The room was dimly lit, and he could see something lying on the bed. He knew what it was immediately. Shit. A note. Tina had gone. He walked to the bed and let out a long sigh, running his hands through his hair in frustration.

Sorry pal, too lonely here alone.
P.S. Flip this over

He turned the page and saw the words in large print.

Turn around.

He did and behind him Tina stood in the doorway, wearing a simple black T-shirt and a pair of tiny red panties.

"Honey," she said in a mock southern accent, "you're home. I just wanted to see how you'd react."

"How did I do?"

Tina wrapped her arms around his neck. "That was either great acting, or you've been seriously thinking about this all night. Thinking about, you know."

And she put her tongue to his mouth and flicked the tip of his lip before the two fell down on the satin sheets together, kissing wildly. He could see the stars above them, and he had to laugh aloud a little at the pleasure of it all.

"So what don't I know about you?"

"Let me show you this one cool trick I learned with a girl-friend of mine."

He laughed loudly, "Oh, please go on."

And she explained the trick in great detail as she applied it.

CHAPTER 6

Sullivan awoke to the sun coming in through a crack in the drape. His watch alarm slurred a beep in the darkness. He hadn't been out long, and in his dreams, the man in the hat was yelling something to him from a distance, but he couldn't get to him. He was trapped in some dark, tar like quicksand. The harder he fought the deeper in he was pulled. As his eyes fluttered open, he could see Tina's head buried in pillows next to him, but the rest of her naked and frankly perfect body was fully exposed. A pair of handcuffs was still attached to one of her wrists, at her insistence, of course. He couldn't believe he was going to leave like this again, but his mind was on overdrive, and that old feeling in his gut told him that the professor was telling at least some of the truth, which meant that he had almost everything wrong. A large clock across the room showed 6:02 a.m., and he wanted to get to the station as soon as possible. He slid to the edge of the bed, pulling his pants back on. As he got up, Tina's voice broke the silence.

"Goin' to catch the bad guys, hun?"

"Yeah, I am."

"Give us a kiss before you go."

And he did. In the low light, he looked into to her eyes for what felt like the first time. They were a drowsy blue. Leaving felt all wrong.

"Don't get killed, OK? This is like the most fun I've had in a relationship so far."

He laughed and picked up the phone. "Hello, wondering if you could send up breakfast for my wife and if we can get a late check out? Thank you."

"Stay, OK?" he said, kissing her again. "Enjoy it."

"Yes, sir, Officer," she said, rolling herself into a ball and moaning in pleasure. "God, these sheets are like heaven," she moaned.

"Yeah, and the bed's too big to roll off too."

Grabbing his things, he slipped out silently to the elevator, pressing his face to the glass again all the way down. The view was stunning. Sunrise. He always loved mornings, while the world was mostly empty still. He did his best thinking then. Patterson had to be the key to the case. He needed information on him badly. He emerged through the lobby, and sure enough his car sat waiting for him just where he'd asked, already running.

"Mr. Cranston, or should I call you *The Shadow*, your car is ready," the young bellhop said with a sly grin.

"Hey, you're not old enough to remember *The Shadow*," Sullivan said incredulously.

"I just googled it. It sounded fake."

He handed the kid a fifty and smiled warmly.

"And congratulations, sir."

"Oh yeah, thanks," he said, realizing that the boy must have realized he'd stayed in the honeymoon suite.

He sped away in the SUV, remembering he'd left his car at Woody's and would have to pick it up later.

Minutes later he rolled into the lot of SDPD. He pulled down the mirror to see his reflection. He looked like he'd been on a bender for days. He yawned deeply and laughed. Young girls were demanding, weren't they? The lot was mostly empty, and as he turned off the ignition, he realized a quick nap would be a great idea. He could wait a few minutes to inquire about Patterson. Showing up this early would set off alarms with Tierney probably anyway, so he climbed to the back seat, which was a hell of a lot more comfortable than that of his own car. He could still smell Tina's perfume, which was something citrus. He loved it. No sooner than he closed his eyes, a thud suddenly caused him to jump back in his seat. Rodriguez had her face mashed against the window. He rolled it down with his heart still racing.

"Are you the one telling people I hang out at gay bars, motherfucker?"

"Oh shit, that guy works fast," he said, laughing.

"I like the bit about Tierney in a dress, but leave me out of your little fantasies, OK? I'm already getting blowback at home over the rumors about us. What the fuck you doin' snoozing here, homey?"

"Had a hot date last night and figured I'd catch up on missed sleep."

"Nice."

"How'd the thing across town pan out last night?"

"What thing?"

"You needed back up, right; Tackett dumped me actually."

"What you talking about? I was off last night too, had a hot date of my own."

"Tackett's not with you?" he said sharply.

"Haven't seen him in a couple of days actually."

"Oh shit, get in. You gotta come with me."

He handed Rodriguez the phone and showed her the message.

"What the fuck is this, man? Who sent this?"

"No idea. He bailed on me, and I thought he went to help you."

"Call his place."

"I am, I am." Sullivan's mind was racing through the possibilities, none of which he wanted to consider. "No answer. Goddamnit!" he said, shouting, punching at the wheel.

"Keep calling. We gotta tell Tierney, get out an APB."

"Yeah, I know."

"Are you sure he didn't just give you the slip or something to go meet a chick?"

"Tackett, a chick? No way."

"If he's not answering at home, we should go check ourselves."

"No, just call and tell Tierney no one has seen him since last night at about midnight. Tell them to look at parking-lot surveillance of the station around that time and to ping his phone. I need to see something for myself first. No APB, not yet."

"Where we headed?"

"To the lake where they found the body."

———

Sullivan and Rodriguez crept slowly through the parking-lot gravel to the edge of Chippewa Lake. The name was a misnomer since the water barely made up an acre. In the past it had been much larger, but time had shrunk it to nothing more than a quaint spot for teenage lovers and late-night drinkers. The banks curved just around the edge of gargantuan trees, California Sequoias. The water was utterly still in spite of a light breeze. It was like a scene ripped out of Sullivan's Richmond, and for a moment he felt a little homesick. Rodriguez squinted her eyes.

"Goddamn, imagine that, a public park and no Mexicans barbecuing."

He didn't get the joke exactly but chuckled anyway.

"Why are we here? We should be back looking for Tack, man. Tierney may go ahead with that APB anyway. He sounded pissed when I told him you wanted to wait."

"We can't look any better than they can. I'm pretty sure the professor is innocent, but I need to see something first."

The two walked around the water's edge until they found the police tape. In a clearing, the spot where Samara Patterson's body had been found floating was visible near some reeds poking through the water. Bugs now plopped on its surface. He bent down to survey the sandy bank.

"These," he said, pointing, "are our divers' tracks. See flat-soled water boots. But what else do you see?" he said, talking, but not looking at Rodriguez.

"Lots of footprints."

"Yeah, but what's missing?"

"I don't know, man. If you see something, spit it out."

"These footprints are heading in toward the bank *from* the water, not out into it. Someone went in from another spot, or they live at the bottom of this lake."

"Looks like just swimmers to me; they're bare feet, could be anybody's.

"Where are the professor's tracks?"

"I don't know; maybe he threw her in over there?"

"Nope. Why not use this spot? The reeds are too high everywhere else. He'd have to be Hercules to toss her in over them. If she floated over here, she was put in the water cleanly somehow, and this is the only spot to do it. But there are no shoe prints going into the water, or even near its edge."

"Yeah, I see what you mean. But how does someone get to the water without leaving tracks."

"They don't."

"Come on, Tackett's in deep shit, but if I'm right, we won't have to find him. He'll find us."

The two ran to the truck.

"Get me Tierney on the phone."

"OK."

She handed him the phone.

"Bob, you gotta hold off on that APB."

Rodriguez could hear a garble of complaining on the other end before Sullivan finally spoke again.

"We'll get Tack killed if we do. I'll explain more later. Just wait one hour more. I have one more errand to run, and then I'll let you do whatever you think is best." He hung up while Tierney was still protesting.

"Where to now?"

"To the good professor's house, in search of treasure."

"What kind of treasure?"

"Old shit, man, very old shit."

CHAPTER 7

"It's a new day asshole, and you got a visitor," came the voice from down the hall.

Downy had finally slept, and in his dream he was on a boat floating across an ocean. His cell was maybe the quietest place he'd ever slept. There was no peace to be had though, and in the dream he'd been overtaken by something like a tsunami. He'd had what felt like an eternity to watch it grow and swell off in the distance. When it finally crashed down, he felt something like relief but then awoke to the awareness of where he actually was. It didn't take Freud to understand what it meant. As he lay silently on his tiny cot, he wanted desperately to believe it was his wife coming to see him, but in his heart he knew somehow it wasn't. The guard opened the door, and sure enough sitting there calmly was Mr. Taro, who rose, putting his hand to the glass before sitting again and picking up the phone.

"Your message has been delivered, and I have good news."

"Yes?"

"Your wife will be coming by today to see you before she departs for her mother's cabin. She was easily convinced to see you, in spite of the slanders and deceptions of your captors."

He noticed again how everything Taro said had a grandiose ring to it. Whoever referred to the police as captors?

"Thank you, thank you."

"I'd consider it a privilege to see her off to the airport myself, if you would feel comfortable allowing a relative stranger to do so that is?"

"It doesn't seem I have a lot of friends riding to my rescue at the moment," he said, holding his cuffs up as evidence of the direness of the situation.

"We know little of our friends until we are truly in need, I'm afraid. Nevertheless, your wife says many have inquired as to your situation and expressed their deepest sympathies and faith in your innocence." Taro paused and leaned in. "I have been thinking of your situation as well and have devised some other options. I will post your bail, of course, but there is another matter that I would like to propose. If you are freed, there would be certain limitations on your movements and that could be problematic for us."

"Us?" Downy said, wrinkling the corners of his eyes.

"There is another way."

"Another way to do what?"

"I must explain to you that I need something from you that I have not yet shared. I only held it back because I thought there would be plenty of time to present my request to you more ceremoniously—"

"What is it?"

"You have come into possession of something that belongs to me, something of great sentimental value to me— a golden laurel to be worn on the head. It was a gift; one I treasure dearly. A black pearl is attached at the base." Taro's dark eyes seemed to glimmer with anger or tears, he couldn't tell which.

"Yes, I have it."

"It doesn't concern me how you came into possession of it. I'm no bounty hunter. I just would like it back. I am willing to pay for it, of course. It has a value in weight, as it is pure, but it means far more to me personally than it ever could to a collector of such curiosities."

"Of course."

"There is...how do you say in English, a rub?"

"OK."

"Someone has taken it from your home."

"Can I ask how you know this?"

"Sadly, money loosens the tongues of even those who take a sworn oath to the law. Where I come from an oath is seen as a treacherous thing for this very reason."

"OK, but how can I help you from here?"

Taro leaned in and locked eyes. He shifted in his seat. "I can arrange, by surreptitious means, of course, for you to leave here this very night and return unnoticed by morning. There is no chance you will be discovered in fact, but you must follow what I tell you to the letter."

"That seems dangerous and stupid."

"It is, but your reward is that I can guarantee your release and freedom from these charges. I can clear your name, and I will. That is a promise. But we must do it tonight, and we must be together. I'm sorry I can't say more, but I will tell you everything very soon."

"You'll have to forgive me that even given my circumstances this sounds like a deal with the devil."

"Ahh yes, that which sounds too good to be true. You're a wise man, Professor."

"You can call me, Noah."

"Thank you. I will, Noah. I don't believe in the devil personally, but I do believe in helping the innocent. I would see justice done."

Downy paused and looked around the room. He wanted out, of course, but not like this; something felt off.

"How do I know you will still post my bail if I leave with you?"

"You don't, but let me tell you I have never once knowingly deceived an honest man, and I suspect you are just such a person. You have my word. I can offer nothing more."

"OK, how do we get out?"

"Tonight when the lights go off, I need you to be in your cell, undressed completely, *fully* undressed. Also, skip dining this evening, have no food. It is most important that your stomach is empty."

"What?"

"It sounds mad I'm sure, but there will be little time.

Arrange your clothing neatly near your bed so that when you return you can put it back on quickly."

"What are you going to break down the walls?" he said cynically.

"There will be no mess and no tearing down any walls. There will be a time to discuss what you see with me this evening, but that time is not now. You can ask no questions until then. I will tell you everything you need to know, but when and only when you need to know it."

"Are you asking me to do something illegal? I mean beyond breaking out of jail."

"Oh yes, yes, indeed. But there is no law that can stop us, nor that we shall ever face, not here in any case."

He sat back in his chair, looking over his shoulder at the guard who waited for him in hallway. "What if I say no?"

Taro sat up straight. "Then I will post your bail tomorrow, and do what I can to help you anyway, but I assure you this is both the most expedient way and the only way I can guarantee your name will be fully cleared. A man with a family and career like yours must surely want to be fully exonerated in such matters as these." Taro put his hand to glass and smiled warmly. "You've made the right decision."

"I haven't said yes."

"You're too smart to say no, Professor Downy. Be ready when I arrive and remember: no food, no clothes, and no questions."

CHAPTER 8

S ullivan stood at the edge of Tierney's desk, pointing to the folded linen he'd placed there.

"Detective, why you have put me in such a situation, or your partner? I really must know. Every minute we waste—"

"It's that," Sullivan said, interrupting. He paced back and forth nervously. "This case has baffled me from the beginning, and, man, that's rare. Every time, in fact, we think we have something sorted, these pricks turn out to be a step ahead. How? We have a mole in this department; I'd bet on it."

"You're not still talking about 1032, I hope." Tierney unwrapped the linen and looked at the golden laurel suspiciously.

"Yes, I am. In fact, I doubt seriously our professor is involved at all, not really, but one thing is clear: Information is trickling out of our department into someone else's ears. But it's not just that. The information is being used against

Downy too. It is a setup, but it's incredibly elaborate, it must be. Why? Why do they need a frame up unless there's something huge at stake? These have to be people of serious financial means, Bob." He stopped pacing, realizing he was basically talking to himself. "That's the answer," he said, pointing again to the laurel. "I haven't sent it to the lab yet, but I'm sure it's real gold. And get this, Charlie Patterson, Downy's friend, was into these relics big time, discovered all kinds of this stuff. It all made its way back to the university collection, including our murder weapon. All but this. I think the reason we can't find the sword is because it's probably halfway around the world by now. There are entire networks of people selling this shit for millions to private collectors."

"So you think Downy is telling the truth then, like it's some kind of goddamn international conspiracy?"

"I think so. This Patterson, it turns out, died under very shady circumstances. Fell off a boat, but no body was ever recovered. We're pulling his file off ICD right now. Downy claimed that Samara had suspicions about his death as well. If he is still alive, he might be the one moving the shit or at least telling people where to find it."

"But why frame Downy, he was his best friend?" Before he could respond, Tierney answered himself, "The daughter."

"Yeah, if he found out his buddy was tapping his daughter, he might have decided to get some revenge in the process."

"So Patterson and this international ring of thieves have Sergeant Tackett?"

"Yeah, and that explains why we can't track his phone. If

they took him, probably he's been taken out of the country already; maybe he's even on the water still, somewhere nearby."

"His last cell ping disappeared near the coast," Tierney said.

"How can we get to him if you're right?"

"I can't say for sure how they're getting information, but I say we release Downy immediately. We can always rearrest him if I'm wrong."

Tierney tapped his fingers on the desk.

"If I'm right, they will want that," Sullivan said, pointing, and we can use Downy to reach out to them; in fact, if that is what I think it is, it may be the only way to convince them to keep him alive."

Tierney folded his hands and looked down. "What do you think it is?"

"I think it's a fake probably, but I'm pretty sure for some reason they think it's real. My hunch says Patterson may have them convinced. He's a specialist in the stuff; probably they trust him."

"What makes it so valuable?" Tierney said, holding the golden laurel up in the light.

"Check the name on the back."

Tierney looked closer at the inscription and let out a sharp laugh.

"We have to make a big deal out of it in the press and talk about how we got it wrong arresting Downy. Make it clear he is a free man, our bad. We gotta make it seem like we're really taking one on the nose. Then we use that as the bait."

"How *you* got it wrong, you mean?"

He smiled like a child caught stealing and stopped talking abruptly. "Yes, Bob. How I got it wrong."

"I told you never to call me Bob."

"I know, Bob. I'm trying."

"Get out; I need to think about this before I do anything else to completely destroy the credibility of this department. Not putting out an APB on a missing cop will surely get me fired, if not tossed in the can myself."

Sullivan turned to walk away.

"Detective Sullivan, I knew the first moment I saw your face I'd regret saying yes to you."

"Thanks, Chief. Me too."

Sullivan wanted desperately to speak to the professor, but now he was with his wife in the visitor's room, talking at last. Instead he walked into the interrogation dark room and looked up at the video monitor, where he could see the two of them. Downy had his hand pressed to the glass, as did his wife, both weeping quietly. He felt a stinging pang of guilt. He was certain he had gotten it wrong with Downy, gotten everything wrong. It had never felt right in fact. There was a quality in Downy that was impossibly at odds with the kind of butchery the crime scene photos suggested. The girl had been sliced both across the abdomen and the throat. She would have bled out in only a matter of seconds, but the two cuts suggested someone double-checking their work, not the haphazard hand of someone driven by passion alone, not someone slashing. It was, from Sullivan's perspective, a very impersonal murder; the cut marks were both precise in their length and depth according to the autopsy, as if the hand of a surgeon had made them, a professional. The medical examiner had even noted that if he didn't know better, he would have sworn the cuts had been made postmortem. It also suggested that the killer had bound the victim in some way, since there was no way she wouldn't have fought back in the face of such a weapon. He held a light to one of the crime scene photos at the water's edge, confirming that the footprints all led out of the water but none into it.

A knock came at the door.

Rodriguez leaned in. "The file on Patterson is up. Come and take a look."

He dashed out of his chair and down the hall, plopping down in front of the computer terminal.

"It's mostly like you said," she said, scrolling down the screen. "But there is one new thing you should see. I got a hit off Interpol on the name Charles Higgs Patterson to this man." A haggard face appeared on the screen. "Professor Jacob Tannehill. Had a huge career in physics at MIT, and then Interpol says he went off the grid for a whole year as a missing person. Showed up again in England at a psychiatric clinic, where he was treated for multiple mental illnesses, and then released in August of 2006. Tannehill got caught up in a sting later that year involving stolen museum pieces— tried to sell some stuff on the black market apparently to an undercover officer. He did no time though; the evidence went missing before a prosecution could begin, but Interpol has him on a watch list still, a priority level 1B."

"Shit," Sullivan said. "That's our link."

"It gets better. Guess who posted his bail?"

"Patterson."

"Yep, in 2006, about a month before his own untimely death."

He jumped in the air at the news. Just as he did, he could see Downy's wife walking out of the meeting room toward him. It was terrible timing. She was being led by a man who stared at him scornfully. As they came closer, the man spoke, "You damnable fools have the wrong man."

"I'm sorry," Sullivan said, lowering his head.

Naomi Downy stood before him silently, but the man's black piercing eyes stared through him, almost in menace.

"No, but you will be, that much I can promise you."

And then the two walked down the hall together, the woman collapsing into the man's shoulder; he looked like her father perhaps. Sullivan wanted to follow them and explain, but he knew it was a bad idea. He had to wait until he could be certain, and saying anything before Downy was released could cause even more problems.

"What's our next move?"

"We gotta set this shit straight and find Tackett."

"I'm gonna go tell Tierney what we found."

"Roger that."

Sullivan's pocket vibrated. He reached and looked. It was a text from Tina. He had almost forgotten about her at the hotel all alone.

That was some wedding night. What did you think of my trick?

He had thought very highly of the whole performance. He considered for a moment and then typed.

Where did a nice girl like you learn to do a thing like that?
P.S. How does it feel to be a married woman?

He hit Send and stared out the window, thinking of Tackett and what he'd said: *Ten thirty-two was cursed and was going to be the end of him.*

Not if he could help it.

———

"We'll release Downy first thing in the morning," Tierney said, appearing suddenly over his shoulder.

"We play it your way for a while. You must know though I'm out on a serious limb here, and if you're wrong on this, you take the fall, all of it. We have to bring Downy in on this too if he is going to help us, but it can't be right away. I want him behaving naturally."

"OK, I'll go get him first thing in the morning, and then we release him with a tail."

"Do you think he will go along? It's a helluva risk if he says no."

"The guy has every right to tell us to go fuck ourselves, me in particular. We need to make it clear to him that he will be helping track down the girl's killer. If my instincts are right, he won't pass on the chance, no matter what he thinks of us."

"What about this agent in London, Clellon Holmes? You spoke to him too, right?"

"Yeah, I did, but how did you know that?"

"Never you mind. It's my job to know things."

"I have no idea if he's involved at this point. We'll have to wait to see which fish are biting after we dangle the bait. He's got serious money this guy, plus the extradition; it could get messy, real messy."

Tierney stared off as if he saw something far away out the window, crossing his arms. It was the first time Sullivan had ever seen him look concerned about anything.

"Chief?"

Tierney looked up at him with a look of surprise. "Yeah?"

"We're gonna get Tackett back, OK?"

"Yeah, I sure as hell hope we can. He's a good cop and a good man. I owe him that and much more. Double down on security for the professor tonight. Somebody has still got eyes and ears on us. I don't want any more disappearances."

"What do we say on Tackett?"

"He's on vacation as far as the world is concerned. I don't know how long I can keep it under wraps though. We have to work fast on this, OK? The longer they have him, the more likely they are to just hit the panic button and—"

He nodded his head in agreement. "I know."

"I'm bringing in Homeland Security. This is getting too big for us. I need some help if we're going after people overseas, and we have to figure out where these goddamn leaks are coming from."

"OK," he said.

"Keep me posted on anything that develops, and watch yourself out there."

"Will do."

————

Sullivan stared at the computer screen at the picture of Professor Jacob Tannehill. A mad scientist if he'd ever seen one. How did he figure into all of this? Why would Patterson, a respected academic, even risk such an association unless he needed him for some reason, some illegal reason?

"Can you take me to get my car? It's still at Woody's illegally parked," he said, looking across to Rodriguez.

"It's down in impound actually. Saw it on my way up, the piece of shit with no door, right?"

"Right."

Rodriguez shook her head silently.

CHAPTER 9

The man could smell the food even before he was awake and was already fantasizing about its taste in his mouth. He could see steam rising from the plate, still warm. As he rose he could also see a note that had been placed by the plate, which read:

Eat very slowly, only half, or you will lose it.

And so he did. His hands shook, and his mouth salivated at every taste; he felt he might tear the bone right out of the meat if he wasn't careful to control himself. He ate rapaciously. First the meat and then a sweetbread, which he then gorged down with the wine, its bittersweet taste making him choke, spilling down the sides of his mouth. Then, he simply stopped, feeling in his gut the weight of the food. He could feel great waves of pleasure coursing through his body. He realized he'd eaten thousands of times without ever tasting the full flavor of food.

He panted lightly in the dim light, looking around him again at the strange surroundings. It seemed as if someone was stacking coins in the middle of the room, each one falling into a giant pile, clinking. But no one was there. The coins seemed to appear and fall out of thin air. Statues sat piled in another corner. They were of faces he had never seen, of gods or goddesses he did not recognize. He was in some foreign land then. But his captor had said he was "close to home," hadn't he? He was a deceptive talker though and clearly not to be trusted. The reasons for his lying were, of course, what really mattered. Discovering a lie but not trying to understand why it was told in the first place was a common mistake; it was not an error he was prone to. He thought of Gnaeus, of the war. It had been won in his head first and then on the battlefield. He had been heavily outnumbered, overwhelmingly in fact, and had the worst position, fighting uphill; and yet still it was his enemy's head that had been delivered to him in a basket. You could see the lack of intelligence in Gnaeus's eyes even then, the milky film of death over them, completely empty. A dumb, dead bear had been his first thought upon seeing him, but he had wept nevertheless, and it had given him no pleasure. He remembered the better times when the two had laughed, their gentle ribbing, the girls, the incredible wealth they had built together. It seemed the fun would never end. Gnaeus was always comfortable when he felt flattered and admired. But any challenge to his sense of personal superiority made him a tyrant, a belligerent fool. He was dead and gone now the dumb, dead bear; yet still somehow he loved him. Thinking about the past couldn't help him though and getting sentimental was pointless.

He could only wait now in any case, as the iron bars of his cell showed no signs of giving way. Then a voice fractured the quiet.

"You there?"

"Yes, I am," he replied.

"We in a well. The coins, a wishing well, no use yelling. No one comes."

"You speak our tongue only a little; where are you from?"

There was a long silence, but the voice had clearly come from the cell next to his. It was a soft whisper, clearly that of a boy or maybe a young woman and a foreigner by the sound of the broken phrases.

"How you get here, remember? How they get you?"

"I was taken, abducted from my home. It was a trap," he whispered. "They killed my nephew I think."

"You speak dead languages with the man, why?"

"What do you mean 'dead'?"

There was a long pause, and the voice came back, seeming to ignore his question.

"We're not alone...others. Two, maybe more."

"How long have you been here?"

"A week, I don't know. They're poisoning us. It's hard to remember. The others here longer, but they don't remember. They barely speak."

"What's your name?"

"It's S—"

A sudden clank broke their conversation. Boot steps could be heard from above them, and both waited in nervous anticipation. A figure suddenly appeared at the bottom of the stairs like something out of a nightmare. He wore a black hood and dark clothing.

"You," the voice bellowed, "your time is up."

The man went to the cell next to his and opened the door. He could hear a struggle taking place, and the voice of whoever was in the cell being muted, strangled.

The man in the hood slung open the cell door, handling his prisoner like a rag doll, dragging the tiny figure away up the stairs. They kicked back uselessly against him. He tried desperately to see who it was, but the low light only gave a glimpse of a tiny shadow. He thought it was a young boy or woman but couldn't be sure. He heard the door at the top of the stairs slam shut, and then the silence came again. It was maddening to be in the dark. He could hear a whisper again, but this time further away. It was a foreign tongue that he could not recognize, a garble.

He could make out only one word, badly pronounced but repeated over and over: "Flamen, Flamen. Priest."

CHAPTER 10

Downy sat on the edge of the cot with his eyes closed, thinking of the look in his wife's eyes when she had first seen his face on set in Rome. He'd been sitting in the corner that beautiful, crisp fall afternoon, taking notes as she played out her death scene for the cameras. Their eyes had locked just at the horrible moment of surprise when Cleopatra's guards and the Roman Centurions had come for her head. She'd been utterly intoxicating, both defiant and vulnerable in the scene. He hadn't been able to take his eyes off of her since. He'd begged her to keep the Egyptian gown from the shoot. She had often promised to wear it for him, though they never seemed to have time for such playful things since they came back to the states. He silently promised himself they would in the future.

He had done his best to explain in the short time they had what had really happened between he and Samara. He could tell on the most primal level that his wife believed the story. He had broken trust with her though and knew it. He would need to spend the rest of his life getting it back, which he was more than willing to do. What he couldn't figure out was why he was even considering Taro's strange offer. The thing to do was to wait it out, of course, to get that union lawyer, but on some strange wavelength, he utterly believed Taro when he said it was the only way to clear his name. Was it because of the glowing letter from the Monsignor? He couldn't explain the feeling rationally, but for some reason he believed Taro. He was already accused of murder; how much worse could it get?

A voice came, breaking his concentration.

"You gonna eat that, boss? That's our best Salisbury steak."

"You can take it," he said emotionlessly.

"Hey, Doc, I gotta tell ya that wife of yours man, whew."

Downy looked at him sideways, without turning his head. "Thanks."

"Show me a beautiful woman though, and I'll show a man tired of fuc—"

"Don't ever talk about my wife like that, you stupid son of a bitch," he said flatly.

"There it is," the guard said, taunting him. "Now see that's the attitude that got you put in here in the first place. I knew that cool exterior was all an act."

"When I get out, you can repeat what you just said to my face. When these are free," Downy said, holding up his hands.

"You ain't going nowhere, so just relax, Professor Frankenstein."

He smiled to himself as the guard carried his food away. It felt damn good to threaten someone actually. He hadn't thrown a punch in years, but at the moment he felt anything was better than just sitting, waiting. He wanted to get his hands on whoever had killed Samara too. Thinking of her made him swell with rage.

Had the vision of Charlie at the bar been only his imagination running wild? It must have and yet everyone was behaving strangely, weren't they? Clellon now too. Why had he spoken so cryptically? He knew he had to get out of the cell to find out the truth and to find out who had really killed Samara. The police weren't doing a damn thing to help him. He heard the suctioned clank of the master cell door at the end of the hall close, pulling all the air out of the corridor. It was going to be lights out in a few minutes. The place was like a tomb, and the silence was almost unbearable. How in the hell would Taro get him out he wondered? A bribe? It seemed unlikely. He lay down and closed his eyes. He was exhausted physically and emotionally, but seeing his wife had changed his mood dramatically. There was a hope he could get his life back; he could see it in her eyes. That wasn't true for Samara though. Downy laid down pulling his arm across his forehead. There was nothing to do in this place but sleep, so he started to doze. His imagination ran wild. He found himself in complete darkness, but then someone spoke in a low voice. An answer came back in the form of a chant. He found himself in a room that looked like an ancient temple of some kind but strangely reminded him of the church services he'd gone to as a boy with his mother, where the pastor offered a prayer, which the parishioners answered back to in unison. The smell of ambrosia, just like his wife's perfume in fact, wafted in the darkness. But there was another subtler smell, like something metallic and burned. In front of him, a tall, muscular man stood at the head of an altar, where a bull's body lay, moving sluggishly on a ledge just above the floor. The beast snorted uneasily, its hooves clacking against the floor in agitation, sensing some danger. The man, whose face was smeared with blue paint, suddenly held something glimmering in the air and swung it to a slicing blow. Blood poured from the decapitated animal's quivering body into a chalice being held by a woman at its feet. She was down on her knees, in silhouette, and bent to catch it, but as the cup filled, it overran the edges; the blood poured down onto her arms instead and then her neck and her chest. Her white gown was now soaked in it. Downy started to sweat. Rhythmic chants came from the darkness, and the woman began to sway in a seeming trance. The muscular man raised his right hand, lowering his head near a fiery pit at the altar, suddenly casting blood into the fire, which erupted into a drowsy blue flame. In its reflection he could see the man's face, which was painted blue, but somehow he looked familiar. His black, piercing eyes raged in the reflection from the fire; he too swayed to the chanting. The girl reached across her chest lurching back on her knees and tore her gown away from her body, seeming to surrender to the trance. She moved her hands, covered in the animal's sacrifice, to her face smearing it into her cheeks. The pace of the chanting became frantic now, and the girl was suddenly surrounded by figures in dark hoods. They appeared from the darkness on all sides, pulling at her body, lifting her into the air. They seemed to consume her, tearing away the final vestiges of her gown, but suddenly the chanting stopped, and they scurried away in fear. The girl lay silently on the ground. He could see her chest rise and fall from the attack, her breasts reflecting in the fire. Across her shoulder was a tattoo with the one recognizable word, *Veritas*, etched into the blade of her back. As she lay on the ground writhing, her head turned suddenly back to Downy as if she'd always known he was there, her eyes locking seductively with his in the low light of the flames.

"Samara!" he screamed.

He awoke on the bed with a start, his face covered in sweat, heart pounding in his throat. He looked all around the cell and without a word began removing his clothing, folding it into a neat pile on the floor next to the cot. His decision was made. Whoever had done this to her must pay.

CHAPTER 11

Sullivan paced back and forth, looking at the clock in the corner. There was much activity in the usually quiet corridors of the precinct. Tierney had apparently gotten his wish, and Homeland Security was now involved in the operation. It was going to mean more resources but unfortunately more complications as well. If he had it his way, he would have kept it in house. He was finished with the case files anyway, so turning them over was no problem, but bringing everyone up to speed was going to be a nightmare. Bureaucracy on a massive scale and wasted time when they had none to spare; men in dark, clearly starched suits stood in the corner with Tierney pointing all around the room, staring in Sullivan's direction. Feds were the worst, and they always traveled in packs. There had been a joke back in Richmond at the station that went, "What's the difference between a federal agent and serial killer?" The answer, according to his old boss Carl Dickson, was "Feds have to get permission to randomly kill innocent people in large numbers." He figured the only real reason Carl had agreed to his transfer in the first place instead of firing him was that he'd secretly been proud of him for cracking the case of the Redneck killer before the FBI could.

His phone buzzed in his pocket. It was Tina:

Is the Joker behind bars yet Batman?

He grinned. Was he falling for this girl? She was a clever one, but he had always managed to go cold, even when things started out white hot with a girl. Work. The job was a huge problem. It was the reason why a one-night stand always seemed the sensible thing to do. He sure wouldn't want to be married to himself. How could anybody else he figured? And so younger, less demanding girls always seemed the most attractive option. They weren't thinking about marriage yet, were they? That was it. They simply couldn't imagine how hellish a life it would be, married to a man who came and went at all hours and really couldn't be counted on to do anything but chase fiends, the low lifes of the world. He thought of the professor now, down in his cell, so far away from his wife—his fault. He'd taken a long look at Naomi Downy in the interrogation video room. She was incredibly beautiful herself, and he sensed sophisticated as well. What was she probably thirty, thirty-two? It was a helluva difference in age with Tina, and he had to admit that a more mature woman was probably what he should be thinking about at this point in his life. My god, he would turn forty-one in less than six months he realized. He'd been playing around for a long time. At some point it was going to start looking awfully tacky and how long could he continue to expect girls in their twenties to find him worthwhile and attractive?

He typed back on his keypad:

Joker is still wild, maybe the Penguin and the Riddler too.

I miss you.

Let's go on another date. A less interrupted one. Soon.

As he was about to hit Send, he realized Tina would want to know about Tackett. It was a bad time to tell her though, or maybe he just didn't want to. He would tell her all about it when he had him back safely.

He started for his things. He needed to get the hell out of dodge before one of the suits laid into him. Tierney seemed distracted for the moment, so he made a run for the door. He decided to swing by the detention block to check in on the professor instead. His spidey sense was tingling a bit, and this would, of course, be a helluva moment for the whole operation to unravel. It made sense to be extra cautious.

As he walked into the cell block, he could see Mark, his old pal, sitting silently at the front desk.

"Hey, my man. How is the good professor?"

"Detective."

Mark seemed solemn, glum. Perhaps the rumor he had spread about Tierney's cross-dressing had already come back on him. Sullivan almost felt bad. It was a lesson worth learning in any case, so he said nothing.

"He skipped his meal and threatened one of the guards, but we got him safe and sound down there."

"Really, I didn't have him pegged as the type to make threats. Somebody push his buttons by chance?"

"Well, it was Mitchell over there who was on duty. You'd have to ask him."

He peered over his shoulder to see Mitchell looking back at them. His uniform's sophistication and his overly-upright carriage suggested he might enjoy his job a little more than was necessary. His hardened expression seemed an open invitation to leave him alone.

"It's OK," he said, smiling at Mark, "as long as he's well protected."

"We're expecting additional agents at the seven o'clock shift change," Mark said, pointing to the clock with his pen. "Right now we got two patrolmen at the front, just watching the gate. Cameras are clear."

"Sounds good, man. Have a good night."

"Hey, Detective?"

"Yeah, man," he said on his way out.

"That was a good one; you got me, Tierney being a cross-dresser. I deserved that, OK? Sorry, you win."

Sullivan smiled. "Loose lips sink ships, Mark. Remember that," he said, walking out the front door but then paused. He rubbed a hand through his hair and then drug his hand along his jaw line, grinding against the two-day stubble.

"Hey, Mark, I thought they had you at the desk over in evidence? You get a demotion or promotion or something?"

"Nah, man. I always work this desk."

"Are you sure about that? Didn't I see you the other night over in evidence; that's where we talked about Tierney, the club, right?"

"I'm right here five outta seven a week, never worked evidence yet, though the boss says maybe next year or the year after."

He rubbed his face as if he were trying to scrub off a momentary confusion.

"You all right, Detective?"

"Yeah," he said, recovering suddenly. "Call me Nick, man."

"OK, thanks," Mark said, smiling with some of his enthusiasm seeming to return.

He made his way slowly down the hall, detouring into the men's restroom before leaving the building. He turned on the faucet splashing cold water onto his face. He reached for a paper towel out of the box to wipe away the water, but it was empty. He looked at himself in the mirror under the fluorescent lighting. He looked tired, damned tired; he was, but he *had* seen Mark at the evidence desk; he was sure of it. Kid must have forgotten somehow; he was working too much probably. He suddenly realized he wasn't alone. He could hear a scratching noise in the stall behind him. It sounded like someone writing on the wall. God, people were weird ass idiots everywhere you went. He lowered his head to see if it was a cop or just some ratty kid. He could see no feet though, but suddenly a pencil rolled out from under the stall. He pushed slowly at the door not sure what to expect.

"Hey, man, we'll only arrest you if you're writing your phone number, OK?"

The door creaked open, but the stall was completely empty, except for the smell; probably a homeless sleeper. He surveyed the whole room, backing up to look for whoever it was. All was silent and empty. He looked back inside yet again, and on the wall inside the stall, he could see the writing:

You aren't where you think you are detective. Bring the waitress. It's the only way to save her. Don't be late.

47 58 87: 5:55 10/22/14

He grabbed his phone and snapped a picture and then reached for some paper towels to wipe his face and then threw them into the wastebasket, walking back into the hall. Oh well, the musings on bathroom walls on the west coast were a little more highbrow at least.

"Hey, Mark!" he yelled again.

"Yeah, Detective Sullivan?"

"You see anybody else come out of the bathroom?"

Mark looked up at the cameras and then back to him. "No, just you and me and Mitchell here now. Everything OK?"

"Guess so," he said, shaking his head.

Then Sullivan walked out the door into the night.

CHAPTER 12

Downy was awake for a few strange seconds before he was aware of someone else's presence. A smell of body odor, pungent, which he had managed to incorporate into his dream, permeated the tiny cell. A man sat opposite him in the corner, one of his legs pulled to his chest.

"How the fuck did you get in here?" Downy said in a tense whisper.

Guy Taro leaned slowly forward before speaking. "You're already breaking your first promise to me."

"OK, how do we get out?"

"We walk. Come on then," Taro said, jumping to his feet suddenly.

He raised himself from the bed, forgetting he was naked, covering himself again in embarrassment.

"Here throw this on."

Downy looked at what appeared to be a very large white sheet.

"Just drape it over yourself; maybe someday I'll show you how to put one on properly."

He realized the cell door was ajar, and his eyes opened wide in amazement.

"We are seriously just going to walk out of here?"

"Absolutely, we are all alone in fact, so you can stop whispering."

The two men walked back through the hall together, but amazingly the giant cell block door was no longer there. In fact the entire station looked as if it were under renovation; whole pieces of rooms were missing, and there were no longer phones at the end of the hall.

"Keep walking, OK?"

Downy suddenly felt uneven; his stomach turned without warning, and saliva rushed up from his throat into his mouth. He bent over to throw up, but since he had had no food, he only dry heaved instead.

"What's happening to me?" he said between gasps.

"You have the sickness. I will give you a pill as soon as we're out of here. It will help, but until the heaving stops you just have to keep moving."

"Where are we going?"

"I don't have time to explain really, but I do believe Woody's makes sense, since you have passed so much pleasant time there in the past."

"Are you crazy? We'll be seen for sure."

"You are absolutely safe with me tonight, Professor Downy. Everything about your circumstances has changed in fact."

The two descended a long corridor, and out of an unfinished door frame, he could see a low moon on the horizon and countless stars, but the night was too big, the stars too bright. In the huge parking lot out front was a grassy, open field where there had been only asphalt for as far as the eye could see. The city, off in the distance, looked dark.

"I don't understand."

"I know you don't. I was you once myself, some time ago."

He suddenly felt his knees buckle, and he fell on the grass, taking in deep, panicky breaths. He was sure he was going to lose consciousness.

"Professor, you must not go to sleep on me. Take this," he said, handing him what appeared to be a sugar cube. "And do not let it come up. We have but one chance at this, and after I have no idea what happens to either of us if we don't get it right."

He looked at the cube and back at Taro. "Are you trying to kill me?"

"Oh goodness, no. Please, it will help."

He put it in his mouth and felt it dissolving, but it stuck in his throat as he tried to swallow. He looked around in every direction, but the city was dark and the skyline too. He bit down hard on his tongue to get more saliva and swallowed again. Taro kneeled next to him and put his hands on his shoulders, starting to slowly massage them.

"Your heart is in a panic at the moment, and your muscles are getting no blood. Try to relax; it will take only a few minutes to ease."

He felt something in his chest like a quivering and then

warmth radiated out spreading to his limbs. He breathed out suddenly realizing that for many seconds he had forgotten to do so.

"Look at those pupils," Taro said, laughing. "Now we're ready for a night on the town."

"Why are you taking me to Woody's?" he asked, but his words seemed to be on delay, and he could almost hear himself after the fact, his voice in a long tunnel, quite separate from his body.

"A certain acquaintance of yours is going to meet us there. I have had a difficult time getting him to sit down with me, but your presence seems to have made him a bit more reasonable on this point."

He stood up on a knee now, feeling his balance return slightly.

"Jesus, Taro! Where are we? What's happening?"

"You, my friend, are intoxicated with a very pure form of a certain tincture. I believe it's called acid."

"Oh shit, you fucking drugged me."

"Yes, but without out it you would end up in a most lamentable state, I'm afraid. I took the same thing only hours ago, and it is a very mild dose, only meant to smooth out the edges, very pure."

"The edges of what?"

"Realitatem. Reality as you say, it's a slippery business, more than I ever imagined. Look, our chariot has arrived," Taro said pointing.

A car's headlights bounced over the edge of the grass, and he could see a taxi sign illuminating a very large cab.

"Come on, get in, and let me do the talking, OK?"

The two men slid silently into the back seat.

"Could you take us to Woody's on Second Street, please?"

The cabbie turned to them, looking them over suspiciously. "Halloween ain't till next week, boys. What gives?"

"Yes," Taro said, laughing, "My friend and I are actors, you see. We practice just over there in the evenings, for a play."

"Whatever floats your boat buddy, no business of mine," he said, driving back toward the highway.

In the darkness he was sure they were lost, but the white ocean surf was on their right, and the highway looked familiar still somehow. They couldn't be far from the jail. He must have been knocked out and brought somewhere different while he slept. It was a trick. His mind twitched at the details of how Taro had pulled it off. Taro leaned forward toward the cabbie.

"My friend is shipping off to fight tomorrow. Would you mind if we share a drink?"

"God bless, go ahead," the cabbie shouted over the roar of the engine. "It's good goddamn luck headin' over now, if you ask me, I heard on the radio the fighting is almost over, but that's not the first time I hear 'em say so. Wars and rumors of wars the Bible says."

"Thank you," Taro said, nodding his head and then holding up a flask. "It's a sweet wine from the country, hand pressed by some of the loveliest girls you might ever meet."

Taro tasted it first. "I'm no drinker, but if I were," he said before savoring a taste.

Downy could see no reason not to and tipped it up

himself. He choked a bit at first but then just let the flavors wash over his tongue. He thought he could feel it creep down all the way to the pit of his stomach. He grabbed again at the flask and swallowed furiously.

"Amazing," he said, and the combination of drink and drugs now had him slaphappy.

"Those girls take a vow to stay virginal, the ones who press it, but that doesn't affect the taste one way or the other I can assure you," Taro said, laughing, putting his hand on Downy's shoulder affectionately.

The cab was clearly on Main now, and he pressed his face to the window. It was beginning to spit rain against the windshield, but there it was off in the distance, the marquee lights blinking in the night, "Woody's Tavern." The cab pulled to a noisy halt in front of the place. The two men pulled themselves out, Taro returning to the window to pay.

"Hey, pal, this is one great tip. Thanks, man. I worked for thirty years, and this one is...I gotta say is the bigges—"

The cabbie was almost coming up out of his seat as they walked away.

"Why does everything look so strange?" he said, stopping to look up, swaying a bit as he stared up at the blinking sign. "The sign's never all lit up like that."

Taro pulled him along without a word through the front doors, and Downy could hear one of his favorite tunes from the jukebox far in the back. Billie Holiday urging into the microphone:

Speak low,
when you speak love
our summer day withers away
too soon...too soon
our moment is swift like ships adrift
we're swept apart too soon...

He turned to see Taro watching him with a bemused expression.

"This music makes you feel good, yes?"

"I love Billie Holiday, man," he said, but his eyes were scanning the room, not paying attention.

Taro leaned in to speak to him. "I get it very well. I hear what she says, though I don't know this music exactly."

"She's moaning for us all, for how fast life is."

"Whaaa," Downy heard himself say, and then Taro caught him by the arm as he fell backward.

"Easy, easy."

He wobbled unevenly against the bar. He couldn't remember seeing the place so clean or crowded. Everyone wore suits, so he reasoned it must be a party of some sort, and it looked like they had made room by clearing out lots of things. The boar's head on the wall was gone.

"I'm OK. Hey, who are we here for? You said I'm friends with—"

He looked to the balcony and could see smoke pouring out of the corner booth.

"I'll go up first," Taro said. "Stay behind me, OK?"

"What's up there?"

The two men walked silently and slowly to the top of the stairs. He could see a man in the corner, smoke rolling out over the balcony, a pair of spectacles just like—

Downy suddenly rushed past Taro.

"Charlie!"

"My dear boy, come and give an old friend a hug."

He locked Charlie in a wild embrace, staring intently, shaking almost violently. "I can't fucking believe it!"

Charlie took a step back, locking eyes with Taro. He had seen the look on Charlie's face only once before in Cairo when they had been held at gunpoint—raw fear.

"You've arrived early," Taro said blankly. "Have I given you cause to mistrust me?"

"And you're right on time as always, Mr. Taro."

Downy walked weakly in a circle around and around, looking his friend over in disbelief.

"What the fuck are you doing alive? How is this?" He squatted to his knees on the floor, putting his hands to the ground to feel it beneath him. Tears streamed down his face.

"I'm not, Noah—not really."

"That's a matter of semantics only though, right, Professor Patterson? Isn't that what you once told me? Tell me how does that semantic seem now?"

"Noah, I'm beyond sorry for all of this."

"Sorry for wh—"

"He would have you believe I am alive, but he would unleash the dead on the living without a care for what it might do."

Downy looked to Taro who crossed his arms, looking unfazed. Charlie's gaze hardened.

"I have been living in exile for all our sakes, as all dead men must, permanent exile."

"Shouldn't we all sit down for a drink, Charles?" Taro said politely. "Three of your scotch, no?"

Taro slid into a booth in the corner, beckoning them to sit down. A waitress appeared as they sat.

"Hello, my dear, could you bring us three of your best scotch?" Taro said, smiling warmly.

"Of course," the girl said enthusiastically. "Hey, I love your toga!"

Downy heard the comment but couldn't take his eyes away from Charlie.

"Oh and one more thing, could you bring us a newspaper if there's one about?"

"Let me check to see. Maybe there's one in the back still." The girl scampered away with a flip of her skirt.

"Have you given him a pill?"

"Of course, it's the polite thing to do. You'll remember you couldn't be bothered, Charles."

Downy sat with his hands clenched on the lip of the table as if he were holding on for dear life, while the rest of the world spun around him. His lips moved in a near silent whisper.

"Can somebody please tell me what the hell is going on? Does he know about Samara?"

He spoke before thinking and immediately regretted it, even in his altered state.

"What about Samara?"

"She's de—" He couldn't even say the words. "She's gone, Charlie. I'm so sorry."

"You bloody fucking monster, you."

Charlie rose up out of his seat and reached for Taro, but the waitress appeared with the drinks, so he sat back down.

"Here ya go, gentleman," she said, "and here's today's paper. War's almost done they say. Can't wait for those boys to come home. I'm so tired of this job, ready for my man to get his ass home," she said with an awkward laugh. "If they surrender tonight, this place is going to go off," she said, looking down to the crowded floor below apprehensively.

"That's perfect, dear, thank you," Taro said, handing the drinks around the table. "Come now, Charles; we all know that Samara isn't in such a bad place really. What is one death when she has so many to spare?"

"Why have you brought me here?" Patterson said pounding his fist against the table.

"I'd like to see everyone get back what they've lost, Charles, and you and I both know what that means."

"Impossible. I will not. What did you do to my daughter, you son of a bitch?"

Taro's hand shot across the table, gripping Charlie's throat before he could get out another word. "Do you think this is a fucking negotiation, you insolent little muppet? I will have my *dignitas*, my honor, and so shall he in fact."

Taro had Patterson by the throat still, now pulling him in closely, almost spitting as he spoke. Downy stood up unevenly, grabbing Taro's arm, pulling it away. Taro fell back and seemed to grow calm, closing his eyes.

"It's as I have always said, Charles. A man never serves his emotions and his best interests simultaneously. I'm going to let you two get reacquainted and read the newspaper, and then we can talk about what to do next. I'll just be down at the bar. Please drink to your heart's content, on me. Charles is quite the extraordinary student of history, as you well know, Professor, but I'll let him tell you his own version of events first. I'm sure it's accurate, from his perspective at least."

Patterson seemed to go limp as Taro walked away. He turned to Downy and looked him over. "Whatever are you wearing, my boy?"

"It's a...some kind of sheet I think. Taro had me put it on."

"I guess he's planning to take you tonight then." Patterson poured the shot in front of him down his throat violently. Then he grabbed the one Taro had left untouched and did the same. "Let me look at those pupils for a moment." Patterson lifted his chin and looked to the left and right. Downy's eyes were as wide as saucers. "Did he tell what it is you took?"

"Yeah, I'm on acid, right?"

"Don't get nervous; it's an absolutely distilled and pure form. Created in a lab and strictly controlled. You won't even have a hangover, so drink up."

"Am I dead, Charlie? Are we both dead?"

Patterson suddenly laughed warmly.

"Oh, no. Do you feel dead, Noah?"

He looked around the room. This place doesn't look the same. He looked down at the newspaper in front of him. He could see half a headline in bold:

AMERCAN FORCES ENTER BERLIN: FURORS
WHEREABOUTS...

"What the hell, is this some kind of movie set?"

"It's good he gave you the pill."

Downy looked bewildered, waiting for Patterson to speak.

"Our first incursion into the timeline occurred on October 29, 1998, two full years before anyone expected it possible. It was a complete success, Noah. At first, we were just sending inanimate objects through and bringing them back. Then we started collecting things, rocks, pots and pans, some coins. Like taking a tiny fishing net into the ocean and seeing what you catch. Then we realized we could send people. It's like a nightmare I can't wake up from now."

"What are you talking about, Charlie?"

"You aren't where you think you are, Noah, not at all."

"I don't know where the fuck I am or how I'm out of jail or got put in for that matter. They said I killed Sam, Charlie; I would never—"

"Look at the date on that newspaper," he said, pointing.

Downy picked it up. "Why did she bring this? It's old."

"It's today's paper. It will take a while for you to accept this, but you've skipped from your timeline to a new one, Noah. It's helpful at first to think of it in those terms, like a skipping record. The needle has landed in a new spot."

"It's the drug, isn't it? I'm hallucinating; you said it was pure. You're dead, Charlie. You are fucking dead."

"No, the drug is protecting you. Without it you'd be unconscious in fact. It helps your subconscious mind adjust. The part of this of which I'm least proud is that I've let you down so completely. I know you truly believed in my genius, as I once did, but I am under no such illusions now."

He put his hand to Patterson's shoulder as if to corroborate.

"You're alive though and that's...what did you mean when you said you weren't really—"

"It was the only way to save everyone after we realized what was happening."

"Who, Charlie? What are you talking about? What was happening?"

"All those things I found, Noah, those beautiful things; the incredible luck of locating the place where Caesar himself fell; I had help. I cheated to get it, all of it. It should have stayed where it was, lost. The past is an utterly dangerous place. I brought back much more than I ever realized. I fucked up so completely, so horribly, and now my dearest Samara. What has he done to her?"

"You're not making sense, Charlie."

"I know what he's capable of—Taro; we all do. That's why we're trying to stop him."

"Are you trying to convince me it's 1944, Charlie?" he said, holding up the paper.

"I won't bother. You'll accept things as you go along. I want you to realize that Taro is doing this so he can manipulate you, Noah. He is incredibly talented at manipulation. You need to hear it truthfully from me at least; I certainly owe you that."

"Please, Charlie, tell me what's fucking happening?"

"It started this year, in 1944, actually—"

CHAPTER 13

Patterson pulled his spectacles up on his face and drew a deep breath. "This year, 1944, a group working on aspects of nuclear fusion discovered something which was then unimaginable. No one knows their identities for sure; they've always existed with the greatest of secrecy. Some say they first came together to protect the secret. Whatever their original intent, there were already men of lesser conscience ready to use what they found. The science, you see, insisted it was possible to jump from one spot in time and appear somewhere else. Time could be adjusted just as easily as space. I'm no physicist, Noah, but that's the essence of it. They dared not give it a name at that point. It would take the work of another lesser known physicist to put the cherry on top. In 1967, a young, ambitious grad student from Harvard physics discovered the code for the MMI, the meta-matrix that governs our positioning in the space-time field. He developed the POND. The name's an acronym. It's called a

Position-Optic Nano Dilator. Later they discovered they could also use existing geologic data to guarantee safe travel. Water levels were easy to measure going back tens of thousands of years. You can't have people suddenly popping up just anywhere. They used the data to determine where the safest passage points could be placed in any time frame. It turns out bodies of fresh water work best. Once that code was deciphered, it was like having a map of everything. Places, space, time itself. His name was Jacob, Jacob Tannehill. At the time, even I refused to acknowledge that his actions were dangerous. But none of us knew how far he'd already gone."

"So you never died on the boat at all with Nazim? How could you let us b—"

"It was a necessary evil, that unfortunate accident, and one that has cost me everything, my very soul in fact."

"So Nazim was telling the truth? He really does believe you're still alive?"

Patterson's eyes registered sudden alarm. "What do you mean?"

"He must think I'm dead."

"No, Charlie, I spoke with him, and he claims to have seen you only weeks ago."

"Christ in heaven, what has the fool done? It's moved again, Jesus."

"Did he see you, Charlie?"

"Whoever he saw that man is likely dead now or the Vestals have him. Noah, I must ask, have you been noticing anything strange, small changes in the things around you?"

Patterson's eyes watered over as he yelled for the waitress to bring two more drinks. "Mak'em doubles."

"I don't know, nothing really."

Patterson looked scattered, confused.

"But now you're here, which means you must return at once, Noah. This place is hell itself. I live here in exile. I am forbidden any future as well. I'm watched at every turn."

"Right now?"

"Yes, the Vestals will come very soon. Taro knows there's little time. But what he's offering you; you mustn't believe whatever he says."

"Who are the Vestals?"

"They're purists, very ancient, maybe they're zealots I don't know, but they monitor the MMI. They'll never let Taro escape. They won't let any of us escape. They believe in the absolute purity of the line."

Downy leaned over the balcony and could see Taro in a crowd of women, toasting and laughing.

"Who the hell is he?"

"I wish there were a simple answer. I only know who he used to be. Now he is the man who would undo everything. He's taken a horrible risk bringing you here. That name Taro is an interesting appellation. You should look it up."

"He said he could help me find out who killed Samara, Charlie. Is he lying?"

"It's me he blames; that's what this little meeting is all about."

"What?"

"He would say I am the cause of her death. Please tell me

she didn't suffer, Noah," he said as tears raced from the corners of his spectacles.

"I don't think so...I..."

"He's a cold butcher, Taro, when he needs to be. I know it."

He saw the waitress approaching with their drinks and noticed for the first time her stockings. They reminded him of the old Betty Page pin-ups. The wood of the tables was untarnished, and the collection of graffiti that had accumulated over the years was missing. Could it be true? Was he really sitting having a drink with his dead best friend in the past? He felt dizzy, mad.

"Tannehill had been using the pond for years already when he made his big announcement. Restraint was never Jacob's strong suit I'm afraid. I didn't question his help finding all those beautiful things either. He led me to what he wanted me to find and then acted as if it had all been my idea. I was a fool. I am a fool."

"All right, boys. Here's four girls in two glasses. I'll be keeping my eye on you two," she said with a wink.

"Thanks," Patterson said demurely.

"Tell you what. Your pal down there sure is making friends with his deep pockets. He's good for it, yeah?"

"Oh yes," Patterson said with a tone of half disgust. "Money is no object with him."

"Thank God. You know sometimes people get all liquored up and make promises."

"Can I ask a rude question?" Downy suddenly blurted out.

"Sure, hun. Go ahead."

"What year were you born?"

"Ah, you had me scared; that's not rude. 1916, hun. Well, am I too old or too young?" the girl said, laughing.

"Neither," he said, smiling awkwardly.

"OK, let me know if ya need anything else."

She was being polite, but he could sense she knew something was amiss with their little party. She looked back over her shoulder at the top of the stairs. Downy inexplicably flashed back to his first time using pot in high school. The realization of how much acting people do just to keep the ball moving in life. How scripted life becomes; how scripted it is. It had made him sad then, but it had also filled him with a kind of empathy. People tried hard even when they didn't believe.

He looked down to the balcony again, and there was Taro, who'd been staring at him for some time unnoticed. He raised his glass in Downy's direction and then handed the drink to a beautiful, young girl who was now on his arm. Taro leaned into her ear whispering, before she turned and blew a kiss in his direction.

"Watch out for the fucker, Noah. He's imminently dangerous and a wanted man."

"What are you doing in 1944, Charlie?" he said, almost falling over with drunken laughter. The scotch was going straight to his head now, and he felt faint again.

"We must never see one another again, Noah. I'm so sorry, my friend, but that is the way it must be."

"Go back to prison, and fight for your life in court. You are innocent, of course. Stay where you are. Samara is...is lost, but you can still live."

"Why can't you?"

"I killed myself a long time ago."

"What did you do?"

"We stole fire from the gods, and now they are very angry with us."

"I'm too high for this, Charlie. Please, just explain—"

"We started jumping around in the timeline, thinking it was no harm. But we got caught, and now we have to stay where we are or risk destroying everything and everybody. The Vestals will catch him soon, and if you're caught with him, you'll be killed too, or worse. He wants to tell you his side of things, to tell his side of the story to the world. Let him. But trust him on nothing else."

Taro appeared suddenly next to them. "Gentlemen, I think our time for revelry has ended. You must say your good-byes. With any luck though, all of us should see each other in the near future. Come, Noah, there is, I believe, a fire escape in the back. We need to disappear, you and I. This bar is filling up with the wrong kind of people."

Patterson lurched to grab for Downy, but Taro stepped in grabbing his collar, brandishing a blade to his neck. "Sit down, my friend. This is no place for your wretched violence."

Taro put the blade back inside his jacket. He smiled. "I abhor violence; I really do and always have. Some men will have it no other way though."

"Turn yourself in, Taro." Patterson said.

"Oh bloody hell, lighten up, Charles. You know how I crave a quick, noble death. It's all I've ever wanted. Let's do it now, and all can be well."

"I won't help you."

"I know that's why I have chosen him, your star pupil. *He* can be reasoned with; I'll bet on it."

Taro pulled Downy close to him as he nearly stumbled again to the floor. He could hear Billie Holiday still crowing on the jukebox:

> *What do I care if it may stahhhm?*
> *I got my love to keep me warm.*
> *I've got my love to keep me warm.*

He had always loved the way she said the word *storm*, as if it were pronounced with a soft "ahh" sound instead.

"I'm dreaming, aren't I? This is the weirdest dream," he said, tottering in front of the two of them.

Taro pointed to the fire escape and simply led him down the passage like they were two old pals off together again. He tried to turn to see Charlie, but his chair was turned over and empty. He had vanished.

"The good news is we don't even have to climb down," and with that he gave him a push through the open window.

Downy opened his mouth to scream, but the wind caught in his throat, and he just floated silently into the darkness.

CHAPTER 14

The man in the cell wouldn't stop repeating the word. Maybe he was trying to remember something important. His pronunciation was off, of course, but it seemed everyone in the dungeon was from parts unknown. *Priest. Flamen.* Was he a priest? The repetition was starting to drive him crazy. He shouted suddenly to the man.

"Shut up!"

The echo carried far off in the chamber, but then there was laughter, a woman's laughter. It sounded like a taunt. He wondered about the fate of the prisoner they had taken away. Then he heard a movement in the corner. There was someone sitting near him, just outside the bars of his cell. He heard the man's boots grind against the dirt but could not see his face.

"I will release you very soon."

"Will you?"

"Yes, I will. What if I told you, you were free? You were just dreaming about running away only a few days ago, no?"

"How do you know that?"

"I know you better than most."

"And yet your face is always hidden. Perhaps you're a god then, who reads men's thoughts?"

"Maybe I am!"

The man suddenly leaped up, becoming furious, clamoring at the bars of his cell. He spat at the cloaked stranger, "What are the terms of my release then? What do you want from me?"

"No terms; you're just free to go and to do whatever you wish."

"I *was* fantasizing about starting over, but I'm...I'm too weary...I won't run either," he said collapsing against the bars of the cell.

"Weary is but a passing state for a man like you. New fascinations will appear. I have a feeling you'll soon be in charge of some army wherever I put you." The cloaked man seemed genuinely amused by the thought.

"Do you not think you have forfeited your own life by taking me in the first place? You must know who I am."

"Life goes on without you believe it or not. Not everyone was sorry to see you go either."

"Yes, but I'm being searched for as we speak. There is none to replace me."

"Gratefully, the people will not have to suffer long your absence."

"Must we always talk only in riddles?"

"No. Let's be clear; when you leave here, you will find yourself in a strange land. But it won't be wholly unrecognizable, and you may start a brand new life my friend. Live as you see fit. Write perhaps. You know the burdens of power, of war. I'd avoid them this time, if it were me."

"Why did you bring me here?"

"Protection. My plans are nearing fruition. We shall not meet again."

"Who are the others, the prisoners?"

"They're refugees like you. I am trying to save them as well."

"The girl in the cell next to me? She was nearly strangled to death. Is that how you save people?"

"Some that I work with are barbarous in their methods, but she is safe now. She spoke to you then?"

"Yes, some."

"I knew her in another place. She is an amazing girl, in fact—a near cipher for our tongue, which is dead to her." The man rose, pulling his cloak further over his face.

"You killed my nephew. Why, he was harmless?"

"So you say. I'd love to see what you do in your new life in any case. I really do love you, my friend." The cloaked man reached through the bars clutching at his hand, squeezing tightly, but ignored his question. "Be safe and live happily. You have earned it."

He stood frozen with his hands against the bars. The man's voice was perplexingly familiar. He turned suddenly, disappearing upstairs into the darkness.

He sat down again to the cold floor thinking of what it all

meant. Why would someone kidnap him only to let him go? Why had they killed his nephew? Objectively, it suggested there was a conspiracy of some sort, but why would saving him but killing the boy makes sense unless his nephew was somehow involved? The boy wouldn't dare. It made no sense whatsoever, especially since he knew his place in the will was secure. He had free access to all of his power anyway, money, influence without any of the burdens. The boy was too smart to take such a foolish risk or throw away what he already had.

Maybe the goal was to remove him from the city permanently. He thought of the old stories of Romulus, the founder of Rome, a boy who'd become king by slaying his own brother Remus. Romulus himself had been lured outside the city by those closest to him, who feared his kingly powers, and then been assassinated. The myth of course claimed he'd ascended to the heavens and become a god in their presence. Poetic murder. Was this the same? Was he to be lured away and then killed like the kings of old? He found the idea of simply being freed unlikely, and yet there had been a great deal of attention to secrecy. He'd seen no one's face that he could recall. He'd had strange dreams of course, in the darkness—the mirror, being chased by his own reflection. The girl had said they were being drugged. It was probably in the food or the wine. How long had he really been down in the darkness?

He heard the man's whispering begin again, but this time there was a new word, put with the first and repeated over and over, "Danni Flamen Danni Flamen Danni Flamen."

CHAPTER 15

Downy could feel a warm breeze against his face as he awakened. There was soft music off in the distance and pillows surrounded him on every side. Someone was playing a lyre, maybe a harp? Lying sideways he could see a man talking with two girls at the door. There were beautiful paintings and colored tile all along the wall, and he could hear the sound of fountains gently flowing outside. He closed his eyes and listened. It reminded him of summers with Charlie's family at the beach house in Santa Barbara. He thought of Samara, just a little girl, smiling as she scurried around to get him anything she could, just to be near him. Or maybe he was in heaven, dead. He'd fallen, hadn't he?

"Welcome to my villa, Noah. I hope you have slept well."

His eyes fluttered open, and he could see Taro standing over him. He was wearing a white shirt now, open and loose at the chest, and a pair of knee-length pants. The distinctive scar across his neckline was much longer than he had noticed before. A belt hung loosely off his waist. The clothing looked distinctly Greek but like stage clothing.

"Where are we?"

"I call it home, but it's just a safe place for us to get some rest and for you to adjust. This is Aurelia and Julianna. They would love to wake you up with a bit of a rub if you can just relax."

The two girls smiled warmly. They were young, beautiful and wore sheer, flesh-colored gowns, one blonde and the other dark. He tried not to look down, but he could see clearly what was underneath, just visible between their legs. He couldn't help but blush. Before he could answer, the girls were on top of him in the mounds of pillows.

"We take it from here boss," they whispered with a laugh, and he closed his eyes again.

"I want to give you my side of the story before we return, OK, Noah?"

The girls laughed gently as their hands ran wildly all over him.

"Remember, girls, this is a married man, so not too aggressive, OK?" Taro's voice disappeared into the music and gush of the fountains as he left the room.

"OK," they said, waving him away.

He closed his eyes again. The girls began to sing softly as they worked but in a foreign tongue, something like Italian but somehow more beautiful.

"What is this dialect?" he said, turning his head.

The dark one spoke.

"Roma, I think you say. He taught us some Angelish, just

enough," the girl said pinching her fingers together. "Shhh now relax, he will 'splain everything to you in time, we are here to pleaser you."

Yes, pleaser me, he thought, *Why not?* Nothing made any sense anyway, and he was tired of fighting against it all. He considered the night before and the possibility that he was either dead or hallucinating still. Charlie. He had seen Charlie, but it might have all been a dream. It was still going on if it was, and it was a goddamn long one. He was on acid. He had fallen out of a window or been pushed, and yet he felt no pain. Why not take the pleasure then?

Far off he could hear laughter floating in from the courtyard. It sounded like a small party. Taro's voice was clear above the others. He sounded like he was directing a play of some sort. That explained the clothing then.

"No, like this." Taro clamored:

> *I could be well moved if I were as you.*
> *If I could pray to move, prayers would move me.*
> *But I am constant as the Northern Star,*
> *Of whose true fixed and resting quality*
> *There is no fellow in the firmament.*

Another, younger voice repeated the lines hesitantly.

"Better, better...keep at it, OK?" Taro said encouraging him.

He recognized the words. It was Shakespeare, but he wasn't sure from what. He suddenly thought of Charlie. Charlie believed Taro had killed Samara? But Taro had freed him from jail. Why? Why had Taro blamed Charlie for Samara's death, and how could he possibly hope to convince Downy, knowing that he and Charlie were best friends? His mind spun at the unanswered questions. He almost fell off into sleep again but awoke with a start, and the girls were now both singing. He had had a massage or two in his life, but this was ridiculous. One of girls leaned into his ear whispering as she sang softly. He could feel her warm breath, which was perfumed, as the second girl reached underneath him, pulling at the muscles of his thighs. The girl singing into his ear was straddling him from behind, and he could feel her thighs moving rhythmically against him, the heat from between her legs pressing urgently. He had to focus on something far away not to become aroused. The cold of his jail cell all seemed a bad memory now. *How could they ever go back?* he wondered. Taro's voice suddenly interrupted.

"Girls, this is a man of both conviction and honor so you may leave now, unless, of course?"

He turned to see Taro who looked at him inquisitively.

"Maybe next time then."

The girls flitted away together without a word, and he finally sat up in the bed.

"We can talk on the veranda. Walk slowly my friend; you've just taken the longest trip of your life I can assure you. The view here really is second to none. It's why I chose it. A bit like your place in fact."

Taro leaned on the edge of the bed like a good doctor, calm relaxed. "There are clothes there for you," he said, pointing. "Comfortable I hope. When you're dressed, please come join me outside." Taro pointed out across the room.

Through every door was a view almost impossible to imagine. Immaculately detailed frescoes dotted the ceilings and walls. He recognized the goddess Diana, her quiver of arrows slung over her shoulder, wild animals fleeing from her in every direction. The colors seemed to move across the ceiling and with them the goddess of the hunt. He had seen other artistic renditions of the same scene, but this was the most spectacular. It ran all the way to the ceiling and wound around the room again in tiny colored tiles. Light flickered from pools beneath. Where the hell were they? Through the veranda doors dramatic mountains loomed on the horizon and a perfect, azure lake ran as far as the eye could see. He remembered Charlie's warning: "Don't trust him."

He rose unsteadily to his feet and started to dress. It looked like costume clothing, but the fabrics were too soft to the touch, clearly not imitations. His mind leaped at the impossible. Was he traveling in time as Charlie had insisted? Charlie had also said he wouldn't be hung over, and he was right. His body felt better than it had in years in fact. There was a tingling in his rib cage, which reminded him of the night before. The music, the impossible meeting, the drugs all mingling into one maddening sense of euphoria.

Through another open door, he could see what appeared to be the troupe of young actors practicing their play. On the veranda, alone, sat Taro.

"It is truly a pleasure to have a man of your curiosity and learning in my home," he said rising to greet him as Downy's eyes enlarged to take in the whole view. A deep ravine cut between the steep cliffs, leading thousands of feet to the ground. "Not bad, is what you say in America, yeah? Have a seat, please."

"Can I ask where we are?"

"Oh yes, the 'no questions rule' is officially revoked—by imperial decree. We are near Parnassus, two days' hike from the nearest village."

"Greece? How?"

"You already know the answer. It is a matter of some fact you know," he said, leaning in, "I am the only person you can call a friend in the whole world. That's hard on a man's reason, his logic. I shall never forget my own reaction to it." Taro shook his head and then raised a glass of tea for him to take. "Please drink it. It's really the best, mildly spiced with fig, dry, but the flavor does something so nice in your mouth and then just disappears."

He stared down to the edge of the Veranda at the forbidding rocks below.

"We're very safe here; don't concern yourself, though, if I push you this time, you'll really hit the ground."

"What is this place?"

"The first Romans are down in that village there," he said pointing off into the far distance at something glowing, "still huddled around fires like savages. The smell alone could kill you, but if it doesn't, they certainly will."

He furrowed his brow and lifted his tea to his mouth, his hands shaking again, as they had the whole of the previous night. "Is this drugged too?"

"Ever so lightly. You can be weaned down to a very little actually. I once made it three whole days without it at all, a personal best."

"Why am I here, Taro?"

"I've thought so long about how to begin this conversation. I had it all memorized; now I can't think of a single word. You know the general outline of my life, professor. I was a man of promise and ability, I think. I achieved a certain level of success among men, in my part of the world at least, unrivaled perhaps. But I was betrayed, and worst of all I survived it. Not by choice, but rather by accident, by cruel intervention."

"Who betrayed you?"

"We can talk about them later, but it's your friend, Mr. Patterson, who I must tell you about. You see Charlie, while he may be your friend and very dear to you, is a thief. That is a fact. He has stolen extensively from me. Beyond the point of reason or forgiveness, I'm afraid."

"What did he steal?"

Taro turned now to look at the setting sun. Its orange glow reflected like tiny orbs in his dark eyes. A tear suddenly traced down his cheek.

"He took my future from me."

Downy had to look away. It pained him to watch another man cry, even a relative stranger.

"How did he do that?"

"He stole my things first, personal things of great value to me, and then he took from me the one thing every mortal man is owed, the very promise of the gods. I had only foolishly wished for it in fact, the night before, and all the while the men who would deliver it were in my very midst, toasting to my successes."

"You promised my freedom and to find the people responsible for Samara's death. What does this have to do with that, Taro?"

"I have already delivered on half of my bargain. You have Samara's killer. Do to him what justice you see fit."

"Charlie, you mean?"

"Yes."

"When you awake in prison tomorrow, you will be a free man as well."

"How?"

"You're innocent, Noah, as much as I. Your friend, Charlie, not so. I think you'll come to see that he is guilty of destroying many lives. I offer atonement and a return to the natural order at least. Now, I need you to keep up your end of our bargain as well—the laurel. It was a gift from those who weep most for my loss, for my memory. The detectives who arrested you have it. Once freed, you must demand it back."

"Who are you?"

Taro rose to his feet without speaking. "They will write about our meeting you know, about this meeting. You are living history even as we speak, Professor Downy. Tell me how does that feel?"

He was speechless. *What was he supposed to say?*

"If I know Charlie Patterson as I think I do, you will see him again very soon. I would say nothing more to prejudice you against him. The truth is always acceptable to me. I shall let you be the judge. When next we meet, I promise to tell you everything he won't. I'll answer any questions you wish in fact. My version of history should be told. I want people to understand me, as you seem to. Your place next time though, OK, in a couple of days. Please have the laurel. I'll bring a substantial donation for the university's loss."

"So I will just reappear in prison, poof, like I never left?"

"Yes, you will. There is one final thing I need to ask of you. The policeman who arrested you, Sullivan, I think he is called, has a partner by the name of Tackett. He's been captured by the Vestals I'm afraid. I can arrange his safe return, but you must never mention me. If I am judging correctly, the police will want your help recovering him. Agree to their terms, and once I have the laurel, he'll be freed. You won't have to involve yourself any further."

Downy nodded his head silently. "What is it you want that Charlie won't give you?"

"Just my life back." Taro drew in a deep breath. "You and I must depart now, I'm afraid. The pond, as some call it, is on the ridge just up there," he said, pointing to a jetty of rocky crags behind them. "Come along, my friend. Time really is of the essence."

CHAPTER 16

Sullivan had parked on the cliffs overlooking the ocean where Tackett had first confided his fears about Case 1032 to him. The thought of sleeping alone in Tackett's house without him had seemed too weird, like an acknowledgment that he wasn't coming back, so he had shacked up in his car yet again. Another night in the back seat, and now it was almost time to head back to the station to release the professor. He grabbed his phone, thinking of Tina. She was definitely too young, but she did have a certain spirit about her. He actually liked her rough edges, and, of course, the fact that she was a complete dynamo in bed was icing on the cake. He punched at his phone's keyboard:

Where are you?
I miss you.
Me

He hit Send before he could take into consideration that it was barely 6:00 a.m. Oh well, if they were going to date, she would have to get used to crazy hours eventually, wouldn't she?

He had dreamed about the strange encounter in the bathroom at the station. There had been someone there; he could feel it, and the pencil, the strange message:

You aren't where you think you are.

It was like the story he'd been reading on account of Tierney's crack about his poor literary habits. What was it called again? *A Study in Scarlet*? Sherlock Holmes had had his own cryptic messages to decipher. "RACHE," in the story, was scrawled on the wall at the crime scene, which was, of course, German for revenge. He reached into the floorboard and picked up the tattered book. Holmes sat in silhouette against a foggy London street, smoking his famous pipe. He had never realized the world's most famous detective had literally been a cokehead. My God, was everyone in law enforcement a recovering drug addict? He hadn't touched the stuff in years, thankfully. He was intolerable when he was high anyway, couldn't stop talking about himself, pacing from room to room, supremely confident of everything, capable of nothing. He'd built a thousand buildings but never driven a single nail when he was on the powder. It was the only unrealistic part of the story. Arthur Conan Doyle clearly knew fuck all about drug addicts.

He looked back at his phone. Tina must still be sleeping. Good. He looked out over the water and wondered where Tackett might be. Was he still alive? He decided it was time to ruffle some feathers, English feathers. He found the number for Downy's agent in London and hit Call. It went straight to voice mail.

"This is Clellon, with Wingate Publishing. Please leave a message."

"Yes, it's Detective Sullivan calling again. It seems there is a bit of a discrepancy from our earlier discussion, and I was hoping you could clear it up for us. You can call me at this number..."

It was afternoon in London, so he would hopefully get the message. Sullivan had a gut feeling he might never hear back from Mr. Clellon Holmes. Guilty people would only talk to you for so long. He had clearly lied about talking to Downy the night of his arrest. Sullivan had checked, and according to the cell-phone records, at least a two-minute call *had* been placed from Downy to his agent. It suggested that the agent had something to hide. He pulled his car into gear and headed toward the station. It was time to set an innocent man free and hopefully get his partner back in the process.

Sullivan had to make his way through a crowd of media to get to the front doors of the station where he saw Mark sitting at his usual perch at the front desk. He looked tired but greeted Sullivan warmly.

"Our man is having his breakfast, and then he's going to be released I hear?"

"Yeah, that's right. Looks like the vultures already got wind of it too."

He had called them actually, an anonymous tipster. It was the only way to guarantee enough coverage. He hoped whoever had Tackett would see it.

"Crazy. I thought for sure—"

"Yeah, so did we. Everything quiet here last night?"

"Yeah, sure. We did have a power outage actually, but thankfully all those cells down there are on a backup generator. They never knew a thing, all accounted for at morning rounds."

"OK," Sullivan said. "Can I get a transfer to a conference room with Professor Downy? We won't need an escort, but I'm hoping to have a sit-down. You can do all his paperwork before we go."

"I'll enter it here. I think Chief Tierney is already expecting you two in room Seven-One-Four."

"Hey, Mark, one more thing. It's kind of a favor. Could you send me last night's surveillance video of the cameras on this floor, the ones near the bathroom over there?"

"Yeah, um, everything OK?"

"Probably nothing, but I saw something...I can't...I'd just like to take a look."

"Any particular window of time, or do you want the whole day?"

"Say from nine p.m. to midnight, basically when I left last night."

"I'll e-mail them as soon as I can."

"Thanks, man."

"Hey, Downy's on his way up if you just want to wait."

He heard the buzzer door opening in the corridor, and out of it emerged Noah Downy still in the custody of the guard from the previous night. He whispered something to the guard whose expression remained stiff, unchanged. He turned for him to remove his cuffs and then gave him a knowing grin as he walked toward Sullivan. Downy looked incredibly fit and well for a man just emerging from one of the deepest, darkest holes in the whole city. He must not have showered either, judging by the smell. His face was beet red though, and Sullivan wondered if he was about to lay into him.

"Professor Downy, can I begin with an apology?" Downy's expression went hard but then softened.

"I'm listening."

"I been doin' this job for many years, and you're the first time I got anything so terribly wrong. I hope someday you can forgive me. It was never personal."

There was a long, awkward pause.

"Somehow, I believe you."

Sullivan reached out a hand for a shake, and Downy accepted it.

"You are absolutely free to go, but I wanted to tell you that my partner on this case has disappeared, we think in connection to the murder of your friend. He's a good man, and I would love to find him. I wonder if you'd entertain the possibility that you might be able to help us. I know after all that has happ—"

Downy interrupted, "Someone killed my best friend's

313

daughter, and if I can help find who is responsible, count me in."

"Thank you, thank you. Come this way; I have a room where we can talk."

"If it's all the same, after you, Detective."

Sullivan smiled, "Yes, of course."

CHAPTER 17

"We believe you have been purposely framed, Professor Downy."

He looked to the table at the linen wrap. He could guess what was underneath before they even showed him. "Why would anyone want to do this to me? To Samara?"

"I wish there were clear answers, but we are only sure of a few things."

"Such as?"

"Your book publisher Clellon Holmes is lying."

"You checked then?"

"It's my job."

Downy nodded with an expression of quiet gratitude.

"Charlie Patterson may or may not be deceased. We suspect he's involved in some way, or at least was. You say you saw him. We're inclined to believe you. Then there is this man." Tierney held up a picture of Jacob Tannehill.

"You know him?"

"Not well, but he was a friend of sorts to Charlie. Tannehill was a gifted physicist early in his career, but he went off the rails—had a breakdown of some kind."

Downy hated lying to the detectives, but he really didn't know what else to say. The supposed truth would get him committed to a loony bin, and in spite of everything he'd seen, he simply couldn't make his mouth say any of the words. *I traveled through time last night, saw a dead friend, met an ancient Roman, a former student of mine actually.* He looked at Detective Sullivan and saw him twitch almost unconsciously, cocking his head with a look of silent incredulity. He already knew Downy was lying; Downy could see him sensing it. He could feel it, as he had during their first meeting back in his office. He had to lie then about being involved with any of his students, Samara being the glaring exception, but it was the same expression: surprise at being lied to mixed with disappointment.

Tierney jumped in. "Look, we need you to test a theory of what's going on here. We believe your friend Professor Patterson might have gotten caught up in the black marketing of rare antiquities. We already know about his reputation in the field. They called him Midas, right? He pulled an unusual amount of gold out of the ground, didn't he? Lucky guy."

"I googled it," Sullivan said, interjecting.

"It may have cost him his life, and some of our detectives' lives as well. It could still cost one of our detectives his. They have Detective Tackett, his partner, but we believe they might be willing to broker a trade."

"A trade for what?"

Tierney pushed the linen toward him. He peeled it away, slowly revealing the golden laurel. It *was* truly beautiful. Downy twirled the black pearl that hung at its base in his fingers.

"I can guarantee you this is a fake," he said, inspecting it closely.

"That's what we thought, but the people who have Detective Tackett believe otherwise."

"Where did you get it?"

"Jacob Tannehill gave it to me as a gift of sorts, but the man's mad."

"Yes, maybe, but we think people associated with him believe in its authenticity."

"And you think they'll reach out to me for it?"

"If we bait the hook right, I think we may catch lots of bad fish. And find Samara's killer in the process. We want to be clear that there is a danger here, a certain amount of risk involved, but you will be monitored at every step."

Tierney crossed his arms, a hopeful look on his face.

"Can you protect my wife? She's at her mother's in Cold Springs?"

"We have unlimited Homeland Security agents at our disposal. We can put agents right at her doorstep until we've nailed the bastards."

"I'll do it."

Tierney and Sullivan jumped to their feet, extending their hands enthusiastically.

"So how do we bait the hook then?"

"Take the laurel with you. There's a back exit we can

shuttle you out in, so you can skip the press conference. I'll be apologizing for your arrest publicly, but more importantly let me say how truly sorry we are now, to you and your wife, your family. It takes a helluva a man to forgive a thing like this and to still be will—"

"Let me ask you one final question?" Sullivan said, chiming in.

"What would cause Charlie Patterson to fake his own death?"

Downy shook his head. "Only to protect his daughter maybe, his family. Money wasn't an issue."

Sullivan nodded. "That guy is your specialty, right?" he said, pointing to the laurel.

"Yes, he is."

"What would it be worth if it were real?"

"The golden laurel of Julius Caesar? It would be utterly priceless."

CHAPTER 18

The man heard a sharp noise and then a creaking, which startled him from his sleep. His cell door was open. He felt raw fear in his gut now. He was walking either to his death or to freedom, and he could get no clear read on which. He pushed the door open slowly and walked to the edge of the steps. At the end of them, he could see bright sunlight cascading in. He peered nervously back toward the row of cells. The whispering had ceased. Had the man finally died or only fallen asleep? There were others as well like the cloaked man had said. They seemed gone now too, so he walked very cautiously to the top of the stairs. By the time he emerged, the light had him doubled over, cowering. How long had he been in this hole? His head pulsed as he squinted to see around him. He was in a vast courtyard. In the center was a dark pool and scattered about were grand statues. Crumbling ruins formed an arc around the edges of the water. Plants and vines grew wild, some of which he had never seen before. They were beautiful but grew in unusual proportions, and their coloring was arrayed in patterns he'd never encountered, even in his many travels.

"Plutonium."

He wheeled round behind him to see a man sitting at the base of one of the statues. "Hades is there," he said, pointing to the pool.

The man was tall and dressed in very strange garments. He had pieces of glass cut hung on wire fastened around his face.

"Who are you?"

"Only one of *your* biggest fans."

"Everyone seems to like me a lot around here, but it's getting hard to believe you're an admirer."

"Yes, it must get very confusing indeed."

The man looked around, still struggling to see clearly. He recognized none of the statues, and he had never seen anyone with something so strange about his face. It was his habit never to register surprise though, so he merely ignored it.

"Let me call your attention to this one," the strange man said, pointing up at the marble statue of a beautiful young woman. She lay in casual repose with a cup, which she held daintily in her left hand, her naked body barely covered by a gown that hung in inviting folds at her thighs."

"I do not recognize her. Is she Diana?"

"Yes, most assuredly, though in her land they call her by a different name."

At the base of the statue was carved a single word: *Veritas.*

"Why have I been brought here?"

"Your people think this place is the very gateway to the underworld. Maybe I'm growing to share that view."

"I know of it, the myth of the gate, but frankly it's a story for scaring children and the feeble minded, nothing more."

He walked nearer the pool of black water and stared in.

"I am not much convinced of it," he said, "old superstitions."

He leaned in to touch the surface of the strange pool.

"I wouldn't put my hand in there. I should have guessed as much. You really are an advanced model, aren't you? Fearless. You know where I'm from men who believe as you do consider themselves enlightened."

"You do not consider them so?"

"No, they are merely vain, unimaginative."

"And where is it that you come from my strange admirer?"

"Far away."

"The man in the hood, are you he?"

"Most assuredly not."

"Do you know him? Why does he hide himself from me?"

"Oh, he's not hiding exactly; he's gone for good now though. He won't be coming back. It's only you and I now."

He picked up a stone from the ground and threw it into the pool. It plopped.

"See, no devils in there."

"None that you can see from here," the strange man said, nodding his head.

"What's that about your face and nose, stranger?

"They help me to see more clearly. The glass just amplifies what you see. Excuse me, I'm being very rude, aren't I? My name is Charles," he said, extending his hand, finally jumping to his feet.

He hesitated for a moment, then grabbed the stranger's hand, and in one swift move felt himself being pulled in closer. Then, a sudden, sharp pang shot through his chest. He tried desperately to speak but found could not. He drew for breath, but none came, only a taste like metal, which filled his mouth with searing heat.

"They call her Samara where I'm from, you fucking dog, and you can't have her."

The man fell to his knees with a sharp groan and looking down could see his reflection in the blade that had penetrated him. His blood poured in a thick pool at his feet. He suddenly felt very light. He was about to say something but felt no need. His eyes faded in and out, flickering from light to dark, and then he was gone.

Charlie Patterson stood over the body, having slowly pulled the sword from the man's chest as he fell. He had to struggle against the bone and gristle to remove it. There was no light left in the man's eyes now, only a look of complete surprise, followed slowly by what seemed a look of acceptance, peace. Patterson paced around the body finally shouting wildly:

"I'll kill you wherever I find you, Gaius! Are you listening, you dog, you whore? Everywhere, every time!"

He looked back down now, and the corpse had taken on an almost-mocking grin, like it knew something he did not. He was taunting him still, so he ran the blade directly into the dead man's mouth, howling like a wild animal as he did so, finally decapitating him in a fury. The echoes pinged across the garden and off the walls of the nearby cliffs. Patterson finally bent over, dropping the sword, still panting from the slaughter. He was completely covered in blood now. He had some of it in his eyes even. He knelt at the base of the statue, tracing his fingers around the letters *Veritas*, tears streaming down his face.

"I love you, my dearest Samara, my sweet, little girl," he said, shaking all over.

He tried composing himself before reaching into his bag for the paper and pen. He started to write:

Sweets, I love you more than I have words to express. Don't be afraid. We will see each other again soon. Right now I am trapped in an impossible situation, but soon I will be able to come to you. I love you.

He tried wiping the blood from the page but only smeared more. He had to get the letter to her as quickly as possible. He pulled another page from his bag and started writing:

Jacob, I need to send a letter. It's the last thing I'll ever ask you to do. I mean it this time. Please get here as quickly as you can. It's Samara; it's her only chance.

W alking up the front steps to his house, Downy could see the bucket, some water and foam still inside from when he and Naomi had last washed the car together. She had laughed at the care he took, since the car was such a relic. Finally, she had simply dumped the bucket over him and at the end on to the both of them. Her tiny, thin T-shirt was soaked through so thoroughly that things had turned very playful, ending in the garage with the door only half closed. He thought of her pants halfway off, one leg at the ankle, their laughter. The bucket looked old and sad to him now. He'd remembered throwing the bucket out he thought. He opened the front door and could see a bottle of his best scotch sitting on the table, the lid off. He had not left it there. Had the cops raided his liquor cabinet too? He walked over to the table and could see a note under the bottle. The writing was instantly familiar. Charlie's.

I had no choice but to do this. Forgive me.

Jesus, he thought. Had Taro been right? Taro had predicted he would see Charlie again. Was this what he meant? It was almost impossible for him to imagine his best friend capable of such a horrific crime. But it was something else about Taro that troubled him even more. Taro didn't act like a man guilty of murder. He was strangely dispossessed of anxiety in fact. Then again, maybe that's exactly how a killer might behave. A sociopath. He'd drugged him after all. That was the only rational explanation to all of this. He looked anxiously around the room. Police tape was still draped across the entrance to the ground floor guestroom where Samara had...he couldn't bear to think of it. He walked to the back patio taking in the view of the horizon. The gray clouds sped past revealing only flashes of blue sky above.

He collapsed into the chair and let out a long sigh. He thought of getting up for a drink, but it felt too good having his eyes closed. The cool breeze had never felt so much like freedom, and he breathed it in deeply. There were cops across the street watching the house, so he felt free to doze, to rest finally. He closed his eyes slowly and awakened in the same room where he had last dreamed of Samara. He could smell amber in the air. The high priest was bent over a pool of water washing his hands now. His back was turned to Downy, who knew he was only dreaming and so floated across the room to get a closer look. The man suddenly turned to him. His face was painted red. He smiled a toothy, malevolent grin.

"What is this place?" he heard himself asking.

He looked into the darkness across the room, where he could see men in chains on the floor writhing in agony.

"She is there," the man said, pointing at a statue. Blood raced down the face of the stone effigy of a beautiful young woman. It was Samara's face.

"Wake up, dear boy. Wake up," he heard a voice repeating in his ear.

He sprung up, and sitting over him stood Charlie. It was now nearly dark outside, so he must have been sleeping for hours.

"Jesus! Charlie, how did you get in?"

"I have been forced to come. Don't worry, the police saw nothing. It's the travel with Taro that has you so fatigued, dear boy. You needn't bother explaining to the cops. You'll go straight to the loony bin."

Downy stumbled to his feet.

"Did you write that note on the table?"

"I wasn't sure I could make it at all or that I'd see you again, so, to be sure, I had to leave it."

"What do you have no choice about?"

"The Samara you had here in your home was not my daughter, Noah," he said soberly. Not really. We're all trying to get back to the point of origin you see, but it's never ending. A fucking box within a box within a box. He always outthinks us." Charlie hung his head, looking defeated.

"Taro?"

"Yes, Taro. That's not his real name, of course. He

borrowed that moniker from an old book. He will come soon to tell you the truth. His truth.

"Why does he think you killed Samara, Charlie?"

"I did. I did it to free her, I swear. There is no life after the Vestals appear, only a long, pointless chase through hell. It ends in darkness, bitter suffering."

"You killed Samara, Charlie?

Patterson stared forward, and one of his hands began to tremor uncontrollably.

"I drugged her first, to sleep. Then I suffocated her with a pillow. It was a mercy killing. I had to use what was available. I had no idea the police would use it to pin it on you. The cutting was after the fact, not my doing. Taro probably did it to lead them astray; he planned to frame you all along, I'm sure. He's cunning, so very cunning."

Downy stood up from his chair backpedaling.

"Then why did he help me get out?"

"I want to tell you how it started. It's still unbelievable to me. Tell me, dear boy, what man of such wealth and power guards his own treasure like a fucking dragon? I never imagined he was on to me."

"Who is he?"

"Noah, do you remember Old Professor Blythe?"

"Hal Blythe? Of course."

"Ah, but you only knew him as an old man, I forget. He was a truly remarkable teacher once. I saw him while he was still in his prime, giving a lecture on Rome that was the most riveting thing I've ever witnessed. I sometimes think my whole career started then, that very day. He talked of Rome as if he were describing a place he had visited on some idyllic vacation, like he had hovered over her in a dream. It was the most sublime mediation on any subject I had ever experienced. He talked of the streets, piss pots flying out the windows, the smell of the alleys, food cooking, people running from place to place. The grind of life, so familiar to our own. He took us to the temples, where he described their already ancient rituals, the sublimation, the mass convocation with the gods, some of whom even walked among them from time to time. You might meet Hera herself in a tavern and be seduced by her some starry evening. Your offspring could claim divine heritage. The gods and goddesses were among them, not above them, not distant: their lush gardens, still wild really. The young servant girls and boys in their dressing gowns, covered in jewels, the great men of importance at the fountain, talking of business, politics, philosophy. A man might have his dinner, put his wife happily off to bed, and then take his pleasure in the baths with the slave girls or boys if he wished. He'd invite a friend over to sell a scheme or two. As evening came, the night sky was as a sea you might fall into. The majesty of it utterly escapes us today. It was the first vast theater. We barely bother looking up now."

"Why are you telling me this, Charlie?"

"Because I could never believe he hadn't actually been there. And I was right."

Patterson snatched at his spectacles wiping tears from his face.

"Not a person in the room at that lecture could speak when he finished. Few of us even left our seats. We erupted in frenzied applause after. It was like a baptism. That one spark has stayed with me all these years, so when Jacob told me he'd been using the pond secretly, I knew it was wrong, but what he offered I simply couldn't refuse."

"What did he offer you?"

"My heart's greatest hope—to see it. Isn't that the lure for us all, Noah, the pull of the past?"

Patterson's look became one of bewilderment. He sighed like a child.

"So he took me to the very doorsteps of the men I had held in my heart as heroes since I was a boy."

"To Rome?"

"Yes, at first we were only spies. Noah, it was the greatest adventure I have ever taken, please understand. It was as if I had been reborn. I was an old man on one final joyride, the ultimate vacation. I can't explain how many ways my heart broke in the bliss of it. I was so alive there. I was among brethren for the first time in my life. Except for you, of course, dear boy," he said, grabbing his arm affectionately. Patterson's eyes swelled with tears.

"What happened?"

"We wanted to bring back some of what we saw. I wanted you, Samara, everyone to see these precious things, to taste them." Charlie held up his hands as if to hold something invisible.

"Taro says you stole from him, Charlie." Downy went suddenly silent, realizing what Charlie actually meant. "Taro is from there, from Rome, from the past?"

"He will come to you tomorrow, and I have agreed to prepare you for him."

"For what?"

"For what he calls 'The great interview.'"

"What do you mean?"

"Tomorrow you will meet with Gaius Julius Caesar my friend, in the flesh."

Downy slapped his hands against knees, letting out a sardonic yelp.

"Charlie, that's insane."

An unexpected noise moved from behind them.

"I'll say."

They both heard a click.

"Stay right where you are, Mr. Patterson."

Detective Sullivan moved slowly around to block the sliding door, pointing a revolver at Patterson. "This is Patterson, right? You can confirm an ID for me, Professor Downy?"

"You tricked me. You staked this out?"

"I had a feeling your emotions might keep you from seeing clearly is all. Nothing personal, OK?"

Patterson looked at Downy imploringly. "You can't let him take me, Noah. Things will be much, much worse."

"You know, Mr. Patterson, I've never heard a defense quite like yours. So, it was basically your daughter's stunt double you murdered and not her, something like that?"

"Gentlemen, I beg you. I simply cannot be apprehended this night." Patterson looked at Downy again and, switching to Latin, spoke slowly. "Serva te constituam Gaius cost."

Then Patterson leaped over the edge of the balcony into the darkness below.

Downy screamed no while both men watched him plummet silently down to the distant trees below. It looked much too far to survive. Sullivan grabbed his radio and called for help from the cops out front.

"Stay here; don't move, and don't go anywhere," he said, locking eyes with Downy. He nodded his head in silent agreement, staring out onto the darkening horizon but could see nothing, absolutely nothing.

CHAPTER 20

When the girl awoke, she realized she was no longer in her bed. Her body was stiff and bruised, but she was breathing normally again. She thought she could sit up now, at least without fainting. She'd only just lay down to sleep she remembered but couldn't because of the noises from the room above. Noah was upstairs with Naomi. Her reaction had confused her. She was both excited and angry at the same time, thinking about the two of them up there alone having so much fun. Then she heard a man's voice in a whisper.

"Danny, Danny Flem, Danny Fleming," he repeated.

"Your name is Danny Fleming," she whispered back.

There was a long pause.

The man's voice came again, now in a whimper. "I'm a football player. I have a wife named Tara Fleming and two kids: Jeremiah and Tommy Fleming." The man sounded deeply shaken.

"OK, OK, how did you get here?"

"I can't remember. I'm losing my memories, but I know I live at 110 W. Lewis St., San Diego CA 921...9211." He sobbed in the darkness.

Then she heard another voice louder and gruffer over his.

"He's a cop; he's been down here ten years he says. Who are you?"

She paused before speaking. It could be a trap she realized.

"I can't remember," she said shakily.

"I haven't heard you before; they just put you in?"

"I think so," she replied.

"But you don't remember your name?"

There was another long pause.

"My name's Tackett; I'm a cop too. Look, we gotta trust each other if we're gonna get out of here, OK? You need to tell me who you are and how you got down here."

She was too frightened to hold back any longer. "My name is Samara, Samara Patterson," she said in a tense whisper.

"Is that so?" the man replied. Now he sounded like the suspicious one.

"Yes, I'm Samara Patterson."

"Is your father by chance named Charles, Professor Charles Patterson?"

"Yes, yes, he is. How did you know that?"

"Oh nothing, it's just that I investigated your murder recently."

"My murder? What do you mean 'my murder'? I was asleep or passed out I think; that's all I can remem—"

"Yeah, but I saw your dead body with my own eyes; you were ID'd by several friends and relatives in fact."

"What, that's crazy?"

"Is it? Come on, who are you really?"

"I am telling you, I am Samara Lee Patterson, and I am very much alive."

It seemed like the man might not answer back.

"Let's pretend that's true. Any idea who took you, Miss Samara Patterson?"

"No, not really. Everyone I've seen, their faces are covered, hidden. I was with friends at their house; we had been drinking. I passed out I think. What do you know about my father?"

"Nothing much; he died suspiciously."

"Yes, it was so strange, the note. You're a cop?"

"Yes, my partner was investigating your...is investigating your case."

The other voice whispered frantically in the darkness.

"I've never heard anyone come back. My name is Danny Fleming, and I've never heard anyone come back; after they take them away, they never come back." He sounded blank and confused.

"Can we get out of here?"

"Yeah sure, the doors are open now."

The girl looked at the door, which was slightly ajar, noticing for the first time.

"We can escape then?"

"Maybe we're gonna find we're in a bigger cage is all. I don't think it was left open accidentally."

"But we can't just stay down here either in the dark, we'll end up—"

"Then we do it together."

"OK."

"Could someone remove that goddamn tape, please," Sullivan said, pointing to the black-suited agents. "I'm sorry you had to come home to that."

"It's OK."

"So, did you have any indication before his disappearance that Charlie Patterson was having mental or emotional problems?"

He thought of the picture of Freud above their table at Woody's. "No, none."

"Any idea where he would go? Did he give any indication?"

"He's been away so long it's hard to imagine." Downy sipped at the cup of tea the officers had put in front of him.

"The problem is, of course, we've lost our only bargaining chip. Any guess why he is treating this laurel as authentic?"

"You heard what he said. My friend is clearly quite ill."

In his mind though flashed images of the girls from Taro's

place. He could hear them still whispering in his ear, and he felt a sudden urge for the bitterness of the tea. The accompanying wave in his stomach gnarled in a knot, and he felt another tremor of craving for it, for the drug. Sullivan nodded silently.

"Who is this Taro he keeps referring to? Excuse me, but are you feeling OK, Professor?"

Downy waived his hand dismissively.

"It's a student of mine actually, just a nutty guy who was trying to be supportive during all of this."

"Do you know his full name by chance?"

"No, he is a new student really; he was in my course for only a few weeks, but he should be on my roster. My secretary—"

"And Patterson thinks he's a dead Roman emperor, something like that?"

He shrugged. "By the looks of it."

"What was it he said before he jumped? It sounded like a foreign language, what was it? Italian?"

"It doesn't make any sense. He said to "keep my appointment" or something like that; it was Latin actually."

"Well, we're combing the canyons and neighborhoods; we'll find him. In the meantime, I need you to stay put. Officers will be here, just outside until we do."

Sullivan rose to leave.

"I'm sorry about your friend, the detective. What was his name?"

"Tackett." Sullivan's stare hardened, and he squinted his eyes ever so slightly.

Jesus, he was doing it again. He couldn't lie to the son of a bitch about anything.

"You know Profess—"

He smiled sympathetically, seeming to ignore the thought. "Get some rest, and I will notify you as soon as we find him."

Downy waited until the door finally closed before falling onto the couch, exhausted. It was true then. Charlie had murdered Samara. My God. He gritted his teeth thinking of it and ran his hands back and forth violently across his face. He wanted a drink immediately. He thought of Taro. Charlie's claim. Julius Fucking Caesar. He was supposed to believe that? He poured shakily into the glass before turning up the entire bottle of scotch. The overflow finally broke his lips from the seal, and the alcohol spewed violently out onto the floor. He could remember the lines now from the actors in the courtyard. It *was* Shakespeare, and it *was Julius Caesar* speaking:

I am as fixed as the North Star.

Of course, it was from the speech before his assassination, Shakespeare's version, when Senators had feigned to beg forgiveness for their kin. They had lured him to his murder on their knees begging for pardon. Cowards. He and Charlie had always shared that sentiment. The speech was the same elevated style, formal. They sounded like words that could have fallen right out of Taro's mouth in fact. He paced now wondering if Taro would actually show up for the laurel, for their meeting. How would he react when he found out he didn't have it anymore? Clearly, it was the reason Charlie had come to take it before Taro could. Could his best friend really have murdered his own daughter out of some deranged sense of mercy?

Downy staggered into the bathroom, catching his reflection the mirror. His face was warm and flush, and his skin looked unusually red. Taro had called it "a lesser side effect of using the pond." He could smell himself as well, a major side effect Taro had called it. His pupils suddenly grew large and black in anticipation. He reached desperately into his pocket for the pill, throwing it in his mouth. Then he turned up the last of the scotch before falling into the fetal position on the floor, his head sliding against the plaster. He saw Taro's face as he faded, painted blue, the distinctive scar running down his neck, a "gift from the war" he had called it. His gleaming black eyes simmered as he stood over the twitching body of the sacrificed bull. It *was* Taro he had seen in the dream. He was the priest with the painted face. The Pontifex Maximus. Samara was his sacrifice.

Sullivan sat in the darkness of the surveillance room, eyeing the black-and-white video of the hallway outside the bathroom from the night before. He'd watched an hour's worth of footage already and found nothing. Rodriguez suddenly appeared, opening the door.

"I can find absolutely nothing on this Taro from the college. I called, and they say there is no record of any such person in Downy's classes. I did google the name though, and something interesting came up. I wouldn't have even noticed except for what you said about Patterson's delusion that he's a time traveler."

"What did you find?"

"Well, the very first piece of fiction ever written about the idea of time travel was a very old Japanese story, even before 'The Time Machine' and all that shit. Guess who wrote it?"

"A guy named Taro?"

"You got it."

"Maybe Patterson has been reading a little more than is good for him."

"Let me ask you something, man."

"Shoot."

"That balcony."

"I know."

"It's forty, fifty feet at least. I only know one kind of person who can make a leap like that and still jump up and run—a crack head."

"It would explain the delusions."

"Yeah, and another thing is that I have been working narcotics for sixteen years. You develop an eye. That Professor Downy looked high as shit to me. Did you see his pupils?"

"Yeah, but that's impossible; I was on him the whole way from the station to his house. I'd have noticed if he took anything—I think."

"OK, whatever you say."

He seemed to reconsider. "I guess it is possible someone gave him something inside."

"What you looking for there?"

"Oh nothing, just a weird thing that happened. I thought I heard something in the bathroom the other night, but when I checked, there was no one there."

"Probably just an echo, you know rectal." She burst into laughter.

"You're disgusting, get out. Let me know if they find Patterson, OK?"

He felt his phone vibrating in his pocket and struggled in

the darkness to get it.

It was Tina. Finally.

Now I know why you aren't married. 6 a.m. Really?

Ah God, Sullivan thought. She really was too young to understand a grown-up schedule.

Another message followed with a beep.

I went ahead and replayed our night while I touched myself...since I was up...

He smiled. Maybe he could imagine such a relationship after all. If it was going to be anything lasting, it needed to be exciting at least. Tina seemed more than capable so far. He swiveled in his chair and almost didn't notice the door to the bathroom slowly opening on the screen in front of him. He lurched in his chair, almost falling, and hit the Rewind button. There, sure enough, on the screen, exiting only minutes before Sullivan had gone in, was a man, a man in a tourist hat. The hat was pulled down so that his face was mostly hidden.

"Jesus fuck!" he shouted.

He rewound the tape frantically, but there was no sign of anyone going in, no look at his face. He must have already been inside much earlier, waiting. He leaped from his seat and ran to get the Chief and Rodriguez. They had their mole. But what did the note etched on the wall mean? His mind raced at the possibilities. Downy was certainly lying about forgetting Tackett's name and probably more. Was he involved after all? He'd practically written his own ticket out of jail, the son of a bitch. He dialed his phone as he ran.

"Yeah, you guys still at Downy's place? Go knock on the door, and call me straight back. I want one person in the house at all times. He takes a piss I want someone outside the door listening."

CHAPTER 23

Downy awoke and could feel the ache in his neck already. His face was stuck awkwardly against the plaster wall, and he had to peel it away before he could even stand up. The drug had given him a long sleep. The skylight suggested it was early morning, and the birds were already cackling away above him. He pulled himself slowly to his feet, focusing on the empty bottle on the floor. He'd downed a dangerous amount and yet he felt no hangover whatsoever, just as Taro had said. The drug had simply erased it. The color in his face had calmed a bit as well. The smell hadn't gone yet; he'd need a bath for that. He splashed some cold water and took a towel out into the main room. He walked to the window but couldn't spot the undercover car anywhere. Jesus, they were probably out getting breakfast. Some protection. He prayed his wife was getting better. He had to call her, of course. As he turned to sit down, he nearly fell to the ground. His antique chair had been moved. As he surveyed the room, he could see all of the furniture was missing, save for two chairs, which he could see sitting out alone on the balcony. Had the police taken everything? He punched his contacts for Detective Sullivan's number and hit Call. The line dialed, but then a recording answered, saying the number was "no longer in service."

"You won't be able to contact them anymore."

"Jesus," Downy leaped at the sudden voice from behind him. It was Taro. "How did you get in my house?"

"Let's stop playing pretend, OK, Professor? The hour is late. The ides are upon us I'm afraid. You can't possibly doubt the veracity of my claims any longer. Your own dear Dr. Patterson told you who I am. Let's be on authentic terms with one another, shall we?"

"You can't be Julius Caesar man; that's crazy."

"You're right; no one calls me that. We Romans prefer our first names just as you do. Call me Gaius, please. I am here to grant you something I have given no one else: a chance at the truth. I want to go on the record before I return."

"What record?"

"I told you we're both about to be very famous, among a select group of people at least. Our audience is about to grow much, much larger though. I have selected you as my own personal biographer, because, as I sat listening to your lectures over the years, I have finally realized you know me better than anyone. You truly understand me I think. It's incredibly flattering."

"Wait, what do you mean over the years?"

"Oh yes. The great thing about your popularity professor

is that one can come and go in your classes almost unnoticed. I had to eventually cover up a bit. That hat is just the worst, yes? Running through time you leave a trail, of course. It's exhilarating to say the very least, and it provides a certain kind of perspective. You can see much that others cannot. These Vestals think they can fix the problem, but it is in fact only I who can. And that's what I want to tell you about; it's what I need you to explain to the world for me, so that when I'm gone—"

Downy walked again to the window, peering out nervously. "So you have been stalking me all along?"

"In a manner I suppose, admiringly, of course."

"Where the hell are the cops?"

"We're a million miles from all that now. No police, no vestals, no ghosts, just you and Gaius Julius Caesar for a once-in-a-lifetime conversation. Tell me, are you up for it? It would seem to me the crowning achievement to a career like yours, if you'll pardon a bad pun." Taro leaped to his feet, suddenly seeming like a giddy child. "You just press the button there according to the man at the shop."

He flicked the device at Downy, who caught the tiny voice recorder in the air. Taro walked out to the front balcony silently. Downy followed him slowly, sitting down in the chair opposite.

"You said 'after you're gone' a minute ago. Where are you going?"

"Back home where I belong—to the dust and to the glory I have earned."

"To die?"

"Ah, what is death? I return to nature, to my true mother. When I listen to the glorious tragedy of my end, as you tell it professor, what better could I ask for?"

"I never called your death glorious. I said it was tragically ironic."

"Ah, but so much better than simply wasting away."

"You'd let yourself be murdered, why?"

"It is in accord with nature. You know you should be recording this. People need to understand what I'm doing and why. It affects all of humanity really."

He pushed the record button, and the red light flickered on.

"You're sure it's working?"

"Yes, it's on."

Taro breathed in a deep breath. "I, Gaius Julius Caesar..."

CHAPTER 24

S ullivan sat silently looking at the picture on his phone, reading the numbers again slowly.

47'58' 87': 5:55 10/22/14

It was clear that the last was a date, today's date; 5:55 PT was obviously the time. He had mapped the latitude and longitude of the first two numbers, and they corresponded with only one location: Chippewa Lake. The very place they'd found Samara Patterson's body in the water. Some coincidence. The message scrawled on the wall had to be from the people who had Tackett. But what had the rest of it meant? "Bring the waitress," it had said. *Could they possibly mean Tina?*

His phone buzzed in his pocket. It was Rodriguez.

"They're closing down the search of the neighborhood. No sign of him."

"Keep me posted, and watch your back, OK? Keep your phone close, just in case."

"You bet," he replied, tossing the phone into the seat.

It was a bad idea to keep the information he'd discovered to himself, but he felt anyone who knew was probably even in more danger. Whoever had written it had outwitted him and the department at every turn. But why would they ask him to bring Tina unless it was for some kind of collateral, some exchange. Yet, the warning that it was "the only way to save her" scared him equally. He was risking her safety either way it seemed. His phone buzzed again:

"Sullivan here."

"Sir, I'm really sorry. We only just realized it, but Professor Downy has managed to get out of the house; we don't know where he is at the moment."

"Goddamnit!"

"Sir, we had every exit and entrance covered; we have no idea h—"

He pounded his fists hard on the steering wheel. Then he pulled his car into gear and sped out of the station parking lot. He looked at the clock nervously and thought of Tina. He thought of Tackett. What was the point of going to Downy's house when he wasn't there anyway? The timing of his escape seemed too much of a coincidence. And besides, he could protect Tina if things went wrong. Maybe it was only a show of good faith they were interested in. Still, the thought of taking her there alone bothered him. How could he do it without telling her? He dialed her number.

"Hey, you," she answered.

"OK, not a lot of time to explain, but let me ask you. Have you ever wondered what it might be like to be a cop, an undercover cop?"

"OK, is this a role-playing thing, dear? Because if it is, let me just say up front. I'm totally into it."

"No, this is serious," he said, laughing. "I may need your help actually, and I have to tell you there is some danger involved, but you'll be safe with me, OK? I promise."

He could hear Tina shuffle the phone. "Oh, this is for real. Are you kidding? I wouldn't miss it for the world. I'm in."

"It's probably nothing in fact, but I have to check to see at least. I can pick you up in half an hour. Be ready. I need to be there right on time."

"Ahhh God, this is awesome! I'll be ready. Hey, do I get to pack heat?"

He laughed. "I have enough heat for the both of us."

"Yes, you do, Detective. I'll see you soon."

He stared into the screen on his phone, looking up to veer around oncoming traffic, and then wheeled the car wildly in a U-turn and started back toward the Aero Club. He prayed he wasn't making yet another mistake.

"I'd grown so tired you see. Conquering the whole of the known world, you know, it...it well, really takes it out of you," he said with a gentle laugh. "Your language is just beautiful by the way. I have been practicing it for many years, and its variations continue to amaze me." He leaned in as if to confide something deeply personal. "It is the simplest expression that one can't forget. You can't say it any better in Latin or Greek actually," he said finally leaning back again. "*It takes it out of you,*" he said slowly accentuating each word. "I am a fan of economy in language, as any successful man must be. Come on, Professor, you must have at least one question for me. Have I not been an object of your intensive study for many years now? You've gotten many things wrong, you know."

Downy readjusted himself in his chair. "You say you are Julius Caesar. How did you get here?"

"I caught a thief in my home. I grabbed him as he fled and then left my world forever."

"You mean Charlie Patterson?"

"Indeed I do."

"So you came through time with Charlie accidentally?"

"I no longer believe in accidents, but I don't think Dr. Patterson imagined me coming along for the ride, any more than I expected to be ripped so violently from my own life. It is violence, you know? He gave me neither remedies to help with the transition nor apologies for his theft. He left me completely alone, displaced from all I knew, my closest relative dead more than two thousand years."

"So how did you survive?"

"There was one place known to me that reckoned to always be there, a place where I could find safety even two thousand years from home. The landmarks had changed much but not entirely. Ancient maps were of great aid to me, once I'd recovered my wits that is, which took many years."

"The Gracchi, the monks?"

"Ah see, you really are a clever boy. Most academics I meet are such dullards. Yes, the Gracchi have passed down so much old Roman wealth as to be virtually impregnable to the changes of time. I wonder often of their true origins. They predate even my own ancestors. A monumental fee was paid in one of your so-called world wars, for the safety of the monastery. My contributions will carry it well into another two thousand years I suspect."

"So that's where you have been all this time?"

"Almost twelve years now, by your count. I try not to think

of my misfortune, but it's hard knowing all I've left behind. It's why I am choosing to return to meet my fate at last."

"What stopped you from going sooner?"

I could continue running from the Vestals and elude them forever probably, through time; it is unimaginably vast —I am tired of the chase."

"Who are the Vestals?"

"They're hunters. Silly people really, a holdover from my own time. They believe in the purity of the 'line' as they call it. They have made a religion out of it almost. Their argument is to do no further harm, to stop the bleeding as it were. How is it you say, 'to put the genie back in the bottle'?" They've consecrated me in a sense, to a degree I never thought possible. I represent the original break in the continuity of the timeline; they call me the First Lord or some such nonsense. All my life people have been giving me titles like this. I've never had much use for them, but I like the ring of it actually. In that regard at least we agree, but they won't allow me to return."

"Why, if they believe in the purity of the timeline? Wouldn't they want you to return?"

"They fear it will annihilate everyone else in this second seam, our seam—an apocalypse they call it. Like restarting a race that's already been run, but wiping out some of the runners completely before it begins. *They* are the runners, of course. They do it for themselves and claim me as their hostage."

"So they want to kill you?"

"Yes, they'd prefer to bring the line to an end and sew it

up forever, I gather. Probably, they'd rather just study me, in a cage, of course; all I can say is that they've forged an alliance with Charles Patterson. A settlement. He gets to keep his life, and I get lose mine again, except without the glory I have earned."

"So you actually want to go back to the ides of March?"

"I choose to die on my own terms in the manner the gods intended. Is that so surprising, professor? It is my final act of contrition. I have no fear of returning to my glorious end. Any other is beneath me."

Downy looked down at the flashing numbers on the tape recorder. They had been talking so intently that he'd almost forgotten it was there. He shuddered as he looked Taro over, noticing now the deep lines cut into his forehead, the light tint of yellow in the corner of one eye, a jagged scar running down his neckline. He looked like a warrior indeed.

"Thank you, for letting me speak in my own defense, professor. I know in spite of all you've seen, it's still so hard to grasp. Alas, reality is so very thin. And our moment is nearly at an end, I'm afraid. I wish there were time to say more, but I must depart. Neither of us can stay here in fact; I need you to make one more trip with me, a final trip home. It is my gift to you, for all you have done in my name."

Downy suddenly felt an unexpected emotion. He couldn't explain it rationally, but he felt its underlying truth somehow. A wave of euphoria raced through his veins, but it was not the drug anymore. Could he really be talking to Julius Caesar himself?

"I still don't understand why Charlie would try to stop you from going back. I know Charlie he would under—"

"Think about it, professor. The answer is almost too easy."

"Samara."

"Yes, of course, he'd do anything to have her back. It's understandable, but it cannot be. I already did what I could for her, but Charlie Patterson is playing for the wrong team."

"If I could just talk to him."

"Don't forget he murdered her with his own bare hands, professor. What happened after the fact was only an attempt on my part to save you from taking the fall."

"So you did frame me," he said angrily.

"Yes, but not to convict you, to save you. Take this," Taro said, handing him a sugar cube. Taro walked inside to the counter and returned with a glass of scotch.

"You'll have your old life back at the end of the day," Taro said, beckoning to him to follow him back inside. He pulled open the sliding glass door, gesturing for Downy to go first.

"You and I will just step into a small crease then."

And as the two men walked inside, all became utter darkness around them.

"We're like fucking Butch and Sundance; look at us," Tina yelped, throwing her hair back wildly in the wind. "Wait no, Thelma and Louise."

Sullivan's ragged El Camino sped down the winding roads that led to Lake Chippewa. "Remember, we aren't doing anything but observing. Any sign of trouble and we're banana splits, OK?"

"You're the fucking cop, man; if there's trouble and we need to do some cop shit, let's do it!"

"Seriously," he said, looking at her sideways.

"OK, fine," she purred demurely. "What are we observing, Butch?"

"That's just it, probably nothing. Let's just say there may be banditos, and if there are, we are going to report them to the cavalry."

"I can't make the news, OK? I left work with the flu. I even fake coughed in front of my boss."

"You won't make the news," he said dryly. He smiled widely, even though he was feeling incredibly anxious.

He rolled the car slowly to a gravely spot on a ridge still a full quarter mile from where Samara's body had been pulled from the water. He reached for binoculars in the glove box and moved himself silently near some tall grass. Tina followed quietly behind. He could see very clearly from their position. There was nothing in the water but ripples from the breeze, occasional bugs swiping at the glassy surface.

"Take these," he said, handing them to Tina. If any people come into view, just give me a whistle; you do know how to whistle right?"

"Wait! Where are you going?" she said nervously.

"Just down there," he said pointing. "I wanna see if anybody's watching us watch them."

"Fucking A. OK, real cop shit," she said, lowering her head, feeling genuinely fearful for a moment. "Some crazy third date shit we got going on here," she muttered as she started quietly practicing her whistle.

He smiled to reassure her as he disappeared down the hill. He pulled a second smaller binocular from his pants and turned them toward her. He scanned in every direction, but it was completely quiet. He looked at his watch. It was 5:41 exactly. There was nothing to do but wait. Maybe they had hoped he would follow this clue and that the real action was going down elsewhere. A diversion. Damn. He turned his binoculars back to Tina. Through the tall grass, she wasn't aware she was being watched. She was a true specimen he thought. *God, why had he brought her?* He shifted his view back toward the water. He would take one more close look, and then they were getting the hell out of there and for good. He started to fantasize about a completely different future than he'd ever imagined. There'd be killers and criminals still, after he put down the badge and the fight would go on, so what? Tina could keep him in bed for at least the next ten years alone he reasoned. He paused for a moment. He was only a couple of hundred feet now from the edge of the lake. But already the taste of that future seemed too pure and good to be real. He was having a moment of absolute clarity, but then unexpectedly his senses flew into overdrive. He could see no one but could feel a presence; he felt like an animal in the midst of a sudden ambush. It was too quiet. He shifted his view back to her, scanning from left to right, but she was nowhere to be seen. He ran back up the hill trying not to panic, but even before he made it to her he could hear her muted attempts at a whistle as she ran into his arms—clearly in a state of panic.

"Bandito!" she finally exclaimed, but Sullivan was calm, reassuring.

It was only Tierney standing at the top of the hill, now walking toward them very slowly, in that damn suit still. What was the fucking chief doing here?

"No, hun, not a bandito," he said consolingly, but then he saw Rodriguez emerging from a patch beyond the trees some distance away. She had her .44 at her waist with both hands on it. Then Sheppard emerged from the opposite clearing, suddenly reaching for his firearm until he saw Rodriguez. He lowered it again when he realized who it was. "What the fuck are you guys doing here, following me?" he said.

There was a moment where he thought he heard Tierney's voice begin to respond, but the sound was drown out by the crackle of gunfire. He had already fast-forwarded in time to what came next and how utterly powerless he was to stop it. They had them all in one place.

The first shot took off of the top part of Tierney's head, and he fell very slowly to the ground, still talking and gesturing it seemed to Sullivan, as if he could barely accept the interruption. The sound of the shot seemed to come after, but that was only because they were still being fired on. Sheppard was on the ground instantly too, but round after round poured into his legs and then every part of his torso. He fired pointlessly into the air and then put his arms over his face, letting out a low groan. His pistol slid limply from his hand. Sullivan yelled for Rodriguez to take cover. She was now hovering in a crouched position trying desperately to locate the shooter, waving her gun wildly from left to right.

"Get the fuck down, man," she yelled to him, but then she seemed to walk right into the bullet, which tore through her neck, exposing a bloody gore, knocking her instantly off her feet.

He could hear the awful gurgling as she struggled to breathe only yards away from him. He was still frozen with his arms around Tina, who had now gone completely paralytic from the shock. He grabbed her like a rolled carpet and dashed to the cover of the nearby tree, trying desperately to free his revolver from his waistband and then raced back to check Rodriguez. She was unconscious, and though he could feel a pulse, it only pumped thick plumes of blood from the gaping wound in her neck. She had already gone completely blue in the face. He thought of his own mother and father, their waxen faces finally at peace in death and simply waited for his turn. He could still see no one. Tina was curled in a ball, whimpering almost silently. He'd led her to her death like a goddamned fool. He would never be able to say how sorry he was. Her life and his would end here. He waited, but no shot came. And Tina finally raised her head again.

In an almost whisper, she was repeating "Banditos, Banditos." Then she tried to whistle.

He stood slowly, looking all around. Too much time had passed. Then he heard the crack of a rifle. His whole body lurched, and he was on his knees again. Then two more shots, but they were far away. No bullet had hit him. He yelled for Tina.

"Are you hit," he screamed?"

"No more banditos. No, I wanna go home; I wanna go home," she said very quietly, like a little girl.

She was talking, which meant she was alive. He stood now, walking in her direction. The gunfire seemed to have stopped. They really had no cover anyway. It was the perfect spot for an ambush. But why weren't they finishing them off?

Then he saw another figure emerge from behind the trees. He couldn't believe his eyes. The man wore a hat, like the ones tourists wear on safari and had his arms raised in the air.

"I have no gun, Detective. I come in peace."

His mind raced to place the face. It was the goddamned guy with Downy's wife from the station, who he'd thought was her father maybe.

"You!" he said.

"They are called Vestals, who killed your friends. I'm awfully sorry for them," he said, looking nervously at the bodies strewn around. "I dispatched them on the hill just there," he said, pointing. "Four of them, the worst of them, but more will come."

"Give me one good reason not to shoot you in the goddamn face!"

Sullivan's hands shook as he tried not to look at the awful carnage surrounding him.

"I might give you many," the man said calmly, "but let's begin with the safe return of your friend Tackett."

"Where the fuck is he?"

"I have him nearby, and we can go to him, but you must trust me if you hope to live or the beautiful young lady over there. You've already saved her once today by bringing her, though it was imprudent to do so to be frank. I knew I could count on your recklessness, Detective."

He lowered his gun a bit.

"If I wanted you dead, I'd have shot you from on the ridge over there, but I don't. I'm on a mission of rescue, and I'm the closest thing to a friend you've got. We have little time before we have more guns on us, I'm afraid," he said, looking around nervously.

Sullivan still held his gun tightly.

"You don't have to give up your weapon, but I'd appreciate

you putting it away. They are foul, unpredictable things in my experience."

He finally lowered it.

"Let me take you to Tackett. He is safe, I assure you, and very anxious to see you, as is someone else you will be very happy to see, I presume. Come, follow me," the man said.

"Wait, who are you? I don't even know your goddamned name."

"Most call me Taro; that will have to do for now."

"Where are we going? What about them?" he said, pointing to his fallen comrades.

"They are quite finished as you can see. There is no time for reflection, unfortunately. She will be killed too, if she stays."

"Let her go," he said, pointing to Tina. "I'll follow you alone. This, whatever all this is, has nothing to do with her." Sullivan surveyed the awful scene before him.

"We need to take a swim together, the three of us. I need you to take off your clothes, all of them and hers. It will be easier for you if you take this," he said, producing two sugar cubes from his pocket.

He pulled off his shirt to reveal a torso pockmarked with scars, the most prominent of which ran from his neckline all the way to the base of his rib cage. He was a man of middle age clearly, but his muscularity was that of someone much younger.

"Come on," he said, "they may appear any minute."

"We're not taking these. Do you think I'm crazy?" Tina said, finally seeming to regain some of her composure.

"I'd be suspicious too, but without them you both die. You're just going to have to trust me. Look, look, I need it too; it will help us later," he said in his calmest voice, slipping a cube into his own mouth. He swallowed with a gulp.

Sullivan looked puzzled. Tina looked at him as if for an answer. He waited, staring at the cube. There was the sudden sound of voices off in the distance.

"They're here; we have no more time," Taro said tersely.

Sullivan swallowed, waiting yet again for the worst.

"Go on," he said to Tina.

"Oh God, I'm going to regret this," Tina said, and they both began to run.

"Where are we going?" he said, catching up to Taro.

"To the bottom of that lake; take off all your clothes, or they will singe right into your flesh," he said, pointing. "There is something I have to show you. Something amazing."

CHAPTER 27

Downy awakened suddenly and could instantly feel a warmth coursing through his veins that he recognized—the drug. He was in a small chamber now; marble busts adorned the perimeter. Holes cut through the stone ceiling shone down beams of light on their faces.

"I come to this room often to talk to them," Taro said, pointing. "That's old Tarquin himself, second king of Rome. By the time he was finished even his own mother wanted him dead."

"Where are we?" Downy said.

His face was burning hot, and he could smell himself now from the travel, like burned meat that had nearly gone bad.

"My private study. The Senate convenes in about an hour. I wish I could take you on the grand tour, but it will be extremely dangerous for you to stay—especially after. I thought it was an appropriate way to finish our talk. It's disappointing, I know. You get to see a whole ten feet of

Rome. Still, she is worth a look," he said pointing across the room.

He rose unsteadily to his feet and approached the bust in the corner.

"Is this?"

"Yes, that is the pharaoh herself."

"It's...it's remarkable."

"It was a mistake putting her in the forum. That statue was perceived as a bit of cosmopolitan preening I suppose, on my part. I only wanted people to see her as I did. I have a weakness for fine things you see. Those men out there sharpening their knives say it's proof of my *true* ambitions."

"Are they right?"

"I'm no king, Professor Downy. I am Caesar."

He traced his fingers around the soft edges of the young girl's face. She had named herself Queen of Kings. She looked like she might speak. Her looks were anything but average.

"She's younger than I imagined, much more innocent."

"She is still but a girl, but a very clever one. I'll never see the lines form on her face; she will stay this way for me always." He let out a long sigh. "Maybe you should go tell them they'll all be dead in a year's time, those bloody senators out there," Taro said. "I'd certainly take one last night with her."

"You're really going to do it then?" Downy said seeming to wake from a trance.

"I want to show you something for posterity, OK, Professor? Please report it accurately." Taro held up his hands in demonstration. They were steady, calm. "I could kill any ten of those men out there with my bare hands if I chose. Instead, I'll give them what they want. If it's an orgy of blood they demand, they may have it."

Taro's eyes seemed seared now in concentration. His emotions were impossible to read.

"It's better that you don't see. I'll bet you're only just now really accepting it, taking me for who I am. It took me years. Being torn from one's own time in the way that we have, it's the most sinister kind of violence. Today, I shall know even more on that subject though." Taro walked to the corner of the room where there hung a purple-bordered cloak. Downy had read about it a thousand times in his books, and here he was staring at it. Caesar pulled it from the mannequin and swung it casually onto his shoulder.

"I have one final gift to give you, professor."

Downy suddenly felt like a child. Here the man was then, great Caesar himself, and he could think of absolutely nothing to say to him.

"This sword was given me by my father, whose history you know well. Venus herself bequeathed it to my family millennia ago. No mortal hand could even forge steel then. It is endowed with great power and tragedy it seems."

Caesar presented the blade to him silently. It felt remarkably light in his hands.

"Keep it safe for me in my memory, and know that you have made this day possible. In a sense, we have saved the world together, you and I." He put his arm to Downy's shoulder and leaned in to embrace him. "God's be with me this day, give me courage." Caesar kept his head buried in his sleeve for a moment and then composed himself before speaking. "That passage leads to a door. Our paths must part here my friend. You cannot travel where I'm headed, and all my work will be undone if you stay."

He looked down at the sword in his hand.

"No one in your own time will ever believe it's real, but you will know."

Downy turned reluctantly to go.

"Run along now, professor. Report of me truly."

"Whom am I supposed to tell who would believe any of this?"

"You need not worry about that. It is the record you have taken that is important."

Downy walked into the darkness of the corridor and paused. He had the sword now, and Caesar was not armed. His heart was thumping in his throat. He could not kill him though, even if Charlie would have. He looked back, but Caesar was already gone. He realized he was in a sense sealing Samara's fate too. She would still be gone when he returned. He quietly opened the door in front of him and could feel the familiar darkness closing in all around. He was headed home for good he prayed and Caesar, finally, to his fate.

CHAPTER 28

Sullivan could see nothing in the deep darkness. He'd been a fool to take orders from someone he didn't know. He could hear Tina's voice.

"The water's gone; I'm not even wet."

A man's voice came from above in a whisper. "Put on these clothes. Continue down the passage, you'll find your friends. I will return as soon as I'm able."

"Wait you can't leave us!"

He heard a door slam behind them. It smelled musty and strange in the room.

"Here," he said, handing Tina what amounted to a large swath of cloth with a whole cut out at the top.

They continued cautiously down the steps until they heard a voice.

"Who's there?" Sullivan listened intently. The voice came again. "Who's there?" It was a gruff, unmistakable voice. "Tackett, is that you?"

"Sullivan?"

"Holy shit, man. I never thought—" He threw his arms around Tackett in a giant bear hug.

"I never thought I'd see you again you—you cranky old bastard."

"OK, don't freak out. I'm happy to see you too."

"Where the hell are we?"

Tackett lowered his voice in a whisper, "I can't say, but it's one of the strangest fucking places I've ever seen. Listen, my new roommate over there on the floor is from our gallery of the dead. She claims she's none other than Samara Patterson."

"What?"

"She's been beaten up pretty badly, but she seems lucid. Knows lots of details about Charlie Patterson too. It's crazy shit; she looks a lot like the girl from our postmortem exam to me."

"How?" Sullivan said, regaining himself. "I have to tell you some really bad news."

"OK."

"Tierney, Rodriguez, Sheppard, they're all...they're gone, man. They killed them all."

"Who killed them?"

"This guy, Taro, who brought us, claims it was the Vestals. Do you know who he means?"

"Taro?"

"Yeah, that's his name. He says something called the Vestals are responsible. Any idea who or what that means?"

"None. No one has said a goddamned word to me since I

woke up here. I was taken at gunpoint while you were inside the station. That was the last voice I heard. Never saw the guy's face, and he sure as hell didn't introduce himself. You're sure about Bob and Rod—"

"Yeah, man, I'm sure, they shot them dead. Ambushed us."

There was a solemn moment of silence between the two men.

"How did you two make it?"

"This guy Taro saved us."

"Can he be trusted?"

"I'm not sure man."

Sullivan rubbed at his face furiously.

"It's just the two of you down here then?"

"No, get this: Danny Fleming is over there in the corner cell. I can't get him to talk to us directly, but when he speaks, he repeats his badge number, address, names of his kids. He's been down here for years I think, since he disappeared."

"Fleming is alive?"

"How did she get dragged into this mess?" Tackett said, pointing to Tina, sounding disappointed. She ran to him finally for a consoling hug.

"She is attracted to deeply stupid men," Sullivan said flatly. "I brought her. I thought it was the only way to protect her. This thing is big man. These people are seriously cold-blooded and calculating. They fucking set us up. Nobody had a chance. We were each lured there under some pretext I'm guessing. They must have been planning it all along."

"Which begs the question of why *we're* still here."

"This Taro says we're under his protection."

"Feels more like we're chess pieces."

"Chess pieces for what?"

The three of them stood together in complete silence.

"Come on, let me introduce you to the dead girl."

CHAPTER 29

Sullivan couldn't believe his eyes. If it was not Samara Patterson, it had to be her twin. The girl shuffled in her sleep. Her eyes fluttered, but then she fell silent again.

Tackett whispered, "She's been drugged I think. She's real weak; she falls in and out."

"How do you think she got here?"

"How did any of us? What kind of name is Taro anyway?" Tackett said, shaking his head.

"It's a pseudonym. I'm pretty sure. It's taken from an old story about time travel, or so Rodriguez—"

"It's Urashima Taro." The girls voice startled everyone. She looked up groggily from her sleep. It's a story about a man who falls asleep fishing one day and wakes up in the distant future. It was one of my father's favorites."

Sullivan leaned in to get a closer look at the girl. The hairs at the back of his neck tingled.

"My partner here says you think you are Samara Patterson."

"I am Samara Patterson. Who are you?"

"I'm Nick Sullivan, a detective. I investigated your murder...I saw your—"

"You're both convinced that was me, aren't you?"

"I'm trained to pay attention to faces and—"

"So how does it feel talking to a corpse then?"

The two men looked at one another nodding their heads, seeming to agree it was impossible both things could be true.

"Can I see your tattoo?"

The girl leaned forward with her shoulder revealing the Latin Script. *Veritas.* Tina suddenly came forward and put a hand to the girls face.

"That's a bad bruise. Are you OK?"

Sullivan and Tackett realized they hadn't been very comforting.

"Do you have any idea how you got down here?" Sullivan said adding a hand to her shoulder, remembering the girl must be frightened out of her wits.

"She came with me." An outline of a man's shadow now stood at the bottom step.

Taro stepped from the darkness and lit a small torch. "I've brought each of you here to protect you, but now we must depart. This location has been compromised."

"Why the hell should we go anywhere with you," Tackett said walking menacingly toward Taro.

"You can stay if you insist, but you'll be dead by supper. The Vestals are now aware of this place."

"What the fuck is he talking about?"

"You know Detective Tackett, you really are quite the blunt instrument. At one point I considered not saving you at all actually. Show me some gratitude. Do as I ask, and you may yet live a while longer."

"Where do you plan to take us?"

"There's a hidden door at the top of those stairs. Once through, I need to entrust your safety to a dear friend. He will watch over you until my mission is complete."

"What mission?"

"My murder has been planned for this day. I must be there to face my assailants. That is enough for you to know." Taro started up the stairs, and each of them looked to the other as if for a confirmation.

"Come on," Sullivan said, "if he wanted to kill us, he's had plenty of chances."

———

The group followed Taro to the door and walked through the darkness, finally emerging inexplicably onto a crowded street corner. They stood in a tiny alley perplexed at the noise, which surrounded them and the mob of people, all dressed in robes exactly like the ones Taro had given them. Taro led the way through the crowd and turned back to them, beckoning them to follow. There was a roar coming from a large crowd nearby.

"Don't get lost, or you'll be lost forever!" he shouted. "It's a mean city!"

"Where the hell are we going?" Tina said, shouting above the fracas, but no one could hear her.

Soon the unruly mass of people had enveloped them, and they could only see the back of Taro's head. He turned, stopping the whole wave of them, creating a tiny lane for them to catch up. The crowd seemed to be following him, but some clamored over the others nearly sweeping them up in the faceless shuffle. The smell of the hoard of people was overwhelming. Taro turned and pointed at an old man who was struggling to get through.

"Artemidorus! These are friends of mine from far, far away. I wonder if you'd tend to them until after my meeting."

"Gaius, I have something for you. You must read it immediately!"

The crowd was circling now, and it was difficult to hear what Taro was saying. Soldiers now appeared clearing away the crowd, which was chanting in unison, some on their knees at Taro's feet.

"Artemidorus, be of good cheer. I shall tend to your words later, I promise. Take care of my friends please, old friend."

"Caesar, please, you must listen; you must re—"

But it was too late. The throng had pushed him past, and he could no longer hear them.

The crowd was now in a near frenzy as he ascended the steps. Perched on top was an old woman covered in filth.

"I know you, don't I?" he said.

She smiled a wicked, toothless grin and stood up at the base of a statue of Pompey the Great. Her face was covered in grime, and when she grinned, her mouth twisted into a horrid snarl. Seeing that Caesar had stopped to listen, the crowd drew together in a tense hush.

"Beware this day mighty one as it has been foretold by the Sibyl's themselves. Beware the ides of March."

Caesar smiled back to her. "I know you from the river, don't I?"

"I know you by the stench of fresh death, *dictatore*," she said hissing through clenched teeth. "I know what ya done."

"We shall see," he said almost demurely.

"Eye, we will see; the day is not yet done, great one."

"Indeed it has barely begun, old woman," he said turning, and with him the crowd once more swept him up.

Caesar flung his robes over one shoulder and leaped up into the causeway, just out of their reach. The crowd broke into great cheers again, and he leaned in to touch hands with some of them. He looked up into the small rotunda of the senate house in wonder at the freshly painted image of the god Jupiter throwing a javelin into a raincloud. He had commissioned it himself. At the top of the stairs, waiting for him was his protégé, Brutus. He smiled closemouthed as Caesar approached. His skin looked drawn and pasty. Sweat poured from his brow.

"Sir, we're so glad you decided to come. There are many inside who wish to honor you waiting patiently. Your great deeds seem only to multiply their affections."

"Dear boy," Caesar said, putting his hands on his shoulders, "let me look on you. Are you unwell?"

Brutus sputtered to speak, diverting his eyes to the ground before a man suddenly appeared, interrupting them.

"We must begin; many are growing impatient. It's poor form to make them wait."

"Yes, yes, by all means, let's begin then," he said pushing Brutus upstairs.

The man who had interrupted them threw an angry side-glance at Brutus, who could now barely walk it seemed.

"Your condition worsens still, Brutus. I fear you've caught the death."

"No, sir, only too much wine at dinner."

They walked into the great hall together among a clamor and Caesar pointed to the atrium.

"Look, there at my new décor, Brutus. What do you think? I chose crimson so as not to be misinterpreted in the kingly purple."

Great drapes hung now throughout the hall, enclosing the space in flowing waves of scarlet. The beams of sun tunneled through making the room seem to sway, almost to breathe.

"I was here only yesterday. You have put a rush on the job, Caesar."

"What do you think, does it not add to the *dramatis* of the place?"

"Yes, of course. They're very elegant sir, very."

"Thank you, my son. You know I have always considered you such."

Brutus's hand began to shake almost uncontrollably, and he thrust it inside his robe to conceal it.

The senators now moved as a throng toward them.

"Go stand over there now, my boy. I see I have petitioners before me."

Brutus fell to the back of the crowd now. It was Casca who approached first. Caesar already knew what he wanted. The release of his brother who had fought against Caesar in the war, not once but twice pardoned already. He would get no reprieve now or ever. Casca fell to one knee reaching for Caesar's robe, the sign to begin the attack, but as he did Caesar stepped back suddenly and spoke in a commanding voice.

"I lay a great plague on your houses villains and bring down the slaughter of the very gods upon you!"

The sound of a mighty war horn bellowed throughout the hall, and all turned in terror at the noise, some dropping to their knees. Then, Caesar pulled a sword from beneath his robes.

"Kill every bloody last one of them!"

The drapes suddenly came down all around them, revealing Caesar's Spanish guard, hidden in the wings, a hundred strong. They moved in one momentous surge into the crowd of terrified senators, who now had nowhere to flee. Caesar stood with his sword in the air crying out. He thought he could hear Professor Downy's crazy music blasting in his ear. Then he started his own cutting, first with Casca.

"Yes," he clamored, "die on your knees like a squealing pig, good Casca." Caesar crouched low and swung upward for leverage. Casca's head flew off his body like a cork popping from a bottle. "Let them drown in their own cowardly blood," he shouted.

But Caesar was looking for just one man—his beloved Brutus. His soldiers knew to leave him alone. Caesar walked through the crowd slowly, methodically toward him. Brutus had a dagger in hand, but it fell uselessly by his side, and he dropped to both knees listlessly. A slow trickle of urine splashed at his feet onto the smooth marbled floor. Caesar laughed in spite of himself. Brutus seemed to be speaking a prayer silently.

"Wretched boy, my misplaced affection." Caesar dropped his sword and knelt slowly in front of him slipping both hands around his throat. He mustered all his strength and squeezed until Brutus eyes nearly gorged from their sockets. Brutus tried to do the same, but Caesar steered him onto his back, overpowering him.

Caesar whispered into his ear forcefully.

"Pray to me, boy. I am your God," and the two seemed locked in perfect rhythm together. He could not tell how many seconds had passed. Then he simply let go.

Brutus's body fell limply to the floor.

The room was growing strangely quiet now, only the last moans of men being killed slowly could be heard. There were tiny yelps like those of whimpering children, pleading, followed by the ghastly rattles of strangulation, a horrible chorus of the dead and dying. Caesar walked over them in survey of the room, checking for the faces he knew so well. There lay each, as instructed, mortally wounded but not yet dead. They could look to one another as they perished, so each would know their own treachery had done them in. Cassius Longinus, who'd begun the conspiracy with his acid tongue, lay in the room's corner having nearly escaped. He had been stabbed in the groin and blood poured from him in a smooth flow, leading down the steps into the great hall.

"Poisonous Cassius, you served me once with distinction. How would you have served me this day? As a cold dish I think, but you first." He leaned in closely to watch the light of his eyes slowly flicker out. Caesar's top lieutenant approached.

"A fair reckoning. All were armed, as you suspected. Your intelligences serve you well, sir."

Caesar seemed to awaken as if from a dream.

"I must go now as planned to the outer provinces, Balbus, further than I ever have been before. Announce this treachery and its conclusion. Nothing can be the same now. We are writing a new history."

"Sir, if I may ask, what of Cicero? He is not among them, but surely his hand is in this?"

Caesar seemed to think for a moment. "Leave him to his books."

"Spare him, sir? I think it is a mist—"

"Deliver to him the head of young Brutus. Tell him to come and collect the rest of those he would deem friends. We shall never see him again."

"Yes, sir."

"You are the best of men good Cornelius Balbus."

"Sir? Thank you, sir."

"Now clear the room for me. I need a moment alone."

Caesar could hear the screaming beginning in the streets outside as the word had already begun to spread. It would be a night full of terror. He walked to the balcony portico and looked out over his beloved city. He could see the *subura*, his old neighborhood, far off in the distance. A sudden dirge of birds bent their flight, turning west into the blazing sun. Some sixty souls were being carried away with them. He pulled the piece of parchment from his tunic. The note from his beloved teacher Artemidorus read:

> *There will be an attempt on your life in the senate house*
> *this day. All are involved and armed. You must return*
> *home at once.*

He crumpled the paper in his hand and gave it a heave off the portico. He felt a strong urge to sleep in his mother's house this night, which was still standing, but there was one final detail yet to be finished—one final piece of history to be written.

CHAPTER 30

Downy awakened with his face against the screen of his sliding glass door. He had returned to the exact spot where he and Caesar had gone through together. He pulled himself up, and as he did the sword slid out onto the floor from inside his jacket. It reflected a glimmering gold and silver. The birds off his balcony were chirping wildly now, as if in appreciation. He inspected it more closely, trying to read the various inscriptions, but they looked foreign, even to him. Was Caesar telling the truth about its age? Nothing seemed impossible to him now.

He walked into his living room, surveying the emptiness. At least the police tape had been removed, a grim reminder of what had taken place there. He and Naomi would have to leave, of course. Nothing could ever be the same in their house. He also realized that by returning he had committed to a world in which both Charlie and Samara were truly lost. It horrified him, but what other choice did he have? There would be no story to tell the police, of course, not that they would believe. What of their missing detective though? He hadn't thought of him, and Caesar hadn't brought him up again either. Perhaps Caesar had released him somehow. He had kept his word on all other matters. It truly pained him to disappoint Detective Sullivan, and in spite of everything he still had a warm feeling about him. And then there was Charlie. Had the cops found him yet? Or worse the Vestals? Or was he trapped forever in the past?

He walked to the counter and reached for his bottle of scotch, but it was gone. Whiskey would have to do: the cheap stuff, Jim Beam. He pulled his phone from his pocket and dialed. He wanted to find out if Charlie had been found, if anything had happened in the search for the missing detective. The line picked up immediately but went straight to an "out of order" message. He looked at his phone to double-check the number. He was calling the right phone. Then he scrolled down to his wife's number. He hadn't spoken to her in what felt like a thousand years. He dialed and waited. She must be frantic by now, not having heard from him. The number rang and rang, but no voice mail ever picked up. Then the doorbell rang, nearly causing him to lose his drink. It was the police no doubt, so he downed his whiskey before walking to the door. So what if they smelled it? He winked one eye and peered into the hole. Outside stood the mailman of all people. He had an envelope in his hand and was already looking through the glass of the side window. Downy opened the door.

"Hello, sir," he said seeming startled. "Are you Noah Downy, Professor Noah Downy by chance?"

"Yes, that's me."

Downy suddenly noticed the mail truck parked at the curb, which was full of passengers; other mailmen it seemed. They were all watching intently through the windows.

"Holy shit, man, I can't believe you answered; when I saw the house was for sale, I thought for sure no one lived here. You just won me a ton in the office pool."

Downy looked confused, staring out at the for-sale sign in the yard. Someone had placed it there mistakenly, no doubt.

"I'm sorry, what's this about?"

The mailman shuffled nervously, seeming to regain his composure. "I'm sorry if...I didn't mean to be impolite; it's just that...well this letter has been around as long as the office itself. None of us believed there'd be...I do need a signature."

He looked down at the extremely weathered looking envelope. His name and address were written on the front in all caps, but there was no return address. Written beneath his name were the words: *Read Immediately*.

"Thank you," Downy said, turning to go back inside.

He could hear the mailman running excitedly back to his truck. Then Downy stopped in his tracks. The sign, the furniture. He'd sent him back to the wrong time. My God, of course! How could he have been so stupid? The drug always made things hazy, unclear. Caesar had made a mistake and sent him back too early. He looked up from the letter and around the room in a panic. They hadn't taken his furniture because it had never been there. They hadn't even moved in yet. That's why there were no cops answering or his wife. It meant Samara was still al—

A voice interrupted him. "I've sent you home a bit prematurely, haven't I?" It was Caesar leaning against the wall, his belt hanging loosely off one hip. He had an altogether different look in his eyes. He still wore the purple-bordered tunic from their last meeting.

"What the hell are you doing here?"

"I had to come back for you, professor. I had no time to get your favorite scotch; I hope whiskey will do."

"I thought you were—"

"I know. For the record, I have still never lied to you. I said my death was in keeping with nature. So then is my ability to stop it apparently."

Downy looked down to the letter in his hands.

"There's no reason to read that now."

"What about your plan? What about the ides?"

"Yes, even now the Vestals are in the Senate house cleaning up after me. Ghastly creatures. They scuttle about like phantoms. I know not what they are. They will come here next, I'm afraid, and that I cannot allow."

"Why are you here?"

"Great movements always require a supreme sacrifice, often equal to their ambition."

Downy looked to the corner where the sword had been. It was gone. Caesar pulled open his robes.

"As I told you, this blade brings great power and *tragedy*." Caesar swung as he always did, in a true, straight line; not with malice but lovingly to release him. It cut through

Downy's throat first and then down his torso. Blood spattered in great torrents around the room as he twirled in agony, hopelessly trying to defend himself. Caesar wanted to give a quick death, so he lunged and stabbed several times, hitting for the heart with each blow.

"There is no future with you in it, I'm afraid, good man, but in your death there are a thousand lives waiting to be born.

But Downy had stopped listening. He was in a light place now where the words seemed muted, inconsequential. He came to rest finally in the room's corner. He was about to say something, but it escaped him. The whiskey was still on his lips, reminding him of home. He was headed there now and felt calm.

EPILOGUE

Detective Fleming pushed at the door with all his strength, finally breaking through. A call had been made that someone heard screaming coming from the house, which was on the market for sale and supposedly empty. Fleming crouched low when he saw the blood on the walls and pulled his weapon. He reached for his radio and called the station immediately whispering,

"We have a situation, a possible 1031 at 381 Latimer Street. Send paramedics and back up, possible homicide, suspect possibly at large, repeat suspect at large."

The room was empty, but through the kitchen he could see to the back patio deck, which opened into a panoramic view of the ocean. He thought he could see some movement and approached with his gun drawn.

"I'm armed and will use my weapon," Fleming shouted.

He made his way silently around the corner but could find no one. The leap was too far for anyone to have risked it he figured. The blood on the walls was still fresh though, of that he was sure, but the house was completely silent and empty. He heard a voice outside announcing SDPD, and then another officer appeared, leaning in cautiously through the front door.

"I was in the area, heard your call." It was detective Jensen. "My God," he muttered, "where did all this blood come from?"

The two men cautiously explored the house but could locate no one. On the table sat an opened bottle of Jim Beam whiskey.

"We can test that later," Jensen said.

"Whose place is it?"

"It's empty, up for sale. We will need to contact the owner."

"Whoever this was is dead for sure," Jensen said, pointing to the wall.

"Helluva place to kill someone too," Fleming said, staring out to the back doors. A flock of birds burst suddenly from the trees below and took to flight. The men peered over the ledge but could spot no one.

"Yes it is," he said. "Yes it is."

———

Artemidorus demanded in a tense whisper to know who it was at his door at such an ungodly hour.

"Thank you, my old friend," came the voice in return. "You have served me well twice this day."

"Great gods, Caesar! You yet live?"

"Yes, my friend, of course, but remember I go by Taro now."

"I had forgotten; sorry, my son."

"How are my compatriots?"

"Well," he said nervously, "it will take the girl a bit more time to wake up. She's been tinctured to the brink I'm afraid, but she will survive."

"Where are we?" Sullivan said, realizing he too must have been unconscious for some time.

The four lay around a tiny fire in the middle of a room with a great opening in the ceiling above. They'd all taken ill after drinking a cup of wine with the old man, to calm their nerves, and then could remember nothing.

Taro stood over the fire, warming his hands.

"That little pond over there will let you go anywhere you want. Dream big, Detective. Your life is one of great fortune, I'd say. You will see sights others could only dream of."

Tackett raised his head groggily, staring into the small fire, watching as the embers moved up into the night sky. Taro drank heartily from a wineskin. He swiped at his lips before speaking.

"You'll find the pond with the help of my dear friend here. The drug has been stored in great quantities at the Priory of the order of the Gracchi. It stands in all time threads I've traversed, so you should always be able to find it. Everything else you need can be found here."

He slung a tiny book at each of them.

Tackett held it up in the light. "What the hell is this?"

"It has maps to the Priory and far beyond. Artemidorus has the medicines you will require for the short term. He can school you in Greek as well. Read the rules of that little book well my friends, and whatever you do read the chapter on avoiding the Vestals. Everything else should be perfectly clear. I've tried to write sparingly, without overcomplicating the topic."

Sullivan held the book up to the light:

On Traveling through Time
By Gaius Taro

Caesar pulled his cloak over his head, concealing his face, and moved to depart.

"Where are you going?" Sullivan said. "You haven't explain—"

"I'm headed to parts unknown, just like you, Detective. I never grow tired of Rome, you see. It's just that it is so full of Romans," he said with a great laugh.

And then he turned and was gone.

THE END

Made in the USA
Lexington, KY
19 February 2019